I0543896

The Christmas Rental

Savannah Hendricks

Grand Bayou Press

First published by Grand Bayou Press 2021

Copyright ©2021 Savannah Hendricks

All rights reserved. No part of this publication may be reproduced, stored, or trans-mitted in any form or by any means, electronic, mechanical, machine language, photocopying, recording, scanning, or otherwise without written permission from the publisher. It is illegal to copy this book, post it to a website, or distribute it by any other means without permission.

This novel is entirely a work of fiction and not created by AI. The names, characters, and incidents portrayed in it are the work of the author's imagination. Any resem-blance to actual persons, living or dead, events or localities is entirely coincidental.

Savannah Hendricks asserts the moral right to be identified as the author of this work.

Savannah Hendricks has no responsibility for the persistence or accuracy of URLs for external or third-party Internet Websites referred to in this publication and does not guarantee that any content on such Websites is, or will remain, accurate or appropriate.

Designations used by companies to distinguish their products are often claimed as trademarks. All brand names and product names used in this book and on its cover are trade names, service marks, trademarks, and registered trademarks of their respective owners. The publishers and the book are not associated with any product or vendor mentioned in this book. None of the companies referenced within the book have endorsed the book.

Library of Congress Control Number: 2021907933

ISBN Paperback: 978-1-7344553-2-8

eBook ASIN : B092RFL1RD

For Film and TV Rights – GrandBayouPress@protonmail.com

Editor: Krista Dapkey - www.kdproofreading.com

Cover design by Savannah Hendricks

Annually, 10% of the proceeds from the sale of this book, and all Savannah's books are donated to dog rescue organizations.

READING IS BETTER WITH A DOG ~ Savannah

For Dick & Jeanette, Ted & Sandy, John & Mary Ann, Bill & Linda, Steve & Sharon, Sandy, cousins John, Kim, Karen, Diane, Mary, Paul, Candace, Patty, and Donna Bertrand. And for the angels: Sharon, Arlene, Linda, and Don

Foreword

*Fishing at Uncle Don
& Aunt Arlene's home
(1988)*

My richest childhood memories are of the times I spent in the Midwest. And when the idea of **The Christmas Rental** came to me, I couldn't think of a better place than Minnesota to set the story. I've lost count of how many vacations I spent on the lakes and the wide-open backyards' of my relatives. It's also why I ask people if they want a "pop" versus a "soda," and when I say "bag," it sounds like "beg."

My parents both grew up in the Midwest, spread across Minnesota and into Wisconsin and South Dakota. So spending time in a tiny fishing boat, hanging from a tree swing, swimming in the lakes, watching horseshoes flying into sand traps, and hearing the laughter floating over the tops of refilled coffee mugs is only a sample of my beautiful memories.

As you cozy up with this story, I hope it brings you the same sense of warmth, caring, and love I've been blessed to have in my life, represented by some of the most wonderful things that make the Midwest such a gem – the people.

Driving the John Deere
on Uncle Dick's farm
(1990)

Contents

Welcome to Oakvale

CAST OF CHARACTERS:

Lorelei Parker - Doctor
Tyler McCain - Real Estate Agent/ bowling alley
Mary Ann Parker - Lorelei's daughter
Cider - Tyler's dog
Richard McCain - Tyler's dad
Arlene McCain - Tyler's mom
Joanne Parker - Lorelei's mom
John Parker - Lorelei's dad
Sharon Miller - owns the café
Sandy & Ted - own Once Upon a Book
Garrison - Sandy & Ted's dog
Diane & Kim - own Thrifty Finds
Don - owns the convenience store
Candace & Chris North - Lorelei's aunt and uncle
Jodi - receptionist/assistant at the doctor's office
Uncle Steve - owns Oakvale Pizza Pie

Chapter 1

Tyler McCain leaned against the window and scoped out the town as he flipped the pen around his fingers. A week ago, when he'd spoken with Lorelei Parker on the phone, she'd sounded like a punctual person. As an emergency room doctor, he assumed she had to be.

After a final glance outside for approaching cars, he turned to the pile of hardcover novels on the corner of his desk. The stack had grown so high if he closed one eye, it reminded him of the Leaning Tower of Pisa. With the holiday hustle and bustle, he'd fallen behind on his to-be-read list.

"Might as well read another chapter while we wait," Tyler stated to his rescue dog, Cider. The mutt continued to snore away on her plush dog bed next to the desk.

Thinking of his pending appointment, he clicked the schedule open on the monitor. Dr. Lorelei Parker was the only name on the calendar for the entire month of December. He spun around in his desk chair but went too far and corrected himself before he could be mistaken for a kindergartner goofing off.

Tyler picked up his cell phone and checked the screen for missed calls, but he knew in the silence of the McCain Rental and Real Estate office he couldn't have missed the ringer if he'd tried. He glanced over at the bowling lanes and chuckled. To this day, he couldn't get over the fact that his office was inside the historic Oakvale bowling alley. With the town's tree lighting tonight, he'd be hard-pressed to find any residents stopping in for a quick game.

Upon entering the building, to the right, was the bowling alley. And Tyler never tired of seeing out-of-towners express looks of confusion when they stepped inside. The real estate office sat off to the left of the lanes in a makeshift space. Over twenty years ago, his parents had remodeled the snack area by removing the tables and bench seating and converted it into an - office. After high school, Tyler worked side by side with his dad, Richard, and mom, Arlene, learning the real estate business.

This morning, he'd spend time decorating the office and bowling alley for Christmas. He started by stringing colored lights around the front windows, before hanging ornaments on the two freshly cut trees he'd hauled back from Paul's Christmas Tree Farm. After securing the wreaths by ribbons to the center of each window, Tyler moved on, weaving garland around the bowling ball and shoe rental racks. The sounds of Loretta Lynn's Christmas album filtered through the speakers. Just as he was about to start singing along off-key, a blast of thirty-degree weather shot through the front door.

"Tyler, what are you doing here? Shouldn't you be out showing Dr. and Mrs. Norths' home?" Richard McCain entered the office, balancing a cardboard box in his arms.

Tyler was his dad's mirror image, tall with brown hair so dark it could be confused as black. Gray hair didn't run in the family until much later than most, and when people saw them from the back, they joked they were brothers. They even sounded similar on the phone, causing callers to ask if they were speaking to Tyler or Richard.

"She hasn't shown up yet. And I need to head over and help with tree lighting prep soon. Hopefully, she doesn't take too much longer to get here." Tyler took the box from his dad and set it on the neighboring empty desk. "What's this for?"

"This Christmas, I'm hiding my decorations for the annual twig reindeer decorating contest from your mom. I think it's how she's one-upping me every year. She sneaks a peek and figures out something better for her reindeer." Richard removed the black gloves from his hands and shoved them into his jacket pocket.

"I think I'm going to win this year." Tyler patted his dad on the back. "Are you sure you want to leave that box here?"

"No peeking, you might be a spy for your mom."

"Good one. I very well could be." He gazed sideways at his dad, playing along.

"We both know—heck, the whole town knows—your mom is the only one to beat."

Cider stood from her dog bed and greeted Richard. The dog's chest was pure-white fur, which only spread to her paws and the tip of her tail, while amber covered the rest of her. She had one good eye (the right) and appeared to be a Brittany mixed with a Saint Bernard. Cider went everywhere with Tyler, from work to any of the shops in town.

As Richard bent down and scratched around Cider's ears, the tag on her crimson collar clinked.

"How's my grand-pup doing today?" Richard asked as though Cider would answer.

"Maybe the Norths' niece will participate in our reindeer contest." Tyler gazed out the window once more. "I told you she's their occupant, right?"

"I'm not sure if I heard it from you, Sandy, or maybe Don. Then again, it could've been the Norths before they left. I do know they have been trying to get her out here for some time now." Richard gave one last scratch to Cider's ears and stood up. "She could give Mom a run for that gift certificate prize if she wins the contest."

"She needs to show up first." Tyler rubbed his chin. "Maybe she's stuck in traffic."

"It would be the first traffic jam Oakvale, Minnesota has ever seen." Richard chuckled and lifted the box off the desk.

"Not here, of course, maybe leaving the city or getting through Booth." Tyler watched as his dad set the box in the corner of the storage closet next to a stack of printer paper and cleaning supplies. He turned his desk chair and faced the window. There was not a time Tyler could remember when he tired of the view from his office or anywhere in Oakvale. Across the street stood Once Upon a Book, the always busy bookstore. On his side of the road, next door, was Oakvale Pizza Pie, followed by the doctor's office and Don's Conveniences along with the pharmacy. Directly in the center of downtown, a Frasier fir grew in the middle of the traffic circle.

Tyler caught his dad glancing around the office with his mouth turned up into a delighted smile. "The decorations look good." He went to his son. "It's a true blessing to have you running the family business"—Richard patted Tyler on the shoulder and squeezed it—"and we wouldn't have it any other way."

"I know, Dad. You don't need to mention it every time you stop by. It's been years now."

"There's nothing wrong with being proud of my son carrying on the family name." Richard gazed around. "Twenty-some years of hard work, we had our ups and downs, but it's still standing. I can't wait to see our grandkids and great-grand-kids running this place someday." A twinkle appeared in his eye when he smiled. "Well, son, I'm heading home. Your mom should be pulling her peppermint chip cookies from the oven any minute." He rubbed his hands together. "I'd save you some, but ..."

"Mom will be lucky if she gets them to cool before they're all gone," Tyler remarked.

Richard opened the door, initiating the return of frosty air through the office. Tyler rubbed his shoulders and shivered.

He sighed and tried not to stare at Once Upon a Book for too long, but his vision always found its way across the street, and he'd become lost in thought while gazing off at it. The For Sale sign rested in the corner of the window nearest the door. When his parents weren't pushing for him to meet someone special and start a family of his own, they were ecstatic to discuss the family business at length. Smiles warmed their faces every time they spoke of their pride in him running it. Not to mention how delighted they were that their dream would continue through Tyler as he handed it down to the next generation. Yet all he wanted sat right across the street. He reminded himself that either way, he would have to give up one dream for another since money wasn't nearly as abundant as the snowflakes outside.

The real estate market in Oakvale had been in a lull the last few months without any new houses being built and having a limited turnover of properties. The only rental in town was Dr. and Mrs. Norths' house for December. The lack of immediate prospects didn't concern his parents; the business always bounced back somehow. The low turnover rate of residents was thanks to the wonderful town and the slower-paced lifestyle.

Outside, the historic curved-metal bowling alley sign still pointed at the front of the building and remained the largest sign in town. The much smaller (but still decent sized) McCain Rental and Real Estate sign hung under the building's façade. Anyone looking for the real estate office was always directed to the bowling alley sign, which undoubtedly could be seen from space.

Back when his parents purchased the abandoned bowling alley, long after the iron ore mining slowed, the town of Oakvale was on the rise of residents and needed someone to sell the vacant properties. The original bowling alley owners hightailed it out of town faster than a toboggan on a ninety-degree, snow-covered hill when their first grandbaby was born. While Tyler earned an adequate income running both of the businesses, the bowling alley provided the lion's share last year.

He'd worked in the building since the age of ten. His first job had been spraying the insides of the shoes, checking them out to bowlers, and putting the balls back on the racks at closing time.

He'd never forget the local bowling club's weekly get-togethers. Or how packed the place had gotten for birthday parties.

Tyler sighed at the memories as he removed his worn-from-childhood, hand-crafted bookmark from his novel. He opened the hardcover far enough to feel the spine crack. Sure, he'd been scolded a thousand times about doing such a thing to a book, but he couldn't help it. To him, nothing was worse than a book that looked like no one had ever read it. Leaning back in the desk chair, his mind became lost in the story.

After a chapter, thirsty for warmth, he picked up his mug and sauntered over to the beverage bar. His dad had managed to salvage the vintage soda shop countertop from Don's Conveniences when the pharmacy area was remodeled. The beverage bar hosted two coffee makers and a hot water dispenser with teas, chocolate, and cider selection. Mismatched mugs for every season from Valentine's Day to New Year's hung from hooks on the wall behind it. A refrigerator sat at the end of the bar, cases of cold beverages lined up inside. At the other end of the counter, an antique register hogged up a bit of space. Of course, it was never used, but it belonged. Residents would hand Tyler cash or checks for games and drinks. The line of bowling balls and shoes were self-serve, which meant Tyler often found himself with little to do. He thought about changing the rules up, but residents were used to it and didn't mind. A sign near the beverage station noted the rules:

Find your shoes and ball size.

Have fun, be respectful.

Return the balls to the rack and your shoes to the return box.

To be honest, the bowling alley could run itself with an honor-system drop box. All Tyler had to do was spray down the shoes and put them back on the rack according to size. And he thought of that every day when he shoved the key into the lock to start his morning at his family's building instead of opening the bookstore's door across the street. A part of him wondered if his parents were more attached to the history behind the building and their time here than the actual business.

Holding the mug with both hands, he sipped the warm cider. Tyler returned to his desk and pulled out a piece of paper. While he waited, he might as well write some ideas down for the twig reindeer contest. After a few minutes, when nothing came to mind, Tyler's eyes glanced over at the closet toward his dad's box. His mom was the feared competitor to beat, which meant looking at what he had in there couldn't be cheating, only making sure at least one of them would have the upper hand.

When Tyler stood up, he checked to make sure no one was coming and walked softly across the floor to the closet. He peeked over his shoulder, squatted to his knees, and opened the cardboard lid.

Chapter 2

T he drive going north on I-35 was beautiful. Evergreens and bare maples lined the road with pockets of perfectly white snow glistening between them. Lorelei Parker tucked a strand of her strawberry blonde bob behind her ear as the radio went to static. Reaching forward, she pushed the scan button until another station came through clearly. As she stretched her back slightly, the welcome sign came into view.

Oakvale Welcomes You! Slow down, and enjoy your time!

"That's exactly why we're here," Lorelei said to her adopted six-month-old daughter in the back seat as she gazed ahead, taking a deep breath. "If only your Gramps and Grams could understand."

After two years of fifty- to sixty-hour workweeks in a constantly moving emergency department at Minneapolis's Metro Central Hospital, Lorelei needed to slow down. Not only with her job but with her lifestyle too, especially now that she had Mary Ann in tow.

As she eased the sedan to a crawl at twenty-five miles an hour, she could almost smell the warmth of friendliness through the car vents. It smelled like cinnamon and pine—clear and colored Christmas lights dressed up the storefronts. Garland with twinkling lights wrapped around street poles, and wreaths hung from each entry doors. The buildings were of different sizes, built from currant and ruby-colored bricks and show windows.

Snow lined the streets, and a giant fir tree sprouted in the center of the town's traffic circle. People with boxes and a few ladders milled around it.

"It's picture-perfect," Lorelei mused.

She and Mary Ann would be in town for the entire month of December, staying at her aunt and uncle's house. Lorelei had placed her condo up for rent back in Minneapolis and had a couple who would be spending a few weeks closer to Christmas there. She wanted to sell the condo but didn't have the courage to set the plan into motion. Her parents dreamed she'd land a spot on the board of directors at the hospital. Lorelei needed to convince herself she didn't need to follow their path, but instead show them that being a small-town doctor was prestigious in its own way and what she wanted more than anything else career-wise. But, after several failed attempts over the years, it would take a Christmas miracle for it to happen.

One exhausted night after work, she'd rocked Mary Ann to sleep while flipping through a magazine with tourism ads for visiting small towns in Minnesota over Christmastime. She took one look at her sleeping daughter and picked up the phone. Her Aunt Candace—her dad's sister—had always stayed in contact with Lorelei even though they had a distant relationship with her dad because of their age difference. For the last few years, Aunt Candace called in the fall to see if she wanted to stay at their home for December and help out with her uncle Chris's tiny medical practice in town while they were away. Her uncle and aunt traveled every year for the entire month, and Lorelei didn't see how they managed to leave the town without a physician for that long.

This time, Lorelei reached out to them, hoping the offer still stood. They'd been delighted by her call and prompted her to follow up with the local real estate agent who handled their rental stays. Although Lorelei found it a little odd, she figured even family should have to follow the same rules from time to time.

She'd spoken with a man named Tyler who'd sounded rather giddy about her taking over. It appeared it couldn't have worked out more perfectly for any of them. Lorelei and Mary Ann could experience small-town life, with Lorelei filling in as a local doctor, and when her parents visited for Christmas, maybe they could see how much she didn't want to be an ER doctor anymore.

"I can't believe how late I'm running," Lorelei murmured as she pulled her sedan into the parking spot in front of the brick building with a gigantic weathered red-and-white bowling alley sign. Of course, if Tyler hadn't mentioned that his office was in a bowling alley, she might've missed it. She glanced back at Mary Ann, still fast asleep from the five-hour ride. Lorelei sighed, hating to wake her daughter.

When her ebony boot hit the slippery snow and ice, she grabbed hold of the doorframe, gaining her balance. *Maybe dress boots were not the best choice.* Opening the back door, Lorelei undid Mary Ann's car seat harness clip and lifted her daughter out.

Gingerly stepping onto the sidewalk, Lorelei eased her way to the office door. She pulled it open and entered. "Hello? I'm sorry I'm running late." Relief spread across her face once she was safely inside.

Glancing around, she didn't see anyone until a person crouched in front of a closet sprung up. He spun around like a preschooler caught with their hand in the cookie jar.

Lorelei reached out her free hand. "You must be Tyler. I'm Lorelei, and this sleeping beauty is Mary Ann." On the phone he'd sounded tall, which seemed odd to conclude, but it was the way his voice carried that made her think he would be, and she was not wrong. Lorelei wondered if she sounded short.

Tyler moved toward Lorelei and reached out his hand, shaking hers. "Dr. Parker, hi. Are we waiting for your husband?" He glanced behind her. "I don't recall per our phone conversation."

"Please call me Lorelei. And no, it's just my daughter and me. I adopted her. Single mom." Lorelei presented a jazz-hand. "Sorry, it's a proud moment of mine."

"It's great; amazing, actually. Parenting is hard work, I imagine." Tyler pointed to an amber-and-white-furred dog who stretched itself up and out of the dog bed. "I know about dog parenthood, but that's it."

Lorelei turned to the dog. "Aww." She placed her hand on her heart. "Aren't you just the cutest thing outside of Mary Ann?" Still holding her daughter, Lorelei knelt to pet the dog.

"Her name is Cider. I adopted her from the shelter over in Booth. You probably drove through it. I mean, of course you did if you came from Minneapolis. We—Cider and I—get out and do things. It's not like we sit around the office, bored all day. But work is work, so it should be a little boring, right?" He sighed and nodded his head.

Clearly, she made him nervous. That, or maybe he liked to talk without taking breaths.

His eyes glanced down at Cider. "I couldn't have asked for a better dog."

"We do have something in common, then. Single adoptive parents." Lorelei sprung up to standing, trying to lighten the mood and make him less nervous. "This place is like something out of the seventies. I love the decorations you've put up in here."

"Thank you. I have the rental agreement for you to sign and review." Tyler moved to his desk and motioned for Lorelei to sit down, his cheeks flushing. "I must admit, I didn't think you'd have to sign one, being their niece and all."

"Right." She placed a hand on her hip.

He nodded and eyed her outfit, his vision lingering on her boots.

"Don't cha know, I'm probably a bit overdressed. Anyway, how great is it that you have a bowling alley in your office—or is it a real estate office in the bowling alley?" Lorelei remained standing.

"Excellent question." Tyler tugged at his earlobe. "I'd enjoy telling you all about it."

Is he blushing?

He glanced over his shoulder and out the window toward town. "I promised to assist with the decorations for the tree lighting. If you have time, I can tell you the story while I tackle the tree?"

"Gosh, no, I don't want to interrupt your day. Sorry, I honestly didn't think I'd be this late. I mean, I would love to hear the story." Disappointment and concern creased Lorelei's face as she picked up the paper off the desk. The thought of her parents' sullen faces as she backed out of her condo's garage filled her mind. Today was supposed to be a happy day, and it only felt like she continued to disappoint everyone in her path. "Just sign at the bottom?"

"That should work. As I said, it's odd you have to sign one, but I guess nowadays, most everyone worries about something." Tyler shrugged.

"Have you read it?" She waved the single sheet of paper in his direction.

"Dare I say no? Usually, we have a formatted one I print up, but your uncle insisted he handle this one for you." Two lines formed between his eyebrows as his golden-brown eyes squinted with confusion. "I figured since he prepared it and was making you sign anything at all that it probably was none of my business. Although, it is my business." He wrinkled his lip like Elvis.

She waved him off. "No big deal, I know you have to be over at the tree thing, and it was my fault for being late." Lorelei signed her name, then handed the form to him. "There you go. I promise I won't break anything, and it will look the same the day I leave as it does today." Holding out her hand, Lorelei smiled and tilted her head a bit. "Keys and directions, then you can get back to your regularly scheduled life."

Tyler removed the key from the desk drawer along with the handwritten directions to Dr. and Mrs. North's home. "Once you've settled in, if you'd like, you're welcome to come back into town for the tree lighting and cider tonight."

Lorelei froze like an icicle. "Apple cider?"

Cider glanced up at her.

"Yes, Sharon's Café provides the best cider and snacks for the lighting."

"I love cider!" they said in unison and laughed.

"That's why you named your dog Cider?" Lorelei pointed.

"Yes, and also because her amber color looks just like apple cider."

Lorelei studied the dog and lowered to pet it once more as it sniffed Mary Ann, now awake. "You're right." Her daughter reached for the mound of fur on the dog's chest.

Tyler leaned in and took a peek at the baby. "Hi, Mary Ann, welcome to Oakvale."

A smile formed on Mary Ann's face as she took in the stranger.

"Thanks again for arranging all of this. I kind of figured my aunt and uncle would want to see me and meet Mary Ann."

"Don't take too much offense. They have been strict with their December travel for as long as I can remember. Maybe they will make an exception and come back before the thirty-first this year."

"True, I do know my dad has mentioned they've never heard from them during Christmastime since they've been married. We'll let you get going. And I promise I won't be late for anything else in this town." She headed towards the door. "What time is the tree thing? And where is it?"

Tyler followed her to the door and held it open. "Right there"—he pointed—"at dusk."

Following his finger, she spotted the traffic circle with the Christmas tree in the middle. More bundled-up people had gathered around, digging through boxes. Mounds of snow had been pushed out of the way, shoveled around the outer edges of the street.

"Should be easy to find." Lorelei winked and unlocked her sedan with the key fob. She skillfully trampled through the snow, scolding herself again for her choice of shoes.

"I put my number at the bottom of the directions, in case you have any issues."

She loaded Mary Ann into her car seat, clicking the harness into place, and shut the door. "Thank you. I'm sure all will be well. Again, I'm sorry we were late. You'd think I would've been early since I couldn't wait to get here." Making her way to the driver's side of the sedan, she rewrapped her scarf around her neck.

"You're here now. Time to relax and enjoy what Oakvale has to offer." Tyler beamed.

"Oh, what about my uncle's office? Are there directions or an address?"

Tyler waved at someone exiting a shop across the street. "Dr. North's office is right there. You passed it on your way into town. The sign in the front yard is buried under snow."

Lorelei glanced over the hood of the sedan and down the street. There, on the corner, sat a two-story home that appeared to have been historic, possibly built in the twenties or thirties based on the design. During college, she'd picked interior design and architecture electives as a way to explore her creativity that didn't involve stitching up wounds. And she often found herself immersed in her knowledge.

"Dr. North left everything at the house for the office. But remember, this is not a big city. He runs things much differently than you're probably used to at the hospital. Nothing fancy or fast-paced. I do hope you have better shoes to walk around in."

"Sure do." Maybe Lorelei would adopt the same rule as her uncle. She opened the driver's door. "See you later for this cider you spoke of and the tree lighting." After buckling up and backing out, she rolled down the window. "Will it be a big turnout? Lots of traffic?"

"Lots of traffic for Oakvale, but not for a city gal." Tyler winked.

Lorelei pressed her lips together to keep from laughing out loud. "Awful soon to be starting in on jokes. We only met five minutes ago."

"We spoke on the phone. Probably should make it fifteen minutes that we've known each other." Tyler waved.

She waved back and couldn't help but wonder how much time she and Tyler would be spending together in the following weeks. A smile twisted up her lips at the edges as she headed toward her aunt and uncle's house.

Chapter 3

W hile he was always excited for the Christmas tree lighting and cider, something about Lorelei and Mary Ann
showing up made it even better. Her voice on the phone sounded sweeter than honey, but in person, there was something more
about her. Lorelei's personality was not what he expected when
meeting a big-city doctor in person. He assumed she would be
stiff and off-putting. Maybe carry a luggage-size purse with gold
embossing. Her fancy boots were a poor choice for the slick
sidewalks, though. During their brief face-to-face conversation,
Tyler became unexpectedly nervous. He hoped it would pass, so
she didn't think he was some fuddy-duddy with nothing better
to do than ramble randomly.

When he returned inside the office, still in a daze of happiness, he noticed the December calendar up on the monitor, and
it hit his heart. Lorelei would not be staying. Just like every other
renter who came to stay at the Norths' home, even though she
was their niece, Lorelei too would leave come December 31. Of
course, all the other renters had been couples; Lorelei was the
first single person. The thought of her sent a slight smile to his
face again.

Running his hands through his hair, he snatched the jacket
off the back of the chair, shut off the lights, and removed the
office keys from his pocket. As he and Cider headed across the
street, the only thing filling his mind was Oakvale's temporary
residents.

Tyler held open the door to Once Upon a Book, and Cider swiftly located her best friend, Garrison, a hound Lab mix.

"Sandy?" Tyler raised his voice.

A curly pile of dove-gray hair peeked around a bookcase a few rows back. "Tyler, over here."

He stepped farther into the store, past the dogs already roughhousing in the open area near the front. Glancing around, Tyler sighed at his dream before him. Ted, Sandy's husband, had constructed every bookshelf. The pine scent still gently lingered, instantly transporting him back to his childhood visits. He'd probably read every book in the children's section. Either because his parents bought him the book for his shelf or because he'd read them while tucked in his favorite corner nook of the store during his weekly visits. Tyler loved books as much as a deer loved a salt lick in the middle of winter.

The children's section remained the same, as had everything else in the store over the years. White lights hung in a canopy over the children's literature section where short bookcases defined the space and several oversize bean bag chairs were nestled in the corner. The rest of the store was divided up into typical bookstore categories with the front of the store reserved for seasonal-themed display tables featuring books of all genres and time periods. Mixed in with the books were Hallmark treasures, from ornaments and mugs to figurines and candles. Sandy managed to keep the dogs from bumping into the area by placing a sizeable ornate rug under the display tables and training them to keep off, like a backward game of hot lava.

The scent of books and peppermint tickled his nose. Christmas lights hung over and around the bookcases. In front of the main window, a train traveled around a flocked tree decorated to the nines.

"I'm here to pick up the ornaments for the tree. Ted said you had a box?"

Sandy finished shelving the stack of books in her arm and stepped out from the aisle. "Yes." She smiled and pointed toward the front door.

Tyler glanced over. "I missed it coming in. Thanks."

"Leave Cider here." Sandy readjusted several hardbacks. "Garrison needs to release some energy."

Cider and Garrison were at opposite ends of a stuffed giraffe, their eyes staring each other down with the tug-of-war game. History provided the dogs could be at this game for a long time, them both trying to one-up each other with a quick move to the left or right.

"Have you spoken to your parents yet?" Sandy approached him and pointed at the For Sale sign.

"You know I'm focused on an obtainable dream, traveling." Tyler's posture slumped. "Besides, we both know I can't ask them. I think about it every day, but in the end, I'm an only child—the only one to carry on the McCain name."

"You could rename the bookstore," Sandy encouraged.

Tyler's mouth hung open. "Your store is the best-named bookstore in all of Minnesota, if not the United States. Maybe the world."

Sandy laughed and glanced out the store's window to view the town's Christmas tree and the residents stringing lights. "You know you're the most qualified local to run this store. You're a walking encyclopedia of book knowledge. Ted's getting restless and running out of things to fix around the house."

Tyler didn't need a reminder. He needed to decide on either finding a way to gather up the courage to ask his parents if he could leave the family business and purchase Once Upon a Book or finally purchase his book-themed travel venture. But the dream of the bookstore kept him from leaping.

Ted and Sandy had announced they were putting their bookstore up for sale back at the end of summer and enlisted Tyler's help. They were in their mid-seventies and wanted to spend their retirement years traveling. If Tyler didn't buy the bookstore, he could travel; if he did, he couldn't. There was no way for him to do both on his income. And outside of the gas station and Don's Conveniences, Once Upon a Book was likely the next busiest business in their small town. Thriving was something the bowling alley and real estate business were decidedly not. Rumor had it Once Upon a Book brought in more money than Oakvale Pizza Pie. Oakvale residents loved to read more than they loved pizza! But so far, no buyers had shown any interest.

Cider bumped into Tyler as she and Garrison continued to tug on the poor stretched-out giraffe.

"I'd better get going and help with the tree. I'm already running late." Tyler lifted the box off the floor and used his back to push open the front door.

"Did the Norths' niece make it in?" Sandy asked, wrapping her arms around herself and pulling her sweater closed as the outside air from the open door reached her.

"Yes, with her daughter." Tyler stood half in the store, half outside. "I already sent them on their way."

"No husband?" Sandy grinned.

Tyler shook his head no. "Don't say it, Sandy."

"A single mom and a doctor. Wow. She's a smart and strong woman. I bet she's cute, too." Sandy pushed her pointer finger to her lips.

"Bye, Sandy," Tyler called as he made his way out the door and toward the Christmas tree.

Chapter 4

The directions on the paper were as straightforward as could be for a small town, and it made her heart cozy with delight. *A right at the Christmas tree, then a left at the stop sign, and follow the road until the trees clear. The house will be on the left.*

"Mary Ann!" Lorelei eased the sedan down the driveway. "It's even cuter in person!"

The tan Craftsman-style home had a white picket fence surrounding the driveway's front section. It was two stories and featured a lovely, welcoming porch with large windows flanking either side of the front door. A sizeable second-story window appeared to rest on top of the porch's roof. Wreaths with red ribbons and ornate bows hung from the fence and were covered in a light layer of snow.

Spruce trees grew randomly throughout the property, as well as bare maples that lost their colorful leaves. Lorelei shut off the sedan and nearly threw the driver's side door off the hinges opening it with such excitement. She drew her robin's egg blue gloves to her heart and beamed.

"It's like something out of a Norman Rockwell Christmas painting!" She took a deep breath, filling her lungs with country air. Lorelei had seen a few pictures of the place in an old family photo album and had always dreamed of visiting. But since her parents were not ones for celebrating a country-type Christmas, and the Norths were never around in December anyway, it had never happened. "I finally made it."

As she made her way to the car's back door, her boots were like ice skates. "Phew. That's dangerous." Using the sedan as a brace, she slid to the back, opened up the hatch, and switched shoes.

Once on solid footing, she removed Mary Ann, who clutched a teething blanket. Snow began to fall, dusting the top of Lorelei's cream-colored jacket.

Sliding the key into the front door, she unlocked it with a click. As it swung open, the scent of warm vanilla and cinnamon hit Lorelei's nose. She set the key on the entryway table and left the front door open. After she made several trips to and from the sedan, dragging in four suitcases while carrying Mary Ann the entire time, she finally closed the front door. Pulling her cell phone from her pocket, she was alerted to notifications lining the top.

"I'll get those in a minute." She slid the phone back into her pocket. "Let's get some heat going and find some place to put you down. You're getting heavy." Lorelei gazed around, standing on the plush emerald green rug.

To her immediate right, through the craftsman archway, sat a room with a fireplace. A plump green velvet couch with matching wing chairs were arranged facing the hearth and built-in bookcases lined the walls. To her left, a set of stairs led to the upstairs. And in front of her, a short hallway led to the open floor plan kitchen and living room.

Locating the thermostat on the wall, she clicked it on, setting it to a comfortable temperature. Lorelei removed her gloves and unbuckled Mary Ann from her seat, lifting her to her hip.

"This is going to be our home for a whole month." Lorelei carried the baby down the hall and into the kitchen. The expansive living room and kitchen encompassed the entire back of the home. Picture windows with wood trim allowed for a view of the backyard from every angle. Another fireplace was on the left side of the room with an L-shaped charcoal-gray flare-armed couch facing it. To her right, the kitchen boasted pine cabinets and a large butcher-block island separated it from the dining area. A bare wood farmers table, with seating for possibly ten guests, filled the remaining space nicely.

Lorelei's entire body slouched as every care and worry left her, melting away into the hardwood floor below. The lingering evening light faded outside as the flakes of snow grew larger.

She glanced at Mary Ann and kissed her forehead as her cell phone vibrated in her pocket. "Baby girl, this is the life we are supposed to be living. Your mommy is exhausted from all the sadness and long hours in the ER." Just as Lorelei was about to check her phone, she shook her head. "Nope. Time to relax."

She found the note on the island and clicked on the kitchen lights. The crimson ink only enhanced the exquisite handwriting, and Lorelei bounced Mary Ann to keep her from fussing while she read through the letter. It detailed the hours for the doctor's office and what to expect as far as workload. But the only phone numbers listed were Tyler's and the practice's—no cell number for the Norths and no indication where to reach them. The letter also welcomed her to treat the home as her own, using everything from sheets to books to the sleds in the garage. Not only was the house beautiful, but it was also spotless. Lorelei imagined someone with a magic wand waving it around, perfecting everything. As she finished reading the letter, she noticed the PS at the bottom: *Please dress up the home as you see fit for Christmas. You will find all the decorations in the garage.*

She flipped the note over, searching for a cell phone number. Nothing. When her eyes traveled around the kitchen, she spotted an old-school phone attached to the wall. Lorelei stepped over to it and lifted the receiver as though it had cooties. A dial tone hummed in her ear. The only number she had for her aunt and uncle was the house phone.

The moment she'd reached out to her aunt and uncle, a relief she hadn't experienced in some time flowed through her veins. Even as she packed up Mary Ann and her items, a chore she was not a fan of, she'd done so while whistling Christmas tunes and dancing around her bedroom. And she didn't think it would stop anytime soon, not as long as the negative thoughts of her parents stayed out of the way. Their disapproval of her doing anything other than living in Minneapolis and continuing her hospital career was loud and clear. Not to mention they already held Ivy League expectations for their only grandchild. She wouldn't allow her parent's judgment and expectation to transfer to her daughter—at least not today.

"We get to decorate the house, Mary Ann. Your first Christmas will be one to remember." Warmth filled her. She'd not given any thought to trimming for the season outside of the condo. In fact, she hadn't packed a single Christmas item, not even her stocking from childhood. The thought of forgetting the stocking hit her right in the stomach, weakening her smile.

"Oh, baby girl, Mommy forgot her stocking. I can't believe I didn't think to bring it." Lorelei hung her stocking every Christmas, regardless of where she lived. "Maybe I should call Gramps and Grams and have them pick it up from the condo when they come to visit. It wouldn't be the same without it. I can't break tradition after all these years."

Unsurprisingly, Lorelei hadn't had time to make or buy Mary Ann a Christmas stocking. Maybe Oakvale had a craft store and she could pick up supplies for one. She used to love to spend her free time crafting.

Hunger ripped through her stomach in the form of a grumble. "Let's get you set up, see what we have in the refrigerator, and figure out supper." She headed to the suitcases, snatched the red one, and wheeled it into the kitchen. Lorelei removed a queen-size quilt she'd purchased from a boutique shop in Minneapolis and laid it out on the floor before setting Mary Ann on it with some toys.

Next, she located a lighter and crumbled up a few sheets of newspaper to shove under the stacked wood in the living room's fireplace. The fire came to life and filled the room with a peaceful glow. She observed the framed photos on the mantel. There were two of her aunt and uncle together and one of her parents with the Norths. Judging by the sixties-style clothing, it must've been taken before she was born.

Moving into the kitchen while keeping an eye on Mary Ann, she opened the refrigerator. The inside was bare except for condiments shoved into a corner of the shelf. Closing the door, she frowned and turned to the stove where a tea kettle rested. She opened the pantry to find crackers, soup, and some canned veggies. On a higher shelf sat several boxes of tea—Earl Grey, English breakfast, and chamomile.

Lorelei frowned. No cider. She would need to pick some up. After dropping a chamomile bag into a mug, she turned her focus to the backyard through the windows. The view beyond was breathtaking, and it drew her closer. Outside, dusk approached and when she turned to check on Mary Ann, a labeled light switch caught her eye: **December Lights**

She tilted her head. Outside of the hospital, she'd never seen a light switch labeled before. *December lights?* She stared at it for a few more seconds before she finally gave in and flipped the switch.

"Oh!" she gasped.

Outside the window, a forest of white and multicolored trees burst to life, glistening from every corner of the property.

"Mary Ann!" Lorelei hurried to her daughter, scooped her up, and without a jacket, hat, or gloves, threw open the French doors and stepped out onto the back patio. "Do you see all the lights?" Pointing across the backyard, Mary Ann followed her mommy's finger, but quickly returned to her teething blanket.

"This, Mary Ann, is why we are here on this adventure." She brought her daughter's cheek to hers and squeezed her tightly.

"Spending time together." In the distance, three deer made their way from behind a set of trees. "Look, Mary Ann!"

Her finger pointed into the distance, but her daughter had returned her focus back to her teething blanket.

"You're right. The blanket wins today. We have all month to deer watch."

Yet, right at that moment, that second, she was reminded that life was far from perfect. This happy little December reprieve would switch back to reality once they were home from Oakvale. No scientific study was required to understand small towns didn't need two doctors. If only she heard back about the resume she'd sent to Booth's physician's office. It wouldn't be Oakvale, but it wouldn't be an ER, either. And she still had to figure out a way to show her parents how great it would be to be a small-town doctor. If she could perform operations in emergencies and make authoritative decisions, why couldn't she stand up to her parents' overbearing expectations? Maybe because they weren't strangers like her ER patients? She valued their opinions, and they needed to be a part of Mary Ann's life. She wanted and needed to make them proud. Maybe because their approval remained as vital as it had been when she'd brought home her first report card.

The soft glow of light from the trees filled the yard, but the joy in Lorelei's heart dimmed as the battle of what to do about her parents raged in her mind. Her cell phone vibrated with another notification, and she tended to them, not feeling any less relaxed than when she was in the city.

Chapter 5

Tyler stood back to admire the placement of the ornaments on the town's Christmas tree. Dusk washed over the sky as the storefront's lights provided a soft glow onto the sidewalks. Closed signs hung in every window as residents assisted with the tree or were still at home bundling up their kids for the celebration.

The spit and sputter of Jodi Hudson's car vibrated from the nearby parking spot in front of the doctor's office, drawing Tyler's attention. Since high school graduation, Jodi had worked as the receptionist at Dr. North's office, so seeing her clunker parked in its usual spot brought a nostalgic grin to his face. Just as he made his way over, with a final choke and hiss of black smoke, the engine gave up.

Jodi climbed from the car and slammed the door as though she wanted to punish it for misbehaving.

"Is it giving you problems again?" he asked, standing next to his friend from sixth grade.

"Hey, Tyler." She pushed long chestnut curls off her shoulder. "It doesn't matter what I do. This pile of metal hates me." Jodi lifted her snow boot to it and gave it a slight kick.

"Well." Because he knew it made his friend laugh, Tyler rested his arm playfully on her shoulder, accentuating their height difference. "It might be time for a new car."

Jodi rolled her eyes. "I can't give up on old Frank. He made it through the snowstorm of '08."

"1908?" Tyler joked.

Jodi slid out from under his arm, causing Tyler to lurch before regaining his posture. "I don't need some shiny new thing. The only driving I do is to run over to Booth to see my boyfriend or for babysitting gigs. I walk everywhere else. Plus, new things are pricey."

"Good point. Have you spoken with Dr. North about a raise?" Tyler crossed his arms and gazed up at the doctor's office, which was nothing more than a semi-converted two-story house. With the practice occupying the first floor, Jodi had been living upstairs since she'd begun working there.

"A raise? He already pays me well, and I don't do much. Some days it seems like Dr. North doesn't even need me there. How about I ask him as soon as you talk to your parents about buying the bookstore?" She shoved her hand at him as though to shake on it.

He waved her off. "No, that's not a fair deal. Your parents' business isn't at stake."

"True." Jodi sighed and stared in the same direction as Tyler.

He lifted the keys from his pocket. "Take my truck."

Jodi snatched the keys and beamed. "Thanks, I'll be back after the tree lighting. I can't believe I'm missing it this year. But Mrs. Keaton needed help with the newborns, and she didn't want them out in the cold tonight."

"Better hurry. You worked today?" he called after her.

"I was getting everything ready for the new doctor, running errands, and organizing Mr. North's office," she yelled back as she popped open his truck door and waved before climbing in.

Tyler returned the wave then checked the time on his cell phone and glanced around. Lorelei had promised she would be showing up with Mary Ann. Maybe they'd had trouble locating the house or there was an issue at the rental. He'd hoped to introduce her to as many residents in town as possible before she started work. Maybe there was a problem with her sedan, although it hadn't appeared to be in disrepair. Before his mind could wander more, a voice came up behind him.

"We're coming!"

The sound of boots crunching over the fresh snow grew closer as he spun around.

"You made it." Tyler warmly greeted Lorelei and Mary Ann with a smile. "And you wore appropriate boots."

Lorelei wore the same cream jacket as earlier but had added a matching wool hat. Mary Ann, resting on her hip, was bundled up like an adorable pig in a blanket with only her tiny nose and eyes exposed. Lorelei held her cell phone in her hand.

"Yes." She snorted a laugh, looking at her boots. "I started a fire as soon as we stepped inside the house. Then I was busy on my phone and completely forgot about the tree thing tonight. Do you know how hard it is to put out a fire in a fireplace when it's just getting started?" Lorelei's eyes questioned.

"Fairly hard." Tyler smirked.

Lorelei took in a breath, puffed up her cheeks, and exhaled. "The house is absolutely magical. Have you seen the lights on the trees in the backyard?"

"Yes, they're spectacular." Tyler waved at his parents as they made their way over to him. "Lorelei, this my dad, Richard, and my mom, Arlene. Mom, Dad, this is Lorelei and her daughter, Mary Ann."

His dad, in a thick jacket, gave a little wave. With her Lucille-Ball-like red hair, his mom reached out, hugged Lorelei, and rubbed Mary Ann's bundled-up arm.

"It's a pleasure to meet you both. Your son has been wonderful to work with, setting up the rental." Lorelei switched her daughter to her other hip.

"Welcome to Oakvale, and happy to hear Tyler was able to help you. Yay, for the family business." Richard shoved his fists up to the sky. "Plus, we're grateful to have you pitch in at Dr. North's office, especially over the holidays."

"Does my uncle usually have trouble finding a replacement? I know it's a tradition for them to be out of town for December." Lorelei glanced around at the town in front of her. Her mouth hung open slightly as if impressed by every little thing she saw.

Tyler couldn't help but stare and wonder what she was thinking. Since he'd lived there so long, he appreciated an outsider's viewpoint. *I wonder how she sees Oakvale ...*

"The Norths leave every December 1st and return every December 31st without fail," Arlene stated, readjusting her plum-colored scarf to cover more of her neck.

"I hope they make an exception this year. I'd love to see my aunt and uncle and have them meet Mary Ann." Lorelei returned her attention to Tyler. "Where do they go? All I know is they travel."

"You don't know?" Tyler found himself staring at her as though he could see her soul through her eyes. "They go north."

"More north than here?" Lorelei's forehead creased. "Canada?"

"I don't know if they have ever said where they go," Richard announced. "I guess no one's ever really asked directly. They've been leaving every December since . . . forever."

"Wherever it is they travel to, must be pretty special to leave all this behind." Lorelei gestured to the gathering crowd around the Christmas tree.

"Come on," Tyler motioned at Lorelei. "I know the perfect spot for viewing the tree lighting."

"Nice meeting you both. I hope to see you around, but not in the doctor's office." Lorelei laughed.

"You'll see us around indeed," Arlene stated and took hold of Richard's hand.

His parents headed closer to the tree as Tyler directed Lorelei to the left of the crowd.

"Should we be moving away from the Christmas tree?" She switched Mary Ann back to her other hip as they made their way to Kim and Diane's Thrifty Finds.

Situated on the corner, the women's thrift shop stood nestled to the right of Sharon's Café. Kim and Diane's Thrifty Finds was a two-story classic brick building with four concrete steps up to the main door. Garland and white lights wrapped the railings leading the way up on either side of the steps. Thankfully, the middle railing was left bare so people could use it when the steps were slippery from ice.

"The sign says Closed." Lorelei pointed.

"It's unlocked." Tyler pushed down on the brass handle and stepped inside the dimly lit store.

Cautiously, Lorelei made her way through the door. "Are you sure? I'd hate to upset someone during my first few hours of arriving in town."

Clear Christmas lights provided the only lighting as the main lights were shut off upon closing. The musty scent of past lives and wood hovered in the air as they stepped farther into the store.

Tyler chuckled. "Yes, Kim and Diane know I always come up here for the tree lighting."

"No one else does, though?" Lorelei followed Tyler past the displays of dishes, picture frames, knickknacks, and records to the back of the store.

"Folks enjoy being around others, chatting it up, but for me, this is the best view. I've been coming up here for more years than I can count." And this was the only time Tyler had ever invited someone with him. The realization hit him as he started up the stairs, and he grabbed the handrail as the thought of it made him slightly dizzy with the anticipation of sharing something special. He'd never taken any girlfriends up here.

When they reached the top of the steps, he pointed toward the window across the way. As they crossed the room, the wooden floor planks beneath his boots creaked and moaned from age. The view of the Christmas tree with all of the town's residents huddled around it came into view.

"Wow, you're right. This is a much better perspective." Lorelei moved Mary Ann to the front of her, resting the baby's back on her chest.

"I'm sorry." Tyler leaned closer to the window and then turned back to her. "I should've asked if you wanted to go into a dark building with a stranger first. We can leave if you want."

Lorelei's eyes remained on the view. "No, this is great. Plus, I've taken many self-defense classes." She winked.

Tyler rubbed his hand over his mouth, trying to cover up his smile. "Should be any minute now. These old windows are pretty thin, so we can hear the countdown."

And as if cued by Tyler, the crowd's echo of "ten, nine, eight" filtered up to them.

"Your first tree lighting, Mary Ann." Lorelei lowered her head, matching her cheek up to her daughter's. "Three, two, one."

The Christmas tree's glowing lights filtered through the windows, and Tyler watched the reflection in the eyes of Lorelei and her daughter. The glow cast shadows off the walls and illuminated the space. Cheering and clapping from below followed.

"It's beautiful, like a painting from up here." She continued to stare at the tree.

Festive colored lights filled out the Christmas tree, and the bright-gold star atop projected beams of glittery radiance from its points. Tyler lost track of how long they stood there, staring at the view, until Mary Ann squealed and kicked her legs.

"Thank you again. This was a wonderful vantage point." Lorelei turned to Tyler.

"You're welcome. Are you ready for the best cider of your life?" He clapped his hands together and then rubbed them.

"I'm ready for cider, but I will be the judge of if it's the best. Speaking of Cider, where is your dog?"

Tyler led the way to the stairs. "She's hanging out with her best buddy, Garrison, over at the bookstore."

"A bookstore allows dogs? This town really is the best."

"Garrison is the bookstore's mascot, so to speak." Tyler held the store's door open for a radiant Lorelei. As they headed back toward the Christmas tree, the smell of snow filled the air, crisp and delicate at the same time. The desire to place his arm around her shoulder came out of nowhere and caused his arm to twitch. *Remember, she's leaving at the end of the month.*

Chapter 6

"You were right. This is the best apple cider I've ever tasted." Lorelei held the steaming mug under her chin with one hand. Her phone rested upside down on the table as she perched on the edge of the chair.

Mary Ann sat in a wooden high chair while Lorelei handed Mary Ann the bottle. Her daughter took in the scene of residents milling about Sharon's Café. The space felt like something out of a historical society museum. Tin squares lined the ceiling that was at least eighteen-feet high. There were only square tables with matching wooden chairs to accommodate customers, nary a booth insight.

Each table showcased a Christmas-themed vinyl tablecloth with a slight bit of fabric backing on its reverse side. A mahogany chair rail ran the interior of the café, garland and lights resting on the thin lip. Classic ornaments decorated two six-foot-tall trees, one near the front door and the other at the cash register. Floor-to-ceiling wood-framed windows flanked the front door, showcasing the Christmassy town outside. The scent of sugar and warm butter filled the air.

"This place is special, don't cha think?" Tyler asked and then took a sip of his cider.

Lorelei realized her mouth hung open in awe of the café, and she bit her lip to close it some. "There is a peaceful feeling here. It's welcoming, as though I've come here every day of my life."

"Does Minneapolis have a café or restaurant that feels homey?"

Lorelei noticed how Tyler leaned back in his chair, utterly relaxed while she continued to sit rigid on the edge of hers. She traced the outline of a snowman on the tablecloth. "Yes, it has many, but I never have the chance to spend time in any of them. Unless, of course, you want to count the hospital's cafeteria as homey." She glanced up at Tyler, his golden-brown eyes staring at her.

"Are you looking for more than a vacation in Oakvale?" He sipped his cider but didn't take his eyes off her.

"My parents love me working as an ER doctor. They proudly paid for medical school specifically because I vowed to become a doctor at Minneapolis's Metro Central Hospital. Don't get me wrong, I love being a doctor. But since adopting Mary Ann, things have changed, goals have changed. For starters, childhood memories of visiting my aunt and uncle who lived in Wyoming on a farm started to pop into my thoughts more so than normal. One hundred acres of pure heaven. They had a rope swing, a pond, a barn, horses, a tractor—you name it. If it was something fun, they owned it. Every time I looked at Mary Ann, I realize I want that for her, all the time."

"So why Oakvale and not Wyoming for your December getaway?"

"It's closer, for starters. My parents wanted to spend time with Mary Ann on her first Christmas."

"For starters? What's after starters?" Tyler leaned slightly forward.

"I don't want to be an ER doctor anymore. Maybe I never did. I'm not sure. My parents are waiting for me to move up the corporate ladder at the hospital. See, my dad retired from Minneapolis's Metro Central Hospital about a year after I started my residency there. His goal was to be on the board of directors. Be the Dean of Medicine, but he wasn't accepted."

"So now he wants to live his dream through you." Tyler rubbed his thumb against the side of the mug.

Lorelei nodded. "Yes, he wants me to be what he wasn't able to be." She drummed her fingers on her arm. "I have zero desire to be on the board of directors. And, my parents are not big on what they call the 'tiny dreams of a small-town doctor.' In fact, that's putting it lightly. The notion of me vacationing here was enough to cause them concern, but leaving my position to be a small-town doctor and raising Mary Ann in a small town would be impossible for them to understand." She shook her head and gazed off.

"But, Oakvale is amazing. It's the best small-town life has to offer. And your aunt and uncle are here the rest of the year. Then again, I haven't traveled much to know. Not outside of a great novel, that is. I have been saving up to travel to all my favorite places I've discovered in books."

"Literary works are amazing time-traveling assistants. Not to mention, it sounds like an astounding trip." Lorelei thought of all the novels she'd read that transported her around the world. "What is your favorite book?"

Tyler glanced at his cider as the steam rose from the green-and-red mug. "*A Far Off Place* by Laurens van der Post."

"So, one place on your travel list is the Kalahari Desert?"

Tyler's face radiated his smile. "Yes, I can't wait to see the beauty of it all."

"They made a movie from it, right?" Lorelei ran her hand over Mary Ann's hair. "I saw the movie, but I didn't know it was a book first."

"Yes, a children's movie, sometime in the nineties. What about you? What's your favorite book?"

Oddly enough, no one had ever asked her such a question, but she instantly knew the answer. "I love so many books, but my favorite is *Main Street* by Sinclair Lewis. You probably haven't ever heard of it."

"I have, but I've yet to read it. And I've probably read nearly every book published from the early years till now. However, a few have slipped through the cracks. Once Upon a Book is like my second home."

Lorelei watched Mary Ann suck from her bottle. "That's what I want for Mary Ann. A place where she can be a kid and explore. A place where I have the time to get to know everyone in the community. My parents think she can't have what they call proper experiences and education in a small town."

"It's hard for me to understand their logic. Small towns provide a community. Not that a city environment can't, but there is something to be said for knowing everyone and essentially having a huge support system. Everyone here is like family. A giant family without room to spare at the table, but we all gather around regardless."

Lorelei set her cider down and reached her hand out, placing it on Tyler's hand. She didn't know why she felt a sudden closeness to him, so she pulled it back and wrapped her fingers around her mug again. "Help me convince my parents of that." She sighed and gazed out the café's window at the town. "I guess it doesn't matter; the rental and job are only for December. Plus, Mary Ann needs her grandparents as much as I need their approval."

"Wait, now." Tyler shifted in his chair. "Your parents, where did they grow up?"

"They both grew up in big cities. My father is from New York City, and my mom's from Chicago."

Tyler chuckled and brought his hand to his mouth. "I'm sorry. I don't mean to laugh." He ran his hand through his hair as if to buy time. "Two big-city folks raised a girl who wants a small-town life."

"It's funny, right?" Lorelei smirked and checked her phone. "Anyway, enough about my problems. Forget I mentioned anything. You have to tell me the story about the bowling alley slash real estate office."

Tyler nodded his head. "Indeed I do. But you might find it easier to relax if you ignore your phone."

She pressed her lips together. "Yeah, it's hard. I'm so used to doing three things at once. It's weird to relax."

"I think after a week here you'll learn to relax. It will drape over you like a cozy sweater. But the bowling alley story would be best if I share it in the place of origin. We can enjoy the Christmas tree and head over there. I'd bet you came to this small town to explore every bit of it, even if it's chilly out there."

Lorelei downed the last of her cider and set the mug with Santa's face back on the table. "You're right." She stood, wrapped her scarf back up, dropped her phone into the baby bag, and unbuckled Mary Ann from the high chair.

Tyler raised a hand in a wave to a woman with straight-as-paper hair wearing a bold green Christmas-themed sweater. "I'll see you around, and thanks for the cider."

She approached the table. "Sorry, it's been busy tonight. I'm Sharon, the owner." After wiping her hand on the cherry-red half apron around her waist, she extended it.

Lorelei shook Sharon's warm, firm hand. "Nice to meet you. I'm Lorelei, and this is my daughter, Mary Ann."

Sharon touched Lorelei's back and then the baby's. She smelled like nutmeg and cinnamon. "You and your daughter come back anytime you wish."

"Of course, I most certainly plan on it." Lorelei beamed.

Sharon gave a quick smile and then turned to welcome a couple coming through the door. The one thing Lorelei noticed since her arrival only a few hours ago was that everyone smiled. Everyone.

As they made their way across the street and around the Christmas tree, Lorelei's pace slowed to a mere shuffle. She couldn't stop admiring the tree, all decorated and lit up. It represented Oakvale. Happy, inviting, full of friendship. Staring at the Christmas tree, Lorelei knew it might break her heart when she and Mary Ann headed back home.

The snow continued to fall in light sheets as though kisses from the clouds. Some residents still milled around the tree, steam wafting from paper cups, conversations light in tone. The sidewalks held those moving about between pausing and chatting with one another.

Tyler unlocked the door to the bowling alley, and Lorelei stepped inside with Mary Ann.

"Want to play a few frames?" Tyler unbuttoned his jacket and removed his gloves, shoving them in the pockets.

"I don't have any place to set Mary Ann down."

"We have a high chair somewhere in the closet. I'll grab it." Tyler made his way from the desk to the side of the office area.

"This town is dog and kid-friendly for sure."

"Little tykes have used it, but I assure you it's clean."

She could quickly grow used to Tyler and his helpfulness. Not that she needed it, she loved being a single parent; however, long workdays proved to be more of a challenge than she'd imagined. There were times when she could use the extra support, and Lorelei couldn't ignore the fact that she wanted someone to share in Mary Ann's first moments. After long days at work or stressful situations, it would be nice to unwind with someone. She found herself as drawn to Tyler as she was to Oakvale.

He lifted a dated wooden high chair from the closet and made his way over to the lanes on the right of the office area. Tyler flipped some switches on the wall next to a beverage bar setup. Before her, four lanes lit up like an airport runway, and the low ceiling shined bold fluorescent lighting down upon them.

"We can have full lights or"—Tyler flipped a few switches—"a Christmas spectacular!"

The fluorescent lights faded, and in their place, multicolored Christmas lights and projected snowflakes spilled over the lanes. Lorelei didn't realize it, but she gasped at the display in front of her. A black light illuminated from the rear of the lanes, sending tiny white snowflakes cascading down each lane's length. Green

Christmas trees waltzed over the shiny lane floors, and carols drifted from the speakers.

"This is the most beautiful office slash bowling alley I've ever seen." Lorelei glanced at Mary Ann, hoping she noticed all that was before her. "Look, baby girl."

Mary Ann's eyes widen at the glow, waving her arms and squealing with joy. Lorelei walked to where Tyler had set the highchair and placed her daughter in it, buckling her up. Lorelei removed her scarf and jacket, placing them on a nearby chair.

"It's been a long time since I last bowled," Lorelei announced, pushing up her long sleeves.

"No worries, I won't laugh at you, promise." Tyler grinned. "I can put up the bumpers for you."

Lorelei waved her hands like she was waving down a taxi. "No, no, no. I'm not that bad." She bumped her shoulder into Tyler's. "I don't think."

Tyler went to the shoe rack and picked out a pair in his size, then handed another pair to Lorelei.

"How do you know my size?" she asked, taking them.

"My first job." Tyler kicked off his boots and laced up the bowling shoes.

Lorelei sat on an orange plastic swivel chair that was bolted to the floor behind the scoring console and removed her boots, replacing them with the bowling shoes. "Looks like you still got it." She glanced up and winked at Tyler.

Stop it! She should not be acting like they were friends; they'd just met. So she couldn't understand why she felt so close to him so quickly. *You are not staying but a few weeks. Don't get attached.* Lorelei couldn't stop thinking about how much she enjoyed being with Tyler under the glow of the bowling alley's Christmas spectacular.

Trying to ignore everything her heart was beating for, she searched for a bowling ball that fit her best. "So, are you going to tell me the story behind this place?"

Tyler snatched a bowling ball from the rack and headed to the second lane before pausing. "Ladies first." He motioned with his left hand.

Chapter 7

L orelei curtsied and lined up with the lane. *She's cute.* Looking at her caused Tyler to smile. She wiggled her shoulders and then wiggled the rest of the way down to her feet. Lifting the ball up to shoulder height, she lowered it down and back in a swing, then released it down the lane. The ball slammed into four pins, knocking them down, leaving the rest to gloat.

"Not bad, it's been years upon years. I think I had braces last time I bowled." Lorelei stepped back toward the ball return and yawned. "So, story?"

Tyler stood, cradling his bowling ball with a slight smile. "When my parents moved here, I was about five. They'd heard about this building up for sale. The prior owners had moved on. My parents' background was . . . is in real estate, they knew nothing about running a bowling alley."

Lorelei's ball slid up through the mechanism, and she readied herself for the remaining pins. She frowned when only one pin tipped over and took a seat at the little desk with the scoring console.

He lined up his shoes and took a practiced stride forward, releasing the ball down the lane. After the ball knocked down all but one pin, Tyler returned to his story. "When they arrived, the residents were vocal about not losing the bowling alley, and my parents didn't know what to do with it. My folks struggled with a decision because they didn't want to upset the town."

Tyler returned to the lane and effortlessly sent the ball to do its job, taking out the final pin with a spare. "But in the end, a compromise made everyone happy."

"I'm glad to hear it." Lorelei snatched up her ball and stared down the lane. "You have way more bowling skills than I do. But it sounds as though you've had years of near-daily practice."

She released the ball and leaned to the right as though the ball would follow her lead. Tyler pressed his lips together to keep from chuckling aloud. The pins tumbled.

"Strike! Yes!" Lorelei pumped her fists in the air and spun around toward Tyler.

Mary Ann fed off her mom's excitement and squealed, smacking her hands on the high chair's tray.

"So, your parents kept the bowling alley and started up their real estate business?"

Tyler went for his ball, waiting for the machine to reset the pins. "Yes, they restarted it up, so to speak. They'd both worked for a well-known real estate firm out of St. Paul and were looking to open their own business and raise me in a small town. They switched up the bowling alley slightly, removing the area that held all the shoe rentals and snack bar, and replaced it with the real estate office. They added the self-service beverage bar and shoe checkout. And it's still the town's gathering place, depending on how busy the pizza place and café end up. Sometimes residents will sit for hours over coffee reminiscing about the past, laughing at stories."

Lorelei went to her jacket, pulled out some toys from the oversize pockets, and set them in front of Mary Ann. "Did you like growing up here?"

Tyler released the ball but didn't stay to watch what pins it knocked over. All his attention remained on Lorelei and the way she glowed from within. Spending time with her created a feeling of joy inside of him. He tried to explain it to himself, but he'd never felt such emotion before, and even with all of his years of reading, he couldn't find the words. *It's only been a few hours, what's up with all the feelings? Knock it off. This is not middle school.*

"Tyler?" Lorelei stood in front of him.

"Yes, I loved it." Tyler turned around to see all the pins still standing. "And I want to raise my family here too." He pulled at his ear, itching behind it. "Did I not hit a single pin?"

Lorelei shook her head. "Maybe I can beat you after all." She smirked and tapped his arm with the back of her hand.

A chill ran through his entire body as though he'd stepped outside without a jacket on. It reminded him of when he read a great scene in a book or saw the beauty in nature—a feeling of peace and excitement at the same time.

"More cider?" He pointed to the beverage bar. "It's not as good as Sharon's, but . . . I can go back to the café and get us some more—if you want, I mean. You don't have to." *Stop rambling!*

"I'd love some, but I'm thinking Mary Ann and I should probably head home sooner rather than later. I still need to unpack, and I'm a little tired from the drive. Plus, I worked sixty-two hours this week, and I'm in need of catching up on my sleep."

"Of course. I'm sure your daughter could use a good night's sleep, too."

Lorelei picked up her bowling ball. "I must sound so old." Her face scrunched. "You're nice to welcome us. I'm sorry." The ball sailed down the lane, taking out all but the three right pins.

"You don't sound old at all. I would say I'm tired too, but I didn't want to sound like a copycat." Tyler grinned.

"But we must finish this game." Lorelei waited at the ball return. "Tell me something about the Norths. I know they're my family, but I don't know much about my aunt and uncle. It's kind of sad. I hope that changes soon."

"Let's see, they always rent out their home every December, and the company—my company, well, the *family* company—has always managed it, except this time. I will say that when your uncle dropped off the contract, I don't think I've seen him smile so grand."

"It's been a few years coming, at least on my end. I'm sure they've asked my parents to visit." Lorelei cradled the bowling ball. "My dad and his sister Candace were never close from what I've heard. There is a ten-year age gap between them and completely different lifestyles. My folks are not big on small-town Christmases. Do you know they asked me if I'd have internet here or if I have to go into Booth?" She laughed and ended it with another yawn.

"We do have internet." Tyler tilted his head. "And the Norths have mentioned you over the last few years. They said how they tried to get you and your parents to come up a few Christmases ago."

"We've been in touch more often since I became a doctor. My Aunt Candace loves to pen letters still and knows about my love for small-town life." Lorelei waved her hand at the thought. "Enough about me, did your parents have to learn how to run the bowling alley? Or does it run itself?" The alley filled with the sound of three pins knocked over by Lorelei's ball.

"It does run itself for the most part, which is why they made it more self-serve. It allowed me to be in charge as a kid. By the age of ten, I could wax the floors and repair and maintain the pinsetter and the ball return."

"Very impressive. At age ten, I was dressing up in party attire and putting on makeup." Lorelei grinned, batting her lashes. She took a seat on the chair and leaned on her knees. "Why are your parents so set on you keeping the business running? It sounds to me like it's not your dream job." Lorelei rubbed her lips together. "I don't mean to sound crass."

Tyler sat next to her. "Not at all, I ask myself that every day. It's because I don't have the guts to confront my parents. And it's the reason I gave up on my original dream of owning the bookstore." He chuckled. "It's not funny, but it's true."

Lorelei giggled. "I'm sorry. I'm not laughing at you." She started giggling again.

Tyler leaned into Lorelei and bumped her arm. "I think you are." He smiled.

She continued to giggle uncontrollably, gasping for breath. Tyler folded his arms and waited for her to stop.

"Okay," she gasped. "I'm sorry. The reason I'm laughing is because we're in the same boat. I can't find the courage to make the life I want for myself and my daughter."

"We're adults. Why can't we be . . . adults?" Tyler inquired, leaning back in the plastic curved chair. "Are you an only child?"

"Yes, and you?"

"Yes, and that's why—because our parents' dreams were forced wholly upon us versus spread over several other siblings."

The bell above the office door rang.

"Ty?" a female voice called out.

"Jodi, hi." He spun around toward the door.

"Here are your keys, thanks again. I—" Jodi froze, her hand outstretched with the keys. "Sorry, I didn't know you were with someone."

Tyler stood up. "No worries. Jodi, this is Lorelei, your new boss."

Lorelei eased off the chair as though trying to gain composure from her laugh-fest moments ago. "Hi, nice to meet you."

Tyler gathered the keys from Jodi as she moved to shake Lorelei's hand.

"Nice to meet you, Doctor," she offered with her brow twisted.

Lorelei held up her hand. "No, please, Lorelei is fine."

"I heard from Dr. North that you work as an emergency room doctor. I'm pretty sure you should be addressed properly." Jodi clasped her hands together.

As long as Tyler had known Jodi, she was easily impressed, which was probably how she'd been suckered into buying her lemon of a car.

"Trust me"—Lorelei lifted her daughter from the high chair—"just because it cost an astronomical amount of money for my degree, doesn't make me any more important or useful than you or Tyler or anyone in this town for that matter."

Great, she's humble, too. Tyler ran his hand through his hair as if doing so would lessen his growing attraction to Lorelei's soul.

Jodi softly smiled and held her hands together. "And who is this little one?" She loved babies, and it took every ounce of her willpower not to snatch them from their parents' arms so she could hug them. Although he'd seen it happen more than once.

"This is my daughter, Mary Ann." Lorelei smiled down at her as she balanced her on her hip.

Jodi reached her finger out, and Mary Ann spotted it, taking hold of it. The smile on Jodi's face showcased how much she enjoyed being around children.

"How do you know Tyler? Oh, are you . . . together?" Lorelei leaned back from Jodi. "I hope it's okay that we were hanging out. He was only trying to show me around town, make sure I met some people."

Jodi placed her hand on her chest and chuckled as she glanced over at Tyler. "No, Tyler and me?"

"Hey, now, Jodi, be a bit nicer to my ego, please," Tyler joked.

Lorelei looked at Tyler and then back at Jodi. "So, you're not . . . ?"

"Dating? Together?" Jodi's voice was high. "No."

"We're great friends. We grew up together," Tyler added. "This is a close-knit community, and everyone is as close as family. Jodi and I—" He glanced at Jodi, rubbing the back of his neck.

"We drive each other nuts. We're like brother and sister." Jodi made a funny face at Mary Ann, and she responded with a belly giggle.

He glanced over at Lorelei. Did her face relax as though she was relieved by this news?

"Yes, I can only handle so much *Jodi* at a time." Tyler winked.

"I think Lorelei understands." Jodi elbowed him.

Tyler rested his arm on Jodi's shoulder and smirked.

She pointed at him. "See, this is what I'm talking about. Annoying." Jodi laughed and slid out from under his arm. "Anyway, I'm your uncle's secretary at the office. I hope you don't find me annoying because we'll be working together for the entire month. And even if you fire me, I'll only be going upstairs. I live in the house, too."

"You seem lovely, Jodi." Lorelei smiled. "And what an amazing commute."

"Once you see Jodi's car, you'll understand she can't handle a commute at all." Tyler prodded. "Unless she could push her car to work."

"And that's why she borrowed your truck?" Lorelei tilted her head.

"Exactly, her car is too amazing even to drive." Tyler nodded and crossed his arms.

"Don't teach Lorelei your ways." Jodi shook her finger at him. "My car . . . it . . . it runs when it wants to, and it chose to take the night off."

"That sounds like a pain. I guess it's a great thing that you live where you work." Lorelei switched hips as Mary Ann drifted off to sleep, her head drooping and wobbling. "If you ever need to run an errand or anything, let me know, and I can take you." Lorelei leaned her cheek on her daughter's head.

For the first time in years, Tyler was grateful for running the family business. Without assisting the Norths with their rental, he wouldn't have been in a position to work this closely with her. Sure, it might sound drastic, but joy spread through him, knowing in a small way his family business still had a purpose. Unfortunately, she wouldn't be staying, and he would soon be traveling for months in an effort to live out at least one dream.

Chapter 8

S he unlocked the Norths' house door and carried a sleeping Mary Ann inside. Thankfully, she'd left the kitchen lights on to guide her through the unfamiliar home. The suitcases remained in the entryway, causing Lorelei to sigh.

"Ugh, unpacking," she whispered and rolled her eyes as she set Mary Ann on the blanket on the living room floor. She gazed out at the merrily illuminated backyard, instantly feeling bad about complaining. Without a doubt, Lorelei knew she could stare at the surrounding forest 365 days a year—decorated for Christmas or not—and never tire of it.

As she lugged the suitcases up the mahogany stairs, her thoughts returned to the stairs at Kim and Diana's thrift store. All she wanted to do was immerse herself in each store in town, studying their history. Lorelei desired to meet everyone and for everyone to know her and Mary Ann. She wanted to wave at them from across the street, share a story or a cup of cider.

After the suitcases were all upstairs and set in the main bedroom, she went down the hall and opened two closed doors. One revealed a guest room with a king-size bed and an antique dresser. When she opened the second door, her eyes lit up. The room held two twin beds and a crib. Under the window sat a glide rocker next to a bookshelf full of children's literature and a bin of toys.

"This is perfect," she said aloud to the empty room. Her shoulders rose to the ceiling in joy as she rubbed her hands together, cupping them and exhaling warmth into them. "If only this house would heat up."

She returned to the thermostat at the bottom of the stairs. It was the same model she had at her condo. The screen showed sixty degrees, but no air, hot or cold, came from it when she placed her hand on a return. Lorelei checked the time on her cell phone, and at just after ten, it was a little too late to call Tyler about what to do. Returning to the kitchen, she reread the note from the Norths, still befuddled by no contact number. It did say any issues should be brought to Tyler's attention. And since her aunt and uncle didn't have a cell phone to reach them at, it made sense.

Lorelei peeked at her daughter, still sleeping on her back on the blanket, as she made her way over to the fireplace. After removing all the wet wood from when she poured water on it earlier, she stacked a set of dry wood in and lit it up. The wood crackled and snapped as the fire spread around each log. She and Mary Ann would need to sleep in the living room tonight in front of the warm fireplace.

Once she'd slipped into her pajamas and brushed her teeth, Lorelei shut off all the lights and snatched a pillow and a blanket off the bed upstairs before returning to the living room. Snuggling up next to her daughter, she covered them both up and propped the down-feather pillow under her head. She had a view of the lighted trees through the French doors on her right and the glow of the fireplace to her left. Her mind instantly went to Tyler and his dimpled smile. She warmed at the way he made her feel, as if she was home, even though Oakvale was far from her condo. There was something magical about their meeting that Lorelei couldn't put her finger on quite yet. It was interesting that they faced the same struggle with their parents. Maybe they could help each other. Maybe she'd be able to help Tyler fulfill his bookstore dream.

Rubbing the chill from her fingers, she turned on her side and gazed at her daughter as the fireplace's glow danced across her face. She wanted nothing more than to give Mary Ann what she felt was the best life possible. Sleep washed over Lorelei, making her eyes heavy as she tried to formulate a plan that might help Tyler and her.

Morning light broke through the house's back windows, causing Lorelei to stir. She rubbed her eyes, grazing her frozen nose. At least it felt frozen as she opened her eyes and lifted her head off the pillow. Sitting completely up, she wrapped her arms around herself.

"It's ice-cold in here." Lorelei made sure Mary Ann was still covered in the blanket and stood up. The fire had all but died out at some point, and the house must have been in the mid-fifties. The clock on the stove read 8:10. She picked up her cell phone, ignored the notifications she needed to answer, and punched in Tyler's number. While it rang, Lorelei stacked the remaining logs inside the fireplace.

"Tyler, hi. It's Lorelei. I hope I'm not calling too early."

Lorelei flicked the lighter under the newspaper.

"No, not at all." Tyler's voice was scratchy.

She bit her lip, knowing she'd indeed woken him up. "The heater's not working, and it's freezing in here. I have the same thermostat, so I don't think it's user error. Is there a repair person I can call?"

"Oofta! I'll head right over. Give me five minutes."

"Thank you, I appreciate it."

After ending the call, a babbling noise drew her attention to the floor. Mary Ann had awakened and rolled over onto her stomach, lifting her head and chest off the blanket.

"I know, baby girl." She scooped up her daughter. "I'm sorry it's cold in here. Tyler is coming to see what's wrong." As the words left her lips, Lorelei's eyes widened. With her daughter in tow, she rushed to the hall mirror. Her strawberry blonde bob stuck out at odd angles; the calculated choppy layers now looked jagged and uneven, some strands forked off in two opposite directions, defying gravity and geometry. Yesterday's mascara circled her eyes like a raccoon.

Mary Ann bounced on her mom's hip as she ran down the hall and scurried up the stairs. With one hand, Lorelei dug through the open suitcase in the bedroom and pulled out a hairbrush. After taming her bob, she opened Mary Ann's suitcase and grabbed the baby wipe bin. Once in the bathroom, she took the baby wipe to her eyes, removing the leftover mascara.

"How does Mommy look?" Lorelei turned to her daughter. Mary Ann reached out her hand, trying to grab at her mom's hair.

There was a knock at the door, and she hurried down the stairs. "Hi, Tyler. You got here quick."

The outdoor temperature, which came inside along with Tyler, didn't seem much colder than the temperature inside the house.

"It's freezing in here." Tyler closed the front door behind him. "Why didn't you call me earlier?"

"I didn't want to disturb you late at night. And I didn't know a repair company to call." She switched Mary Ann to her other hip and looked around Tyler. "Where's Cider?"

"I left him at home. I didn't know how keen you'd be to having a dog in the house."

"You can always bring Cider. I love dogs."

"Thank you, that's great to know." Tyler removed his gloves. "If I can't fix it, we can call Don."

"Does Don own a heating and electric repair business? Should I have called him instead of you?" Lorelei asked.

"No, the Norths were specific about you calling me first. Plus, they don't have a cell phone or a way to contact them. However, they usually leave Don's number."

"Seems odd. But it makes sense that someone should be reachable if a problem arose."

"Don runs the convenience store, but he is the handiest man in Oakvale. If he's not able to fix it, then we will need to buy a new . . . whatever is needed. But Don can fix just about anything."

Lorelei headed down the hall, stopping at the edge of the kitchen. "Would you mind watching Mary Ann for two seconds? I need to get her playpen out of the sedan."

"Of course." Tyler held out his hands for Lorelei to place her daughter in them.

After she handed Mary Ann over, she threw on her jacket and scarf and snatched up the keys. Upon returning inside with the playpen, she heard Tyler talking about the thermostat to her daughter. "Let's see if we can fix this for you and your mommy before your fingers start falling off from frostbite."

Lorelei passed them and set up the playpen between the kitchen and living room. "You seem great with kids," she called down the hall.

"Other than the bowling alley, my first, what I call real job, was hosting the children's story time over at Once Upon a Book. I read every picture book in the store for sure."

Lorelei pressed her lips together to keep from making an *aw* noise aloud. "And your handyman skills, where did they come from?"

As she approached Tyler and her daughter, all the blood surged to her heart, causing it to hammer. He had Mary Ann facing the thermostat while she chewed the handle of a screwdriver.

"To be honest, I'm the least-handy man in all of Oakvale."

Before she could even ask, Tyler replied to precisely what she was thinking.

"Don't worry. The screwdriver is clean. I always clean all of my tools. I have a neat-and-tidy disorder." He turned to Lorelei. Her daughter kicked her legs as she sat atop his left arm, his right clamped around her like a seat belt.

"Sounds as though you have a truckload of great qualities, Tyler." She lifted Mary Ann from his arms. "So, you and Jodi never dated in school?"

It was not any of her business, but it slipped from her mouth before she could reel it back in. Her feet stopped like she'd approached the edge of a cliff. "I'm sorry, forget I asked." She pivoted around, facing his direction.

He glanced at the floor and then back up at Lorelei. "I don't mind, and yes, we did date in high school."

Her lips formed an O as she nodded slightly.

Giving his hand a wave of don't care, he said, "I think it was three dates, and we discovered we had nothing in common other than Oakvale and decided to stay friends. And she's a great friend."

A smile formed on Lorelei's face. As soon as she realized she was blushing, she spun around and set Mary Ann in the playpen. Then she brought her attention to her cell phone. She scrolled through and responded to a few of the text messages from some ER nurses back home. The room around her faded as her shoulders tensed with each continued minute tapping and swiping through the cell phone screens.

Get off your phone! Lorelei thought as she set the cell upside down on the counter and rolled her eyes at herself.

"Do you know what's wrong with the thermostat?" Lorelei called from the kitchen, where she'd started preparing the coffee maker. She double-checked her hair in the reflection of the microwave door, fluffing it up with her fingers.

Why am I having this concern about how I look around Tyler? she questioned herself, taking a deep breath. *Focus, you met him a day ago. You're not staying.*

"I think I need to go up into the attic." His voice was closer than she expected, and as she spun around, they were nearly nose to nose.

"Hi." Tyler's voice was as smooth as melted butter in a hot pot.

Lorelei swallowed. "Hi." Her cheeks instantly flushed.

In an attempt to get her cheeks to return to normal, she opened cupboards, making sure to hide her face under the guise of locating the mugs. "Want some coffee?"

"That sounds great, but let me climb up there and see if I can figure out what's wrong first. It's too cold in here for you and Mary Ann."

Lorelei reached out for the countertop as a wave of calmness washed over her. It didn't take but a few seconds to realize the calm wave was a release of responsibility. Someone else to shoulder the weight of a problem for her and Mary Ann. Her daughter started to fuss in the playpen as Lorelei prepared her formula. With a warm bottle in one hand and a coffee mug in the other, she set them both on the coffee table, picked up her daughter, and sat on the couch. In front of them, the fire crackled as they enjoyed their warm drinks. Outside, snow fell in tight, tiny crystals. Leaning her head back on the couch, a smile formed on her lips. This is what small-town life was all about. A helping community, not checking her cell phone every five minutes, no running around keeping up with a constantly busy schedule. Regardless of her fast-forming crush on Tyler, she instantly appreciated the sense of friendship.

"Well," Tyler said as he entered the living room, "looks like we're calling Don." He wiped his hands on a small blue cloth. "At least the fireplace is warming up this area a bit. You both look cozy." He leaned over the couch and smiled at them.

"We are, join us. It's far too early to be up and about." Lorelei began rising from the couch, her mug empty. "I need a refill, and I'll grab you a cup."

"Stay there. I'm already up." Tyler took her mug to the kitchen.

"Thank you. I like it black."

"I like mine black, too." Tyler refilled her mug and poured his own before sitting next to Mary Ann, who was propped up in a nest of pillows, holding her bottle.

"Thank you," Lorelei said, taking her cup from him.

"I do wish you'd called me as soon as you realized the heat wasn't working." He sipped from the mug. "Hopefully, Don can fix it."

As Lorelei shook her head, a large crash came from upstairs. Springing up off the couch, she nearly spilled her coffee as she jumped a foot in the air. "What was that?" she asked, raising her voice to be heard over Mary Ann's cries due to the commotion.

"Stay here. I'll go check." Tyler swiftly exited the living room, his coffee steaming as it sat on the end table.

Suddenly, Lorelei wanted to be back in her tiny condo, where she knew where every noise originated. Picking up Mary Ann, she swayed her gently on the couch, calming her tears.

"It's okay, baby. I'm sure it's nothing." Although it sounded like something to Lorelei—it sounded like someone or something was upstairs. Tyler had been up there only minutes before, so he would have seen if something was there. *Right?*

"It's okay! But it's not okay!" Tyler's voice echoed down the stairs.

Lorelei stood from the couch, taking her daughter with her. As they rounded the hall to the stairs, Tyler descended them, along with an extra burst of fridge air.

"We need to call Don for two things now." Tyler brushed snow off his shoulders.

"Why is there snow on you?" Lorelei's brow creased.

Tyler stood at the bottom of the steps, his hand on the banister. "There is a slight hole in the roof."

"Hole? *Slight*?"

Tyler glanced back up the stairs and then back at Lorelei. "Bowling ball size."

Chapter 9

"**Y**ou definitely have a hole." Don stared up at the snow coming through the open roof.

"I don't understand." Lorelei turned to Tyler. "You were up there, and you didn't see anything right before it happened. How did it manage to happen through the attic?"

"No attic in this spot." Don pointed. "See, this here roof angle . . . and over there, that angle, that's where the attic stops." He sported a red plaid ear-flap hat with matching scarf and jean overalls.

Tyler glanced over at Lorelei as she held Mary Ann, rocking her and probably trying to calm her nerves, too. While it was not her house, he could see Lorelei clenching her jaw—in less than twenty-four hours, she had no working heat and now a hole in the roof of her aunt and uncle's house. The noise they'd heard was not the snow but the ceiling's drywall collapsing into a vase of dried flowers. The vase set off a domino effect, leaning against a vertical stack of books which took out the classic double-bell alarm clock which toppled off the side of the dresser into the copper trash can three feet below. While downstairs, all Tyler and Lorelei had heard was a loud crash.

"You can fix it, right, Don? I mean, it's snowing inside." Lorelei brushed the snow off her nose.

"Yep, I can." Don remained focused on the hole.

Tyler patted Don on the back. He'd taken about thirty minutes to arrive after Tyler called. Don had finished ringing up the customers at this store, flipped the sign to Closed, and then bundled up to make the short drive out to the Norths' home. While Don was skilled in all things repair, he never succumbed to stress or troublesome situations. Which meant, while he could help, he didn't have the urgency of most. Things were done and done well but at a leisurely pace.

Lorelei's eyes jetted to Tyler, and she elbowed him.

"Don, what can I do to help? Bring in some supplies from the truck?" Tyler placed his hand on Don's back.

"That'd be nice." Don peered back up at the hole. "I'm trying to think what we'll need."

"It would be great if we could have you look in the attic at the furnace, too, since the thermostat is on the fritz." Tyler directed Don, ushering him out of the room.

"Yep, it is a might bit chilly in here. Let's get the stuff for the ceiling, and then we'll tackle the heat problem." Don's feet shuffled down the steps.

Tyler followed behind but turned back over his shoulder to Lorelei. "It's going to be okay," he mouthed.

He saw her pinch her eyes closed as though she might be wishing for a miracle. And he completely understood. As he helped Don unload supplies from his truck, Tyler couldn't erase the image of Lorelei when she'd opened the door this morning or the way he felt the second he was with her. His mind focused on how she walked with graceful but freeing, almost childlike steps, her genuine smile, and how he already recognized when something frustrated her. Never in his life had he paid attention to how someone walked before. Even thinking of it now seemed odd. Yet, the thought of how her shoulders squared up with confidence and her feet, joyful with each step, caused his dimples to appear.

"Tough break for Lorelei. This house has never had an issue that I know of, and now two things fail." Don fastened his tool belt around his waist. "I'll fix everything, and she'll be able to enjoy the house. And maybe you two can spend some time together."

Tyler's mind was lost on Lorelei, and he nodded his head in agreement without listening completely to Don's words.

"You should have her and the baby head into town today. The house will take a while to heat up once the issues are fixed. It might be good if she met more of the residents before she starts work come Monday."

Tyler pulled himself from his thoughts of Lorelei. "Sorry, Don, I only caught the last part of that."

Don placed his hand on Tyler's shoulder. "Less than a day, and you're already daydreaming about her."

Tyler waved off the comment. "No." Although, as the word lifted his mouth, it sounded more like a question. "She's only here temporarily. Regardless, you and I both know there's not a vacant house in town. Plus, Oakvale only needs one doctor."

As Don and Tyler reentered the home, Lorelei popped her head from around the kitchen wall. "Don, would you like any coffee?"

"No, thank you. I had three already this morning. It's nearing lunchtime." Don headed up the stairs.

Tyler checked his cell phone. Two minutes to ten. Don always closed the convenience store from eleven to eleven thirty so he could enjoy a nice leisurely lunch and read a few chapters from a book. Tyler knew this because most of the books Don read ran about thirty chapters. And he noticed every fifteen days Don would exit his store, cross the street, and headed into Once Upon a Book. After a good ten minutes, Don would leave the bookstore with a satisfied smile and a new book in hand, heading back across the street. Tyler also knew Don didn't read after work or on the weekends, or he would finish a book much sooner. Thinking of how much he knew about each Oakvale resident based on their book habits sparked a fire inside him. Tyler had developed a special skill, but he wouldn't win any game shows with it. Sharon loved sweet romance and cozy mysteries. Jodi devoured thrillers. His mom loved anything with an animal in it, and his dad a huge nonfiction fan. The townspeople often asked for book recommendations, and he used his skills readily to help Oakvale residents who were big booky fans. *Not to be confused with bookies.* And those hungry readers were what made Once Upon a Book a continuously thriving business.

"I can manage this alone if you want to head into town with Lorelei and her daughter." Don popped open his toolbox on the bedroom floor.

"I introduced her to a few residents yesterday. Unfortunately, I need to head over to work and get everything up and running. By the time everyone finishes their weekend chores and errands, they will be looking for something to do." Tyler itched at the morning scruff on his chin. Typically, he shaved his face before leaving the house each day, but in his mad dash, he hadn't taken the time.

"Good point, Tyler. I'll give you a call if anything comes up."

"Thanks, Don." He smiled and made his way downstairs to Lorelei.

Upon entering the living room, he found Lorelei and Mary Ann wrapped under a large throw blanket facing the fireplace. Her right hand was outside of the blanket, her thumb scrolling on the cell phone's screen.

He cleared his throat, and she tossed the phone next to her.

"I need to learn how to ignore my phone, or I'll never relax." Lorelei turned to Tyler. "How does it look?"

"Don can fix anything, even if he doesn't spring into action immediately," Tyler stated. "He did make a great suggestion. How about you head into town with Mary Ann and get to know everyone and look around the stores."

"It would be warmer than here." Lorelei's smile was weak but visible. "Will you be joining us? Maybe show me around my new office, too, unless you need to stay and help Don."

Tyler gasped internally. *Oofta!* Somehow, he completely forgot he needed to show her around the doctor's office before

Monday. "Yes, I have the keys at my office, but no, sorry, I won't be able to join you." Though he wanted to! "Whenever you're ready, stop by to grab them. I'm heading home to pick up Cider, then straight to the office." He rested his hand on the edge of the couch. "Bye, Mary Ann, I'll see you and your mommy later."

"You're leaving already? You can't stay to finish your coffee?" Lorelei pivoted her upper body on the couch.

At that moment, he finally understood why being an adult sucked at times. He would love nothing more than to spend the day with Lorelei and Mary Ann. In fact, he couldn't recall the last time he'd strolled around town enjoying the day. "Did you need me to stay?"

She opened her mouth and then brought her finger to her chin. "No, I guess not."

"You can trust Don. Your stuff is safe. And he can lock up when he's finished, drop off the key with me, and I'll track you down in town." Tyler pushed his hand into his pocket.

Lorelei batted her hand. "I'm not worried about any of that. Self-defense classes, remember." She stared at him as though she had something else to ask or say.

"Are you sure there isn't anything else?"

Running her hand over her neck, she removed the throw and stood up. "Nothing at all, thank you for everything. I'll get ready. Heading into town sounds like a great idea. Do you think I need to put the fire out?"

"No, but let Don know so he can make sure it's out before he leaves. He should be here a few hours, and by then, it'll have long died down." Tyler headed to the front door, but the weight of whatever Lorelei was holding back remained with him.

"See you shortly," she called from the kitchen. "Thanks again."

As he started up his truck, he couldn't help but pause, staring at the house. Between his heart and his mind, it felt as though a string was being tightened. Could he be missing Lorelei? Because it sure felt like it. The string drew tighter, and he took a deep breath, trying to loosen it without success. He was nearly certain he couldn't miss someone he'd only known for a day . . . could he? Reluctantly, he put the truck in drive and headed to work.

Chapter 10

T he heat blasted through the sedan's vents as Lorelei
turned onto the main road into town. Her fingers were
nice and warm by the time she pulled into a slanted parking
spot in front of the bowling alley. She noticed Tyler's truck and
saw the lights on inside of the office. It'd stopped snowing for
the moment, but the clouds warned it might start again at any
minute. Thankfully, with the sidewalks cleared, she could use
the stroller today.

Leaning over the steering wheel, she spent a few moments
taking everything in. Without the modern cars parked along
the road, the town looked the same as it might have in the
1950s. Lining the sidewalk, glittery green Christmas trees were
attached to light poles, while wires running across the streets
held oversized cherry-red bells and twisted silver garland. Every
storefront had multicolored lights running along the borders of
the windows.

After she loaded Mary Ann into her stroller, she waved at
Tyler, who happened to be milling about inside, Cider at his
side. He waved back. She wanted to give him his space to work
on whatever he needed to get done, and after all, she had seen
him less than an hour ago.

Lorelei wanted to explore the town with Tyler, as he could
surely tell her stories and provide a rich history. Plus, she'd
dressed up for her meet-and-greet, donning tights, boots, and a
long sweater under her jacket. But the boots slipped a bit, even

with the snow cleared off the sidewalk. Her outfit went perfectly with her coat which had the perfect pocket for easy access to check her phone.

Tyler had already stepped up to help out a ton and had proved to be a great host. He's probably friendly to everyone. Don't mistake his kindness for something romantic, she told herself.

Tyler stood in the doorway to the office, his hand holding the door open. "Hey, do you want me to take you over to the doctor's office now?"

"No, you work. Mary Ann and I can check out a few places. I don't want to interrupt your day." Lorelei adjusted her robin's egg blue scarf, shoving the loose end inside her coat.

"You're not." He smiled, and his dimples showed. "But my limited adult responsibilities are calling. I have yet to check on the pinsetters."

She glanced down the street, trying to keep from staring at him, but she couldn't—she was drawn to him like a favorite memory.

"How about we meet for lunch? Not a Don-time lunch." He chuckled. "What about at one? I can meet you over at the doctor's office, and by then, Don should be all done and back with the key. Then we can head over for lunch at the pizza place." He pointed to Oakvale Pizza Pie, the building next door.

"That sounds perfect." She gripped the stroller's handle with both hands.

"It's a date," Tyler chimed. "I mean, not a date. It's a specific time, but not a date, like a couple going on a date. It's a set time and place."

"Sounds like a date to me," Lorelei warned as she bit her lower lip to keep from smiling.

"No." Tyler shook his head. "I didn't mean a date, it sounds like a date, but we only met yesterday. Clearly, it can't be a date." His cheeks were as pink as radishes.

Lorelei stepped forward as she pushed the stroller in front of her. "See you at one for our date," she called in a joking tone.

"Fine! I guess it's a date!" Tyler exclaimed.

What had she done? What had gotten into her? She glanced over her shoulder to see Tyler grinning before he stepped back inside his office. As she continued on her way, she passed Oakvale Pizza Pie. Snow covered the tables and chairs in the outside sitting area next to it. Ahead of her was the lighted town Christmas tree in the center of the traffic circle. Once she crossed the street, Once Upon a Book was in front of her. The glow from the windows cast a soft and inviting atmosphere as they displayed hardcover books for all ages on a low shelf the length of each windowsill with greenery and Christmas lights weaved around them. Beyond the display, she saw people scanning the bookshelves and chatting. She spotted a set of preschool kids running in a circle around the front of the store. A woman opened the door, stepping outside, and held it for Lorelei and the stroller.

"Thank you." Lorelei beamed.

"You're welcome, dear. Strollers are only useful gadgets when you don't have to try and maneuver them through doors. Have a wonderful day."

"You as well." Lorelei pivoted her upper body back toward the door.

"Welcome, come on in." A short woman with curly gray hair approached her. "You must be Lorelei." She leaned over the stroller, her fuzzy crimson sweater blinked with Christmas lights in the shape of a tree, catching the infant's eye. "And this must be Mary Ann. Well, aren't you the happiest baby?" She stood up straight and thrust her hand outward. "I'm Sandy, my husband, Ted, and I own the store."

"It's nice to meet you, Sandy." Lorelei shook Sandy's firm hand, probably from all the book moving. "I've heard wonderful things about your store from Tyler." Lorelei wigged her feet in her boots as her right foot cramped up, causing her to regret her footwear.

A mixed-breed dog, possibly half hound, half Labrador waddled over, so she got on her knees. "Hi, there." Lorelei let the dog sniff her hands. "You must be Cider's best friend."

"Meet Garrison," Sandy stated as she waved goodbye to another customer leaving the store with a toddler in tow.

"Wonderful to meet you, Garrison." Lorelei stood back up and took in the bookstore. The smell of paper and wood danced in her nose. As calmness washed over her, her eyes blinked with sleepiness. Light filled every inch of the store without being harsh. She noticed the string of lights near the far-right corner and located the children's section.

"I see you already spotted what you were looking for. Go, have a look around. We can chat before you leave." Sandy stepped out of the way.

Lorelei pushed the stroller past the romance, mystery, and fiction sections, trying hard not to stop and get lost in the shelves. "Look at all these books, Mary Ann." Her daughter kicked her feet against the stroller as she chewed on her finger.

As Lorelei browsed the children's books, she pulled a few from the shelves and stacked them on top of the stroller near the handle. She had only brought one book for Mary Ann from all the chunky board books she had at home because she hadn't wanted to overpack, but of course, she realized now that one could never have too many books. Glancing over at the corner, she noticed a framed photo on the wall. As she moved closer, Lorelei recognized it was Tyler sitting on the floor with kids all around him, and Cider was in the mix, too. In his hand, he held a picture book, but she couldn't make out the title.

"The kids always love story time with Tyler." Sandy came up from behind her.

"I can imagine they do." Lorelei continued to stare at the picture, smiling. "Does he still come to read often?"

"Yes, all I have to do is ask, and there he is, sitting on the floor again, reading a story." Sandy wrapped her arms around herself. "I wish he would talk to his parents. Oh well, none of

my business. Let me know if you need any help locating a book."
She turned and headed back toward the register.

Lorelei stacked several books on top of the stroller and made her way to the adult section. Every time she went into a bookstore, she needed to restrain herself from buying all the books she could carry. She ran her hand over the embossed covers as she located one that caught her eye. Picking it up, she flipped it over and read the back cover blurb. Lorelei added it to the mound and continued to seek out another book. By the time she made it to the register, it felt as though she was pushing a stroller with twins in it.

"This is all . . . for now." Lorelei piled the books on the counter for Sandy to ring up.

"Some great choices. You're welcome to stop by anytime, especially for the Christmas reading." Sandy pointed at the flyers next to a cluster of poinsettias on the edge of the counter.

Once Upon a Book presents its annual O Come, All Ye Readers. Enjoy hot chocolate and apple cider. Story time for the kids. Pine cone decorating contest for all!!

"This sounds so fun!" Lorelei beamed. "Mary Ann and I will be here."

"Great. You must come to our Kiddo Story Time, it's every Sunday afternoon at two. It will give you a chance to meet other parents and maybe set up a play date or two for Mary Ann." Sandy placed the books into a paper bag with a tiny rope handle.

"Does Tyler read for that one, too?" Lorelei asked, hoping the answer was yes.

Sandy shook her head. "Sorry, you're stuck with my husband or me on Sundays."

"I didn't mean it like that." Lorelei's heart stuttered a beat, worried she'd come off as snooty.

Sandy smiled. "I didn't think you did. If we could have Tyler reading every Kiddo Story Time, we would." She winked. "But he does help out plenty."

"How long has the bookstore been for sale?"

"Not too terribly long. When Ted and I decided it was time to retire, we figured Tyler would jump at the chance. We've been openly discussing it for some time, and he mentioned he's been saving up for the occasion. But his fear of leaving his parents' business overruled. That's when he decided the money would be better spent on something that didn't affect the family's legacy—his book-settings trip. Which I understand, but ..." Sandy sighed and gazed off over Lorelei's shoulder, no doubt at the bowling alley. "His passion is here. Every resident sees it and knows it, but somehow his parents have no idea. We don't speak about it in front of them."

"Of course, I won't say anything, either. I can understand where he's coming from. I'm in a similar situation. I think when we look at something from the outside, we see the easy interpretation of it but forget the personal aspect."

Sandy tilted her head and looked at Lorelei. "You put it perfectly. I really should mind my business." She handed the shopping bag to Lorelei. "Maybe, if you two are going through similar situations, you can help each other out."

Lorelei thought about the statement as she put the bag into the stroller's bottom carrier basket. "Should we? I started to go down that road with him, but he seemed set on the travel plan." She'd fallen asleep thinking about the possibilities last night, but that was a mere musing, not something she should overstep or intrude on in his life.

"Only because Tyler feels that's his only option." Sandy walked out from behind the counter.

"But we don't know each other at all. We just met. It's not like I'm a high school friend or a long-lost relative. Giving unsolicited advice is usually not taken well. It's not like I'm his best friend Jodi." *Oh no, how did Jodi's name slip out!*

"Jodi and Tyler are great friends. But don't feel jealous."

Lorelei placed her hand on her chest. "Me? No, I'm not jealous. Jodi is very nice. I met her last night briefly." Oh no, she was definitely jealous. "I have no reason to be jealous. I'm only here for a month."

Sandy smiled into her coffee mug before she took a sip.

"I mean, I wish it could be more than a month, but . . . well, it's not that easy."

"Maybe you could work together and find out. After all, how do friendships start, but by working as a team for something great?"

Chapter 11

After situating Mary Ann's stroller out of the way, Tyler held the chair out for Lorelei, and she sat down. Residents were packed into every inch of Oakvale Pizza Pie. A low wall at the entrance provided a spot to hang stockings, and there were plenty, each with a special touch to show they were handcrafted and not some quick décor. There was no sign displayed, but every local knew it was a seat-yourself type of establishment.

"Is it always this busy?" Lorelei leaned toward Tyler, her head popping over the top of her laminated menu.

"Always, especially on Sundays. Once church lets out, it's a mad dash to make it here and snatch up a table, afterward many head over to the bowling alley. And Pastor Bill has been known to sneak out the back of the church to make it here before everyone else." Tyler grinned.

"Well, it must be great." Lorelei returned her focus to the menu. "Does this mean we need to eat fast so you can get back to the bowling alley?"

"That's the great thing about a small town. They'll linger until they see me heading back." Tyler weaved his fingers together. He didn't need to review a menu.

The Oakvale Pizza Pie hadn't changed its menu. Ever. As Tyler glanced around, he noticed Lorelei was the only one with a menu in hand. All of the other tables' menus rested between the glass containers of red pepper flakes and Parmesan cheese on the table.

Tyler could tell Lorelei what was on the menu without even looking. There were the standard choices of pizzas, a make-your-own pizza, stuffed ravioli with three different fillings, classic spaghetti, and the best garlic bread in all of Minnesota. Then, further down the menu, were fancier options for what he considered special occasions or dates. Since he could remember, the restaurant's scent had never changed either—a mix of melted cheese, garlic, and ripe tomatoes.

"How's Cider?" Lorelei's voice floated out from behind the menu. "I miss her."

"My parents have her today. They love to watch their granddog. My mom is probably making Cider homemade dog biscuits as we speak. They're itching for human grandbabies."

Lorelei peeked over the menu. "What a great thing. That's awesome." She smiled and returned to the menu. "Everything sounds so good. I can't decide. Any suggestions?"

"They make everything homemade. The sauce, the cheeses, the pasta. You can't go wrong, and we can always come back and try something different next time."

Lorelei's eyes spied over the menu.

"I mean, you can, or we can." Tyler looked over at Mary Ann, thinking, please don't let her see my flush face. Why does it feel so hot in here?

"I like the idea." Lorelei blushed. "And that makes it easy. I'll order the first thing on the menu, and next time, I'll order the second item on the menu."

She slid the menu back between the condiment shakers and reached for her cell phone.

He glanced at her and she set the phone down, her shoulders sank, and she folded her arms. "I'm still trying to learn to relax. Even when a doctor is not working, they still seem to be working." She pushed herself back into the chair. "I look forward to you showing me around the office. My office? I must admit, it will be a drastically different work environment than I'm used to at the hospital. I don't know what to expect."

"I think it will make for a nice *relaxing* job for the month. Of course, it's flu season, but I'm guessing it will still be a lot better than the hospital"—Tyler waved Uncle Steve over—"and I don't know anyone around here with the flu."

The owner approached the table. He wore his classic button-down shirt, always in a shade of blue. An off-white half apron wrapped around his waist, holding straws and order pads. Even though Uncle Steve owned the restaurant, he worked as hard as all of his staff.

"Hi, Tyler and . . ." Uncle Steve turned Lorelei.

She pivoted in her chair, reaching out her hand. "Hi, I'm Lorelei, and this is my daughter, Mary Ann."

"The niece! The doctor!" Uncle Steve beamed. "It's wonderful to meet you and have you both in town for the month. I'm the restaurant owner, and your uncle usually has me deliver a few lunches a week, so feel free to request the same. Just give us a call, and I'll run it over."

Lorelei glanced at Tyler and then back to Uncle Steve. "Wow, that could get me in some trouble for sure." She laughed. "Thank you, Steve."

"Call me Uncle Steve. Everyone does." He removed the pad of paper and pen from his apron. "You know what you want to order?" Uncle Steve asked.

"I'll have the mushroom ravioli and some garlic bread, please." She licked her lips.

"My usual, Uncle Steve, thank you," Tyler stated.

"What about your daughter?" Uncle Steve asked, giving Mary Ann a smile and a wave.

"I brought her a bottle. She isn't on solid foods yet." Lorelei gasped. "Oh, but I don't have any warm water to mix it with."

"Perfect, even the youngest gets to order," he emphasized. "I'll have some water warmed and brought out for her bottle. And what about to drink for both of you?"

"Sparkling cider?" they asked in unison and beamed at each other.

Uncle Steve hurried off to the kitchen's swinging doors.

"That's nice of Steve—*Uncle* Steve. Mary Ann would have shrieked and chucked her bottle if I tried to give her a cold one." Lorelei glanced around. "He must be someone's uncle?"

Tyler leaned back in his chair. "No relation to anyone in town, but everyone calls him that because he's like the town's uncle."

The Pizza Pie's wallpaper from the early eighties—mini orange-and-blue flowering buds—ran down from the ceiling until it met the dark-stained chair rail, which encircled the restaurant. Since this was the first time he'd brought an out-of-town visitor into the restaurant, it was also the first time he considered it from an outsider's perspective. He'd never really noticed the wallpaper or thought too much about how small black-and-white photos of people who'd eaten in the restaurant over the years hung from the walls.

"Uncle Steve will return with his camera," Tyler warned.

"His camera?" Lorelei's forehead wrinkled.

Tyler pointed around at the photos. "Everyone who eats here gets their picture on the wall at some point or another."

Lorelei gazed around, turning left and then right in her chair, taking in the entire restaurant. "Then your photo must be up here." She continued looking around.

"Yes, there's a horrible photo of me with my parents. But"—Tyler leaned forward—"I had braces, so you can't see my face below my nose because I hid behind a slice of pizza."

"Where is it?" Lorelei beamed.

Tyler shook his head. "Mum's the word."

"I see how this is going to work." She nodded her head. "How long do you think it will take me to find it?"

Tyler's eyes glanced up at the ceiling. He knew exactly where the photo hung, and he didn't want his eyes to wander in the direction and give it away. "You'll never find it." Tyler's neck craned up as far as it would go, but laughing caused it to tilt back down.

"I guess I have my work cut out for me." Lorelei grinned.

Uncle Steve hurried his steps from the kitchen. He always seemed in a hurry for such a laid-back town. "Here's the warm water for your daughter, and I can take your photo now or before you leave." Uncle Steve stood at the edge of the table, his camera in hand. "I'm sure Tyler filled you in."

Lorelei nodded. "Yes."

"Let's have you hold Mary Ann," Uncle Steve instructed as he took the lens cap off the camera. "Tyler, I want you in this, too."

"You already have one of me," Tyler warned.

"Don't be a poor sport." Uncle Steve waved him to lean closer to Lorelei so he could get them all in the shot.

Tyler inched closer to Lorelei, who held her daughter between the two of them. As the flash went off, Tyler's heart filled with emotion. He couldn't help it. He was delighted to have this moment captured. While his face held a smile, contentment traveled throughout his body, giving him a sense of peace, a comfort, like a fire on a cold night.

"I think it'll look great on the wall," Uncle Steve stated. "Let me bring out your dishes. And drinks!" He pivoted and walked off. "Where is my head today?"

"I'm excited to have our picture on the wall. This town is . . . lovely. It's like a big knit Christmas sweater." Lorelei removed a bottle with powder at the bottom of her purse.

"You're correct." *Maybe she'll find a way to stay.* "It's magical even when it's not the Christmas season."

Lorelei shook up the water and formula in the bottle and handed it to Mary Ann. Her daughter took it in her tiny hands, eyelids already heavy. Unable to hold the bottle entirely on her own due to her sleepiness, Lorelei helped hold it up for her with one hand.

Watching them brought comfort to him, like when a song's words sent goose bumps down his arms. It was as though everything around him blurred, and he only saw her and Mary Ann.

His heart thumped against his chest so loud he swore everyone in the restaurant heard it. While he'd admit he found Lorelei attractive, there was also something more powerful happening. No matter how long he spent with her, it wasn't enough. He wanted to hear about her childhood, her life, her dreams and goals.

"I hope this isn't too forward . . . ." Lorelei opened the paper napkin and set it on her lap with her free hand.

Tyler didn't know what she might be about to ask, but he knew he would say yes to whatever it might be. Just then, Uncle Steve returned with their warm dishes of food.

Lorelei's eyes widened as he set the plate in front of her. "Smells amazing, Uncle Steve."

"Be sure to flag me down if you need anything else. Oofta! Drinks!" Uncle Steve hurried back to the kitchen.

Tyler rubbed his hands together. "It doesn't matter how many times I eat here, every dish is like a new experience." In front of him was a twelve-inch pizza, its crust plump and toasted. The mozzarella cheese perfectly melted over the marinara sauce. The prosciutto and pepperoni sprinkled over the top ideally golden.

Every inch of him hoped Lorelei felt at home here, as part of the community—even if she'd only been in town for twenty-four hours. When he thought about it, he couldn't understand how he'd attached himself to her as quickly as he had. There was something about being around her that caused him to feel half his age and like a kid on Christmas morning.

Uncle Steve approached the table once again and set the drinks down. "Enjoy."

Tyler lifted a slice of pizza. "You wanted to ask me something?" He took a bite.

Lorelei cut one of the raviolis in half with her fork. "Yes." She pressed her lips together. "I wanted to see if maybe we could work together. I can help you, and you can help me."

Tyler continued to chew, unsure of what Lorelei wanted help with. "Work together?"

Lorelei blew on the ravioli and then took a bite. "Wow, that's . . . wow."

Tyler nodded. "Right?"

She took another bite and then a sip of sparkling cider. "My parents are coming to visit on the twentieth, and I'd love to convince them of what a great place Oakvale is to raise a baby. Show them how important a small-town doctor can be in a place like this. As a local, I would greatly appreciate any help you could provide me with to showcase my point." Lorelei forked another ravioli. "And, I'd like to help you present your dream of owning the bookstore to your parents."

Tyler continued to devour his slice of pizza as he pondered Lorelei's offer. *How bad can her parents be to have raised such an amazing woman?* But confronting his fear of disappointing his parents plus having to decide on using his savings for only one dream seemed impossible.

Could he help her if he didn't have the courage to stand up to his parents? He finished the slice and wiped his fingers on his napkin. "I want to say yes. I do. I mean, I can help you out with your folks for sure. But my situation is different."

"Different?" Lorelei tilted her head.

"Your situation, although similar, is not about terminating a family business. Plus, I can't have both—it's either the bookstore *or* my book travel trip. And I made up my mind a year ago that I couldn't give up the family business."

"Oh." Lorelei slouched and leaned backward. "But it's your dream. The bookstore is amazing. Sandy and I spoke, and I could tell she wants you to take over."

"You spoke with Sandy?" Tyler took a sip of cider. The bubbles refreshed his mouth.

"Sandy was the one who mentioned we could help each other. I don't mean to step on toes. I know I'm new and temporarily here, maybe." Defeat filled Lorelei's eyes, and her lips fell into a frown. "Never mind, I overstepped." She glanced at Mary Ann, whose bottle was about to slip from her lips as she was fast asleep amongst the noise of the restaurant.

"No, you didn't overstep. I don't see how I can do that to my parents." Tyler picked up another slice of pizza. "Which is why I haven't. Plus, I don't want to give you false hope about your abilities to move here. There aren't any houses on the market currently and we already have a doctor."

"But it doesn't have to be *this* small-town, any small-town." Lorelei rubbed her hand on her glass. "I mean, how do we know unless we try? We both have obstacles, yet they are not unobtainable. Think about them as you would skiing. There are beginning, intermediate, and advanced runs to take. None of them are possible unless you start on the beginner's slope."

"The thing about my family's business is not about sales, but about keeping the name going. If I leave to run the bookstore, my family's legacy ends. It's a failure not to keep it open. The bowling alley is a separate matter."

"But you said owning the bookstore is your dream, and your heart's not in the family business." Lorelei wiped the marinara sauce from the corner of her mouth. "It's not like it will disappear. Someone else can take over."

Tyler nodded as Uncle Steve sprinted from the kitchen.

"Your garlic bread." He set it on the table, next to Lorelei's dish, before heading back to tend to another table.

Lorelei covered her mouth with the napkin as Tyler noticed her cheeks plump out at the edge. "Uncle Steve cracks me up." She lowered the napkin. "He does feel like a fun uncle. I see why everyone calls him that now."

"Look at you fitting right in." Tyler leaned back in the chair.

"I've seen a few kids in town. Are there a lot?" Lorelei asked, ripping off a chunk of garlic bread.

Tyler thought. "There are some, not a lot. After graduation, most of them move to Booth or to attend college in another state."

"Any Mary Ann's age in town?" She glanced over at her daughter, still fast asleep.

"Yes, I can introduce you, but they'll most likely come into the doctor's office. Lots of runny noses this time of year, and we don't have a hospital, but—"

"Booth does? Gosh, I would say Booth is trying to one-up this town every chance it gets." Lorelei's eyebrow raised and she grinned. "Oh, where is the day care center here? I didn't see it on the way in."

"Day care center?" He didn't know why he repeated what she'd asked other than the business sounded out of place in Oakvale and tripped him up. "We don't have one. We're a dog-and baby-friendly town. Besides, Jodi can watch Mary Ann. She spends every free second babysitting half the towns' kids."

"Jodi, my receptionist? My daughter needs childcare." Lorelei slumped back into the chair. "How'd I let that slip my mind?"

Tyler reached his hand out. He sensed the disappointment oozing from Lorelei. She needed this town, but she had yet to learn their ways. "You're not in the city anymore. You're in Oakvale. And if you want, I can watch her, too. Or my parents."

Lorelei's body language changed, and she sat up straight. "I can't impose on people I don't know, and where do people place their kids when they work?"

"School. Friends. Family. Neighbors. And you know people. You know me, Jodi, Uncle Steve, my folks, Sharon, Don, and Sandy. I would say you know quite a few residents." Tyler raised his pizza slice to Lorelei, who picked up a bite of ravioli with her fork.

"I don't *know them* know them." She shoved the bite into her mouth.

"Then I guess we better make sure we change that. For Monday, bring Mary Ann with you. Jodi will be beside herself with excitement. You might have to pry your daughter from her at the end of the day."

"Baby fever?" Lorelei asked as she glanced over at her sleeping daughter.

"I'm not sure. She's had it since high school."

He could tell she was thinking by how she gazed off behind him, as though the answer was hidden in the wallpaper. When she refocused her vision on him, she said, "Well, at least I have a plan for Monday."

"Don't give up on Oakvale so quickly. Remember, you can't leave town until you find my picture on the wall." He beamed before taking a bite.

Lorelei raised her little finger in the universal gesture of a pinky promise. "And I'll convince you why you need to follow your dream—the one you want the most—and come clean with your parents."

Tyler set down the rest of his slice, wiped his hands on his napkin, and clasped his hands together. He wanted to say no, but her enthusiasm was contagious. "Well, if we are going to pinky swear on it, then I guess I have no other option."

Their little fingers locked. The deal was on, but the plan had yet to be set.

Chapter 12

T he snow continued to come down like diamonds from the clouds as Lorelei and Mary Ann arrived at the doctor's office for her first day. No matter how odd it felt to bring her daughter with her, she smiled as she walked in and found Jodi digging through a box on the reception desk.

"Hi, Lorelei." She popped her head up. Her chestnut ringlets bounced back into place. "Oh goodness, you brought your daughter!" she squealed at such a volume that Lorelei winced.

Jodi nearly skipped over, lowered her head, and used her pointer finger to try and tickle the infant. "Can I hold her?"

"Yes, of course."

"It's an honor to have you here. Usually, we're high and dry for help come December. And look at you, wearing scrubs, aren't you just the cutest." Jodi took Mary Ann and squeezed her into a hug.

Please don't squeal again. "Oh, is it not alright to wear this?" Lorelei glanced down at her blue-gray scrubs. Yesterday she'd overdressed, and now, somehow, she'd underdressed.

"You're allowed to wear whatever you want. Dr. North always wears jeans and a button-down with flair."

"Flair?" Lorelei tilted her head.

"You know, holiday-themed or tropical, something fun for the kids and the young at heart."

Lorelei nodded at the thought.

"I didn't want to say anything in front of Tyler, he would have called me baby crazy, but having Mary Ann here is just the best thing ever."

"You and Tyler are close." She didn't mean to prod, yet it slipped out before she could catch it.

"If you consider a mouse and cat close, then Tyler and I are close."

Although Tyler and Sandy had made it known Jodi was only a friend, the confirmation provided Lorelei with a sense of peace. "Oh?"

"Tyler and I have a lot of fun together, as friends, but we're incredibly different in so many ways I've lost count over the years. I'm dating a guy in—"

"Booth?" Lorelei jumped in.

"Yes," Jodi's eyes lit up like a Christmas display. "How'd you know?"

"Because everything seems to be happening in Booth. Maybe I picked the wrong small town."

Jodi placed her hand on Lorelei's shoulder. "Not in the least. If this man and I end up working out and getting married, he'd better be alright with moving here because Oakvale is the best town ever. Plus, Booth doesn't have me, and I can watch Mary Ann anytime you need."

"Thank you. It's weird bringing her to work. I think it's great, just different." Lorelei walked farther into the office. "I brought her playpen, but I'm afraid it will be a lot of lugging around every day to and from the house."

"We have one here. I set it up for you in Dr. North's office."

Her uncle Chris's practice operated out of a converted historic home, and it was boldly obvious. Not that Lorelei objected. The entry hosted a wood-burning stove and hardwood floors. A receptionist desk of rich cherrywood and mismatched waiting room chairs filled the room. Nearest the fireplace sat a deep-brown leather chair big enough for Santa to greet children in and a small antique end table. Lorelei followed Jodi past a kitchen and mahogany staircase leading to the second floor, down the short hall in the back to a room.

"I need you to let me know the rules around here since this is also your home," Lorelei stated.

Tyler had given her the tour and history yesterday before lunch. The reception and lobby area was once the front room, and the fireplace was still used daily in the winter during operating hours. The kitchen cabinets held most of the medical supplies and the all-important coffee maker. The two closest bedrooms were waiting rooms and the third the office. Tyler mentioned that the house had been updated in the 1970s before the family relocated to Miami, and that was when they'd turned it into the office space. The upstairs was Jodi's residence, so they hadn't gone up there since Jodi wasn't home.

Jodi entered the office first. "Gosh, don't worry about dropping in on me. I love visitors, being alone in this big place can be rather lonely. I only use one room upstairs, anyway. The other two are collecting dust."

Lorelei walked into the room but kept her coat on as she approached the desk. The fireplace out in the waiting room would take a while to warm up the back rooms.

"Mr. North has a thing about the cold. He doesn't seem to be bothered by it a bit." Jodi rubbed her hand on her red knit sweater. "If you like, I can run over to Don's and see if he has any space heaters. I have an extra one upstairs if you need it."

"Thanks, but I'm sure this place will warm up in a little bit." Lorelei took a step toward the door.

Jodi provided a weak smile.

"Tyler showed me around yesterday, not upstairs, of course. You must have been with your boyfriend."

"Yes, I was at his house in Booth. I helped him decorate for Christmas." Jodi glanced around, still holding Mary Ann, who busied herself with Jodi's necklace.

Lorelei laughed and plopped down in the lush desk chair. "Do you enjoy living where you work?"

"Once I'm upstairs, I sort of forget about work. I guess because my job and this town are peaceful and laid-back, I don't have anything I need to detach from at the end of the day."

"I need a few lessons on learning to relax." Lorelei checked her cell phone, leaving Jodi to stand there without anything to do.

Jodi continued to look at Mary Ann. "You mean like you're doing right now?"

Lorelei froze her fingers over the cell and clenched her teeth. "Yes." She set the phone down on the desk.

"I can help you, if you wish." Jodi perched herself in a chair opposite Lorelei.

"Help me?"

"Please don't take offense to this, but your body is tense. I can see it when you walk like you have a rod holding you up. And it's pulling your shoulders to your ears."

Instantly, Lorelei pushed her shoulders down and back with her muscles. "I guess they are kind of tense. But I'm wearing scrubs." She pointed and pulled at her top.

"Scrubs are a bit formal." Jodi dramatically batted her eyelashes.

"How? They're basically pajamas."

Jodi snickered. "Yes, but fancy doctors and nurses wear them. Oakvale is lovely and nice, but it's not scrub fancy."

"Point taken." Lorelei leaned forward. "Alright, I'll take you up on your offer."

Jodi sprung up in the air on the tips of her boots and beamed. "I'm excited. It'll be fun. Like sisters getting together."

Leaning back in the chair, Lorelei picked up her phone. Jodi cleared her throat and shook her finger at the doctor.

"Right," Lorelei set the phone down, "starting now." She took a deep breath. "Do you have my appointments for today?" She glanced around, no laptop in sight.

"Only three." Jodi waved her off. "And don't bother looking for a laptop. Everything here is by hand, all medical records and appointments."

"What about a day planner?" Lorelei asked.

"That, we have." Jodi smiled and hoisted Mary Ann toward Lorelei.

She took hold of her daughter as Jodi pivoted. "I was about to decorate the office for Christmas. I'm several days behind. If Mrs. Wilson comes in, I'll be in trouble." Jodi called behind her as she scurried to the reception area. "She has Christmas decor up year-round. You must stop in and see her house."

Lorelei hurried after Jodi as she held the baby tight to her hip. "I can't believe only three appointments for today."

Jodi started to pull garland from the box on the desk. "We might have a few drop-ins."

Lorelei leaned against the frame of the wall. "What does my uncle do with the rest of his day?"

"Dr. North is an avid reader and makes the most wonderful wooden toys. If he's not with a patient or walking the town checking in on folks, he's buried in a book or carving wood. He spends some of his time by the woodstove with his feet on the hearth." Jodi pointed to the oversize leather wing chair. On the opposite wall, a built-in bookcase housed books from floor to ceiling. "You can help me decorate if you wish."

Lorelei didn't want to offend Jodi, and she cringed before she said, "Thank you, but I think I'll spend some time in the office, get a feel for the patients by reviewing their charts and assessing the doctor's stuff." Lorelei turned without a response and headed back down the hall. *Doctor's stuff . . . what was this, kindergarten pretend play?*

"Wait," Jodi warned. "Hand me your cell phone."

"But what is a nurse or doctor needs me?"

Jodi pointed at Lorelei's pocket. "Because you're in Oakvale, not Minneapolis."

Lorelei huffed and handed Jodi the cell phone before storming back to the office. She set Mary Ann in the office playpen and was about to sit down in the plush executive chair with nailhead trim when her daughter let out a wail of a cry.

"It's okay. Mommy's here." She went over and hoisted her daughter up into her arms. "I guess being stuck in a playpen all day isn't the best thing." She kissed Mary Ann's forehead and placed her in her lap as she returned to the office chair.

"Baby girl, how wonderful is this place?" Lorelei held a teething toy in front of Mary Ann's grasp while her eyes explored the office. The wall directly opposite the desk showed off a forty-something-year-old collection of thank you cards. To her right, shelves of tiny carved trinkets. On her left was a picture window with thick red drapes. She took Mary Ann with her and walked over to look outside. As she pushed back the drapes, Lorelei spotted a patio with a small wrought iron table and two chairs safe from the falling snow. A wooden fence sat just beyond the deck.

She glanced at the clock on the wall behind the office chair. It was not even nine thirty in the morning. Lorelei wanted to run over to the Oakdale Pizza Pie and see if she could find Tyler's picture, but they wouldn't be open yet.

"Jodi!" Lorelei called but headed down the hall anyway.

"Yes, boss lady?" Jodi stood on a stepladder as she hung Christmas lights over the front door frame.

"Do you happen to know where the photo of Tyler is at the pizza place?" Lorelei sat in the wing chair with Mary Ann, warming up by the fire.

"I do, but he already told me not to tell you." Jodi beamed.

Lorelei gasped. "That stinker, how'd he even know I would ask you?"

"Tyler can read a person like he does books." Jodi climbed down from the ladder to grab another decoration from the box.

Lorelei leaned forward in the chair. "If you see his love for the bookstore, and I do too, how do his parents not see it?"

She might have been overstepping, yet again, but they'd pinky sworn to help each other, and all she was doing was research.

"Richard and Arlene are the nicest folks in town." Jodi paused, resting her hands on the edge of the box. "But their family business means a great deal to them and the future McCains."

"Yet if they're the nicest, shouldn't it be easy for Tyler to tell them what he wants?" Lorelei bounced Mary Ann on her knee as she started to fuss.

"That's probably why it's so hard for Tyler to tell them. Just because they're nice doesn't mean they want to see the obvious."

"But what about his book travel thing?" Lorelei's brow creased, creating lines across her forehead.

"We both know he is using that as an excuse. He has pretty much accepted that it won't happen, which is why he saved up to travel the world for half a year."

"Well, the good news is, I'm going to help him," Lorelei boasted.

"And just how do you plan on doing that? I don't mean to snow on your Christmas parade, but I don't see how you can help Tyler overcome what he has been hiding for so long and suddenly give him courage."

Lorelei slumped in the chair. But before she started to feel too defeated for herself and Tyler, the front door burst open. Snow drifted in and stuck to the entryway rug.

"Why, Mrs. Wilson, are you alright?" Jodi went to the woman with curly pearl-colored hair and glasses from the 1950s.

Mrs. Wilson clutched at her tan corduroy coat oddly. As she unbuttoned it, a tiny kitten of smoky gray popped its head up.

"I'm fine, dear. It's Mittens. I think she's sick." Mrs. Wilson caught the view of Mary Ann, and her cheeks plumped up. "Is this the new family in town? The Norths' niece?"

Lorelei remained seated with her daughter. "Yes, I'm Lorelei, and this is Mary Ann."

"What a precious baby. Once Mittens is feeling better, you must swing by my house. I can show her all the lovely Christmas joy my home has to offer."

"We'd enjoy that," Lorelei replied.

Mrs. Wilson glanced around. "Jodi, where is the rest of the Christmas décor? You're aware it's after the first of December, correct?"

Jodi placed her arm around Mrs. Wilson and quickly led her down the hall. "I'm working on it right now. Let's get you and Mitten's into a room, and the doctor will be right with you."

When Jodi returned, Lorelei asked, "Why is Mrs. Wilson in a room with a kitten?"

Jodi held out her hands for Mary Ann. "Let me take your daughter while you see to Mrs. Wilson and Mittens."

"I'm a doctor, not a veterinarian." Lorelei's eyes widened. "What am I supposed to do with Mittens?"

"Oh, Boss Lady, Mittens is fine. Mrs. Wilson relays problems she's having through Mittens. So if Mittens has a stomach ache, it's Mrs. Wilson. If Mitten's paw hurts, Mrs. Wilson's foot hurts." Jodi patted Lorelei on the back. "You'll get the hang of this." She smiled. "Honestly, she wants someone to talk to without feeling vulnerable."

Lorelei's heart swelled with delight. Actual time to chat with a patient was almost too good to be true. Her smile radiated through her as she went down the hall to the exam room.

Chapter 13

"If you keep pacing, we'll have to add a fifth bowling lane parallel to the windows," Richard declared.

"Sorry, Dad, it's just—" Tyler paused, leaning against the window where he could see Lorelei's parked sedan in front of the doctor's office.

Richard reached out for Tyler's shoulder and squeezed it with one hand. "You can't be . . ."

"No, Dad, I can't like someone I only met a few days ago. And she's not staying. Sure, she's the first person I've connected with since Meg . . . ." Tyler shoved his hands in his pockets. *But it doesn't matter.*

The coldness from outside seeped through the thin windows of the bowling alley. Meg was his high school sweetheart, and he thought his future wife. After their senior year, she packed up and left for college in California. She'd kept in touch for a while, but Tyler found it best for them both to move on with their lives.

"You and the doctor would make a nice couple, and you know your mother already likes her." Richard's car keys jingled in one hand as he held his travel mug of coffee in the other. "And you know how badly we want you to marry and start a family."

"Dad, too soon," Tyler whined. "Anyway, she can't stay even if she wanted to. I mean, there are no long-term jobs, and after speaking with her, I found out her parents don't want her to raise her daughter here. I don't need another heartbreak caused by this town."

"Another?"

"Never mind." Tyler shook his head.

"When love is meant to be, it finds a way." Richard straightened the mugs in the beverage area. "And I thought her uncle was planning to retire?"

"I'm not sure about Dr. North retiring. I'd heard a rumor, but it was short-lived because he didn't want to leave the practice to just anyone."

"Well, she is family."

"So, maybe he was waiting for her all along." Tyler didn't want to state the obvious, but Lorelei had no place to live. And no one in town had mentioned moving out, not even Sandy and Ted after they sold Once Upon a Book. "Lorelei asked for my help. I guess her parents are coming to town to visit for Christmas, and she and I—" Tyler paused. He almost let it slip that Lorelei was going to be helping him out, too. "She wants my help convincing them that being a small-town doctor is her dream, even if it's not *this* small town."

"How do you plan on going about that? Can Mom and I help you out?" Richard took a seat in the chair opposite Tyler's desk and stretched out his legs.

Tyler strolled over to his desk chair and reluctantly sat down as if taking an eye off the doctor's office would cause Lorelei to disappear. He folded his arms and leaned forward on the desk.

"There's the reindeer contest and, of course, the O Come, All Ye Readers event that would be a great way to show Lorelei's parents about our close-knit community." Tyler picked up the Norths' signed rental agreement to finally file it away when he spotted a sentence. He tilted his head much like Cider does when she looks like she's questioning something.

"Everything alright?" Richard asked, taking a step forward.

Tyler leaned forward and reread a paragraph of the contract. "It says Lorelei is to host a Christmas feast."

"What?" Richard took the paper in his hand and read it. "Why it certainly does. That's rather odd."

"Why would the Norths put this in the agreement?" His dad handed it back to his son.

Tyler shook his head. "I have no idea, but it's in two days." Tyler covered his mouth as he gasped. "Oofta!"

"She doesn't know?" Richard's eyes bulged.

"I didn't even know." Tyler sprung from the chair. He snatched his coat off the coatrack near the door and hastily wrapped a scarf around his neck.

"It's not like the Norths will hold her to the contract. They're not even here," Richard reminded him.

"I have a feeling Lorelei follows everything to the letter."

"You might be right." His dad shoved a hand into his pocket. "I think Oakvale is exactly what Lorelei needs, and maybe Oakvale needs her. She does seem a bit tense, always on the go."

Tyler threaded on his gloves and nodded his head. "She has a lot on her plate to unwind from."

"Indeed. You'd better go and speak to her. I'll stay here and man the fort." Richard made his way to the beverage area, pulling the lid off his mug. "I'll keep Cider company, too."

Tyler swung open the door as the frigid air and snow came drifting in. "Thanks, Dad. I'll be right back."

He made his way up the street as the wind and snow battled his every step. The snowflakes tickled his face, and his boots slipped as he passed the pizza place. He paused at the crosswalk, checking for cars. Once Tyler reached the path to the front door of the doctor's office, he grabbed hold of the railing to aid him. But as he pivoted to head up the ramp, his feet went out from under him. Attempting to brace himself, he wrapped both hands around the railing. However, holding onto the handrail only caused Tyler to appear as though he were trying out for a ballet recital. Pirouette and plié. He knew these words thanks to all of the picture books he'd read at the bookstore's story time.

Keeping his hands still wrapped around the railing, Tyler swung underneath the bar and landed with a thump in the snow. He raised himself by pushing his elbows into the snow, but he only fell flat again.

The snowflakes started to cover Tyler's coat as he lay on his back, catching snow in his mouth.

"Tyler!" Sharon called out.

He lifted his head and spotted Sharon, bundled up in her bright-pink coat and hot-pink scarf and matching hat, dashing across the street. She leaned over him, blocking some of the snowflakes.

"Tyler, honey, are you alright?" Sharon asked. "I saw you putting on a show with some tricky footwork over here."

"I think I might have bruised a few things. But I'm sure I'm alright. Just need a minute to stand up."

"You stay put. I'm going to go get the new doc." Sharon shuffled up the ramp without slipping even once.

Pushing himself up on his elbows, he finally sat up completely, although his back was already sore.

As he brushed the snow from his hair, Sharon and Jodi emerged from inside the doctor's office. "What did you do this time, Ty?" Jodi raised an eyebrow and grinned.

"Don't be jealous of my moves." Tyler reached up for the railing.

"I've seen your moves at our Under the Snow prom. Everyone saw your moves. It explains why you're on your bottom right now."

"Sounds like someone's jealous she didn't get a dance with me," he said.

"Yes, soooo jealous." Jodi reached out her hand.

"Ladies, thank you. I'm alright." He eased himself to his feet. Grateful Lorelei wasn't seeing him at this very moment.

Jodi got on his left side, Sharon on his right, and they brushed snow from the top of his coat. Then, they linked arms with him as he crept up the ramp, trying to hide his fear of slipping again.

"Tyler, I'm sorry. You know how hard it is to keep the path clear with all this snow falling nonstop," Jodi stated, letting go of him to open the door.

"Not a problem at all." Tyler internally rejoiced at the sight of Dr. North's faux leather chair. "Where are Lorelei and her daughter?"

"They're both back with Mrs. Wilson," Jodi said as Tyler lowered himself into the plush chair.

"Mrs. Wilson does love babies as much as cats." Tyler reached his hand behind him, massaging his lower back where the pain warmed. "I think I'm alright. Let's not tell Lorelei."

Sharon folded her arms over her chest. "Fine, have it your way. I need to get back to my customers."

"Thank you, Sharon." Tyler relaxed back into the softness of the chair. "And, Jodi, thank you. Do you know how much longer Mrs. Wilson might be? I have an urgent matter I need to discuss with Lorelei."

"The doctor—I mean Lorelei—should be finishing up shortly. Mrs. Wilson has been back there for over half an hour." Jodi placed an ornament from a nearby box onto the Christmas tree and stood back before adding another. "I've never seen her chat with Dr. North for his long before."

"Thank you again, Doctor," Mrs. Wilson's voice traveled down the hall. "Don't cha know Mittens is already feeling better." A grand smile formed on her lips as she reached the reception area.

"Mrs. Wilson, Mittens, wonderful to see you both." Tyler eased out of the chair, reaching for his back.

Lorelei appeared behind Mrs. Wilson with Mary Ann on her hip. She was dressed in scrubs and wore running sneakers with neon-orange laces.

"I'll get you squared up, Mrs. Wilson." Jodi stepped behind the desk.

"Good morning, or mid-morning, Lorelei," Tyler stated, holding his back.

"Tyler took a little slip outside." Jodi peeked around Mrs. Wilson at him. "He might have hurt his back."

He waved her off with his free hand. "No, it wasn't anything. I'm a Minnesotan. I can handle the snow. I did need to speak with you, Lorelei, if you have a moment."

Lorelei nodded. "Sure."

"Privately," Tyler whispered. He didn't want Jodi and Mrs. Wilson to see Lorelei flip out if she did that sort of thing when he told her the Christmas feast news.

"Oh." Lorelei's mouth went from a smile to a frown, a wrinkle creased between the bridge of her nose. "Sure."

"Do you need me to take Mary Ann?" Jodi asked.

"No, I need to get her to nap for a bit, thank you, though." Lorelei headed down the hall to her office.

Tyler closed the door halfway behind him. He didn't want Lorelei to feel as though he was trapping her in the office.

After Lorelei laid Mary Ann down in the playpen, she took a seat behind the desk, and Tyler took one of the patient chairs opposite her. "Are you sure your back is feeling alright?"

"Oh, yes. Okay, remember how neither of us read the rental agreement before you signed it?" Tyler continued to whisper. He wanted to model quiet behavior in hopes of keeping Lorelei calm. Yet, she worked in an emergency department. Technically, she shouldn't frazzle easily.

Lorelei nodded, her face confused in thought. "What'd I miss? Wait, I don't have to cover the cost for the roof repair, do I?"

Tyler leaned forward. "No, of course not." He gently cleared his throat. "See, your uncle and aunt added a small thing you have to do. I mean, you can skip it. I don't think they will find out until they return. But you seem like a stickler for rules."

Lorelei's hand went to her neck. "I do?" She titled her head. "Of course I do." She brought her hand to her forehead. "There's nothing wrong with following rules. They keep people safe, and I'm a mom. A role model."

Lorelei stood and paced the small office. She wrapped her hand around the back of her neck.

Tyler ran his hand through his hair. "It's not a big deal. A-a-a Chr-rr-ristmas feast, to be exact," he stuttered.

"A Christmas feast?" She paused, tilted her head. "I have to throw a dinner party?"

Tyler scooted to the edge of the chair and placed his hands on her desk. "The contract says you need to throw a feast and invite residents of the town. I have no idea why your uncle and aunt are doing this, but of course, they aren't here to enforce it."

"That's not bad. I mean, I wanted to decorate anyway, and the Norths left a note about using their decorations. And I'd love to meet more residents. I mean, it's only a feast, how much work can that be, but I think you mean potluck …where everyone brings something, right?"

Tyler swallowed; the noise echoed in his ears.

"When is this little potluck I'm having?" Lorelei beamed, unaware of what was about to come out of his mouth.

"It's not a potluck." He presented the rental agreement to her.

Lorelei read it over and looked up. "It specifically states I need to cook, from scratch, a Christmas feast. Turkey, mashed potatoes, stuffing, gravy, rolls, and green bean casserole. Plus pie for dessert. And I must decorate to the nines."

Tyler drew a deep breath. "The Norths have always wanted their renters to connect with the town, but never something like this before. Maybe by hosting a feast, you can have a real sense of what living here will be like?"

Lorelei fell back in her chair. "Wow, that's bold. I guess I don't know my aunt and uncle enough to say if this seems out of place. But I can handle it. I mean, they must've wanted me to do this for some reason, although it's far from relaxing. When is this monstrous feast?"

"In two days." Tyler winced.

"What?" Lorelei screeched as she scanned the document.

Mary Ann started to cry, and she rushed to pick up her daughter.

"I'm sorry, we both should have read it before you signed it." Tyler clenched his teeth. "I assumed it was just some basic agreement."

Lorelei attempted to calm her daughter, but it looked like she was trying to soothe herself with all the rocking as well. Knots twisted in his stomach. The pain in his back from the fall seemed like nothing compared to the burden on her face. "It's not your fault. Neither of us expected this to occur. And I would have signed it regardless."

"It's not a big deal. I can help you. We can do it after work tonight," Tyler offered.

"Thank you so much. I'd be grateful for any help you could give me."

Yet, worry remained creased in her face. "There is a slight problem with the feast requirement." Lorelei rubbed her hand over her daughter's hair. "I don't . . . really . . . I've never cooked a turkey . . . or made the bean stuff." She half-smiled. "I can make mashed potatoes."

Tyler placed his hands on his knees and squeezed. He indeed wanted and intended to help Lorelei, but he wasn't sure how to break the news that he'd never cooked a turkey before either.

Chapter 14

"I 'll unload the groceries if you'll please grab all the decorations?" Lorelei pulled three boxes of stuffing mix from a grocery bag. "The note said everything's in the garage."

Tyler hoisted the last of the grocery bags onto the kitchen island. Yet again, Lorelei found herself staring at Tyler, losing her thoughts in the smile forming on his face. She noticed snowflakes resting on the shoulders of his black jacket and over the top of his hair. *He could be a Hallmark Keepsake ornament.*

"Everything okay, Lorelei? You zoned out for a second there." Tyler stepped toward her. "It's been a long first day of work. Maybe you should rest with Mary Ann, and I can finish putting everything away."

Lorelei blinked hard. "No, it's . . ." *Just that she could not stop thinking about him.* "Maybe you're right, a long day." She ran her hand over her shoulder. Of course, she had no idea why it'd felt like a long day. She'd only seen four patients. It was nothing like her regular days of intense, life-threatening injuries or the myriad of patients filtering into the hospital for care. She didn't even have to deal with traffic, a busy grocery store, or rushing to the day care center to pick up Mary Ann before they closed. In fact, she'd enjoyed a leisurely lunch with Jodi in the kitchen, caught up on some medical articles, and helped put birdseed in the feeders on the back patio.

Mary Ann kicked her feet in the high chair as Cider sniffed her way around the kitchen. The sun, although hidden by the clouds and snow all day, had set outside the windows as the landscape disappeared into darkness. While the heater and roof's hole had been repaired, the house remained chilly, and Lorelei shivered.

"Why don't I start a fire? We can't very well decorate for Christmas without one." Tyler spun around, facing the fireplace.

He noticed she was cold. That's so sweet. "Out of wood inside. Please tell me some is stacked someplace," she glanced toward the back patio. "Under cover."

Tyler pivoted back to the kitchen, then toward the rear French doors, and then the fireplace. "There should be some outside on the patio."

"We have so much to do." She took both hands and ran them through her short hair. "It's okay. We got this." Lorelei straightened her posture. "I'll get the groceries and wood. If you could please"—she pointed at Tyler—"handle the gathering of decorations." At the clap of her hands, they both pivoted to their jobs.

After unloading the groceries, she placed a bowl of water on the floor for Cider and heated a bottle for Mary Ann, who'd started to fuss. With her jacket and scarf still on, she passed Tyler on his way in with another load of boxes he was stacking up behind the couch. She exited through the half-open French door as the icy wind tickled her cheeks.

A nice pyramid of chopped wood rested up against the patio under the windows. Lorelei lifted the small gray tarp protecting the logs from the dampness of the snow, but when she reached into the pile, a gust of wind caught hold of the tarp as though it were a kite. She shrieked and grabbed for the tarp, catching the edge of it, and held tight. Tyler appeared at the French doors, standing boldly in front of them.

"Let me help you," he stated. "I heard a gust of wind hit the house."

"Not my screech?"

"Oh, I heard that, too," he laughed and closed the door.

She sighed and shuddered at the cold. "Could you please hold the tarp, and I'll collect the wood," Lorelei directed.

He took the tarp's edge from her, and she stepped sideways under his extended arm. Stacking six logs into the crook of her arm, she wobbled under the weight.

"Are you sure I can't help you?" Tyler asked, one hand reaching out for her.

"Of course." Lorelei fake smiled as snowflakes touched her lips. She reached the French doors and attempted to stretch her hand to the doorknob while supporting the stack. Out of the corner of her eye, she spotted Tyler covering his mouth.

"Don't laugh! Help," she whined.

"You said you were fine."

The log on top of her stack started to slide, and as Lorelei reached for it, she lost her grip on the entire armful, and the firewood crashed at her feet. She hung her head, but together they collected the logs, three each, and upon standing up straight, they paused, aware of how close their faces were. Between the Christmas lights casting off the forest of trees in the backyard and the lights shining out from inside the house, Lorelei was able to see the features of Tyler's face perfectly clear. While she could picture him in her mind at any moment's notice, she enjoyed being this close to him. With him near, she felt such comfort, a true feeling of trust. Not to mention, her heart skipped beats and sped up, too. She knew it was more than an attraction to Tyler's attractive masculinity, but to his actual soul, his heart.

"It's a windy one tonight," Tyler mentioned, without taking his eyes off hers.

"Yes, the fire will be nice." Lorelei found herself staring into his eyes, then at his lips, and then back at his eyes. A soft smile formed on his face, and she copied in response. Tyler didn't smell of cologne, not like it wafted off of every man she'd dated in the city when the wind blew in her direction. *How lovely, he doesn't dip himself in scents.* It pleased her more than she thought it might because she never thought about it until now.

"Are you cold standing out here?" he asked.

"Yes, very." She nodded her head.

"We should probably go inside." He placed his hand on her arm and held the logs under his other.

"Yes." Lorelei squeezed her eyes shut as though to break the spell of his magic over her. "Yes, yes, inside." She pivoted and opened the door.

She needed to stop having these feelings because she and her daughter's future were undecided, and the last thing she needed was a broken heart. After placing the wood into the fireplace, she gathered up some newspaper and wedged it underneath as Tyler set the logs he carried on the hearth.

"Was that all the Christmas decorations?" She stroked the match and caught the paper on fire. Pushing herself up off her knees, Lorelei checked on Mary Ann, who'd sucked down most of her bottle. Cider laid next to the high chair. Her head rested on the edge between Mary Ann's feet.

"Yes, all the boxes I managed to find." He glanced at the five jumbo boxes labeled Christmas Decor stacked behind the couch.

"I know we have a million things to do, but I'm starving. Want to share the frozen pizza I picked up?" Lorelei headed into the kitchen, stopping to unbuckle and pick up Mary Ann. She wrapped her up in her arms.

"Frozen pizza? Why don't I run out to get pizza from Uncle Steve's place?" Tyler suggested, poking the fire.

"What do you have against frozen pizza?" Lorelei snuggled her face against Mary Ann's cheek.

"We have Uncle Steve's pizza—Oakvale Pizza Pie." Tyler rested his hand on top of one of the Christmas boxes. "You can't tell me frozen is better."

"You're right. I can't. I had the ravioli. *You* had the pizza."

Tyler pushed his lips together, muffling a laugh. "Fair. I guess that means we can have frozen pizza tonight. Unless you're up for heading into town."

"I would love to, but clearly, you forgot I desperately need help decorating this place and getting everything prepared for the Christmas feast." As the words left her lips, stress settled into her stomach. Maybe it wasn't hunger pains but an overwhelming feeling that she may not be able to pull off an Oakvale tradition.

"Remember, you don't have to do this." Tyler's voice brought her out of her thoughts.

"I know, but I want to, even if my uncle and aunt never find out. I think it's important to do something for the community, and it will be a great sense of neighborliness."

"Together, we'll make it happen, so wipe the worried look off your face."

She pressed her hand to her chest. "I don't have a worried look . . . it's hunger."

"Then toss that frozen circle in the oven, and let's start decorating." He reached his hands out for Mary Ann.

The baby leaned toward Tyler and happily accepted him holding her as Lorelei preheated the oven and opened the cupboard, searching for stemware.

"Since you won't be driving for at least a few hours, can I pour us a glass of wine?" She rested her fingers around the cupboard's handle. "Or, I do have some sparkling apple cider in the fridge."

"No contest, sparkling apple for sure." He beamed like a five-year-old about to get three scoops of ice cream on his cone.

Lorelei placed the frozen pizza on the oven rack, then filled two wine glasses with chilled cider. As she cupped the glasses by the stem and headed into the living room, she paused. Before her, Tyler had opened one of the boxes and held a small reindeer carved from wood. His voice was soft as he described the statue to her daughter. Lorelei leaned against the edge of the island, staring at the beauty in front of her. The fireplace glowed around them, and as she sipped the cider from her glass, every second of the task ahead melted away.

She knew how great it would be to raise Mary Ann here and how much she needed to slow down and stop having her life taken away from too many hours at work. And she wanted to be more personable with patients, have a better understanding of their medical history. *Not because of Tyler. No . . . maybe.* And she needed to help Tyler achieve his dream, too. The plan rested in the back of her mind all day, trying to place itself front and center every time she thought of him. Only she didn't have a solution yet.

"Do you want me to take her back?" Lorelei asked as she approached to hand him his glass of cider.

He took the glass but leaned his head back. "Of course not. I'm sure you could use a Mommy break."

She smiled shyly. "Thank you. Now, I know we need to decorate, but we can't forget about the plan. Think of all the fun things in town you'll miss if you're gone on your trip. All the newly released books at the bookstore."

"I would miss out on many things over six months."

"I mean, if you're going to support me to confronting my parents about my dream, and you pick your dream runner-up, then it contradicts the argument, doesn't it." She crossed her arms and tilted her head.

"Okay, point taken."

"Great. Do you think during the feast would be a good time to talk to your parents about the bookstore? All the residents around might make it easier. They all seem to agree on how great you would be running the bookstore and would support you."

"I said 'point taken' as in I'd think about it. While you do make a valid point, it could be embarrassing if it backfires." Tyler managed to take a sip of the cider without Mary Ann's grubby fingers touching the glass.

"You're a tough holiday nut to crack. I guess you might be right, like when a guy proposes during a gathering and the woman says no." Lorelei bared her teeth. "What about during the reading? The Christmas reading Sandy mentioned you do every year for the kids."

She took a seat at the edge of the fireplace hearth while Tyler set his cider on the coffee table and sat on the couch with Mary Ann. His brow furrowed as his eyes wandered the room.

"You'll be in your zone, your happy place." Lorelei leaned forward. "Reading to the children will energize you and give you the strength. When you have attempted to speak with them about it in the past, have you been at work?"

Tyler nodded and turned his attention to a silent game of peek-a-boo with her daughter.

"So now you won't be faced with the weight of the family business around you. When you're in the bowling alley, you're attached to everything there—everything you and your parents have become. Being at the bookstore will remove the connection element for your folks. I'm pretty sure I'm rambling now because I'm starving." She gulped the cider.

"I just don't know," he hesitated.

"I know you can't have both, but even if you had all the money in the world, it wouldn't help you speak honestly and openly with your folks." Lorelei sighed. "I don't want to pressure you. If you decide on the bookstore, Mary Ann and I will be your moral support. You can even hold her as your support baby."

Tyler glanced up from his peek-a-boo game. "It would make it a lot easier if I had support baby. I didn't know I needed it, but now that I know about it, I must have it. A support baby." He chuckled. "And what about your parents?"

She tapped her finger just above her lip. "They're coming on the twentieth."

"Also perfect. That's the night of the reindeer decorating contest. The town will be in full celebration mode."

"Reindeer what?" Lorelei tilted her head.

"Every year, the residents get together and decorate a reindeer. A fake one, not a real one." Tyler sipped his cider while

Mary Ann drifted to sleep on his chest. "Kind of like a snow-man-making contest or gingerbread house contest."

"Sounds like a lot of fun. Where is it going to be?"

"We take turns having it at residents' houses. We held it at Sharon's Café once, but everyone ended up eating cookies, and it took hours to complete." Tyler took a sip of cider.

Lorelei's eyes widened. "Let's have it here!"

Tyler turned on the sofa. "Are you sure?"

"Absolutely." She beamed. "Home field advantage must have some pull."

"You'll need it if you want to beat my mom. She's won five years in a row."

"Wow." Lorelei leaned her head back onto the sofa pillows. "You think that's a good time to—? I'm sorry, but how is that going to be the best time to convince my parents that being a small-town doctor is great?"

"By then, you'll know almost all the residents, and they'll all know you and Mary Ann. It'll give your folks a front-row seat to see the community we have here and maybe ease their worries."

Lorelei nodded in agreement. She didn't want to put a damper on the mood, not with the strong smile on Tyler's face. Maybe the reindeer contest would show her parents Oakvale was great, and then she could figure out if her uncle would indeed be retiring and hope a home went up for sale.

Thankfully, the timer for the pizza buzzed, and she withdrew from her thoughts. "I think the plan for my parents will be tricky, but we have plenty to do in the meantime." She removed the pizza from the oven with the assistance of an oven mitt and the flattened pizza box.

Tyler stood, a sleeping Mary Ann still on his chest. "Can I put her down?"

"Oh, sorry, yes."

He pointed to the stairs.

"Yes, in the crib upstairs is fine, on her back, of course."

Tyler nodded and headed up the stairs with Cider by his side. Lorelei located a knife and sliced the pizza. By the time he and Cider returned, the pizza rested on two plates, and she'd refilled the wine glasses with more sparkling apple cider. They stood on either side of the island, leaning over as their elbows rested.

"Not too bad, I guess." Tyler finished chewing his first bite.

"I'm excited to try the pizza at Steve's place. Maybe we could meet up for lunch?" Lorelei wiped her mouth.

"Absolutely."

"Why don't they call it Steve's Place instead of Oakvale Pizza Pie?"

"Great question." Tyler raised his eyebrows. "The restaurant has been standing since the thirties, and the original owner wanted to see it with the same name. He feared that if he named it after himself and retired, the name change would prevent customers from coming in due to new management. He wanted to make sure that everyone enjoyed it for decades without feeling like a new owner would destroy a tradition. So every time it's sold, it's was written into the contract agreement. And thus, it remains Oakvale Pizza Pie."

"This town has a thing for contracts." Lorelei shook her head.

"It's just how we like it. Now, where's the turkey?" Tyler asked, taking another bite of pizza.

"I put it in the freezer."

Tyler nodded. "Should it be in there?"

"It came frozen, so I figured it's like a pizza. Preheat the oven, cook from frozen. Don't cha know, a turkey takes a long time to cook? Probably because it's frozen."

"I should call my mom to double check." Tyler glanced at the refrigerator.

"What happened to teamwork?" Lorelei pouted.

He stared at her, and she felt the heat rising in her cheeks from it. They started to laugh. She covered her mouth. *He's even cute when he laughs.*

"There is something about per pound with the bird," Tyler added.

"That's for how many people it feeds."

"How have neither of us ever cooked a turkey before?" Tyler reached for his pizza crust scraps and tore off a piece.

"My parents always had a chef prepare our holiday dinners, or we'd have a reservation at a restaurant. Big city life and all." She shrugged her shoulders. "But you and your family?"

"I always had other things to do when my mom was in the kitchen. My goal in life was not to become Mr. Crocker."

Lorelei, about to take a sip of cider, thankfully paused the glass to her lips because she burst into laughter.

"It wasn't that funny." He tore off another piece of crust.

"Speak for yourself." Lorelei gathered herself.

He raised an eyebrow. "We should probably finish up supper and start decorating. This place will take hours, and we both have work tomorrow." He looked around. "And you don't have a tree." Tyler tossed the remaining crust onto the plate.

"Trees. I want to do two trees. This place is too grand for only one tree."

"Two?" Tyler asked.

"Two." Lorelei held up two fingers and grinned.

Chapter 15

"Yes, two trees. It's a must!" Lorelei glanced back at the clock on the stove. "Are there any corner tree places still open tonight?"

"Corner tree places?" Tyler perched his lips and raised an eyebrow. "You mean tree farms?"

"No, like a small little corner tree lot. All cut up and ready to haul off?"

"Nope," Tyler stated, trying not to laugh. "We don't have those."

Lorelei rolled her eyes. "How am I supposed to know that?" She picked up her wine glass, stuck out her pinkie, and batted her eyelashes. "I'm only a city girl trying to fit in."

Tyler tugged at his earlobe, a nervous tick he developed as a child when he needed to keep his thoughts, good or bad, to himself. *She's so cute!* "I'm giving you a hard time. But regardless, the tree farm closest to Oakvale closes at dusk."

Lorelei's shoulders slumped. "What can we do? Oh"—she leaned over the box of decorations—"artificial trees."

He raised both hands high in the air. "No, no, no. That's a Christmas sin. Second, no store in town carries plastic trees. You would need to go to—"

"Booth."

"You're catching on quickly." Tyler went over, poked at the fire, and laid another log on top. Then he gave Cider a few pets while she was curled up on the edge of the living room rug with her chin resting on Mary Ann's stuffed dog.

Lorelei dug through the decoration box, removing lights and a ceramic Santa. "I'm sure no one will notice." She glanced up at Tyler.

He didn't say a word, and he continued to stare at her as she removed several small wire Christmas trees in gold and silver. The way her short hair fell over the side of her face and how she tucked it back behind her ear, only for it to fall out of place again, made his dimple crease.

"I can feel you staring at me. What did I do?" Lorelei glanced out of the corner of her eye at him.

His heartbeat double hopped as he caught his breath. Clearing his throat, he pressed his lips together. "No, you didn't do anything." *You're beautiful and spending time together is like reading a favorite book.*

"Artificial trees are not as bad as people make them out to be. They're my recommendation for patients with allergies." A smile warmed her face as she set the wire trees in a cluster on the coffee table. "I can run to the store and pick up two tomorrow."

"If you are heading into Booth for trees, you might as well stop at the tree farm and get the real ones."

She rubbed her chin. "Wait, I have work tomorrow and still need to make this feast. I don't have time to pick up trees." Lorelei squeezed her fists together and punched the air. "Maybe I can't do small-town life."

Tyler went to her and placed his hand on her shoulder as she sank into the sofa. Being close to Lorelei, he caught the scent of something floral with a hint of peach. He wished he could change Lorelei's current state of mind.

"Hold on now. I can help watch Mary Ann anytime you need. I can run to the tree farm for you and help you cook the feast."

"Thanks for offering, Tyler. But you have your own life and things to do." She rested her head on the back of the couch and glared up at the ceiling.

"I'll close my office tomorrow. Come to think of it, why not close your office tomorrow, too?"

"I can't close down the doctor's office." Lorelei slapped her leg. "I've only been working one day."

"That's what's great about running your own business. Your uncle's practice is not the emergency department. You can close for one day, especially when you're hosting the Christmas feast. Do you have any standing appointments tomorrow?"

Lorelei glanced over at him, then back at the ceiling. "No, actually. I checked the calendar, and I'm completely free tomorrow unless there are walk-ins. I'll go stir-crazy. Today I cleaned the entire kitchen at the office, even though it didn't need it. Then I dusted every book my uncle has on his shelves. But what if someone needs medical attention?"

"They can call you. Plus, we all know it's a slim-to-none chance someone is putting a house up for sale tomorrow, and no one will be in for bowling since they'll all be heading over here for the feast."

She didn't respond. Her eyes scanned the living room before she stared off out the window.

"What are you thinking?" he asked. He picked up the ball of multicolored lights and began unraveling them.

"I'm thinking . . . I'm thinking of how too good to be true it all sounds."

"I understand you're used to Minneapolis and all the hustle and bustle of the hospital. But let Oakvale prove to you that when things start to crumble, we all step in to help each other. Even miracles happen."

When she grabbed the other end of the lights, their fingers touched, and Tyler's eyes shut before slowly opening again, as though he was capturing the moment for later. Maybe he jumped the gun with Lorelei, thinking something could come from her being here. She had a point. As of right now, he didn't know what the end of December would bring for either of them. It would be best to push his feelings aside. Yet, every time he tried, his mind reminded him of something else, another reason not to give up. *For her dream.* Lorelei and Mary Ann belonged here. He could feel it like hot cider keeping him warm on a cold day.

"Let's focus on getting through this feast first." Her fingers lifted off his. "Wait, you have Christmas trees up at the bowling alley."

"I have two." Tyler continued unraveling the lights.

"You have two." She smiled. "Can I borrow them just for the feast?"

"What about afterward? Don't cha want a tree for you and Mary Ann?"

"Of course I do. It'll be her first Christmas." Lorelei shook her head. "Wait, what about ...?" She glanced toward the backyard.

Tyler shook his head. "No, you can't cut any of those down."

"Would they *really* miss two of them? Don't cha know, I'm only trying to problem solve."

"Let's take off work tomorrow. I would love to go tree shopping with you and Mary Ann." The thought of a tree-hunting adventure filled his mind, and he smiled.

"Fine, I'll take off work." She shook her head and crossed her arms. "But no, you're helping me too much, I can't ask you to do all of this. I can't be frivolous."

"You're not frivolous. You're celebrating the holidays. Plus, I'd love a day off from sitting in a desk chair and staring at the world across the street."

Lorelei sighed, undoubtedly in defeat. "Alright, in that case, I can't think of a better helper to . . . help me." She grinned. "I've never been to a tree . . . forest before."

He covered his mouth and laughed. "You've never been to a Christmas tree farm? Ever? Even as a child?"

As she shook her head no, Lorelei bit her lower lip, stifling a giggle. "It's funny, right? That I've never been before." She placed a hand on her hip. "No, maybe it's sad."

He crossed his arms and leaned on the edge of the couch. "No, it's different. I mean, I've never bought a tree from the grocery store parking lot. It's the opposite for us both."

"Do you want to experience a grocery store tree lot?" Lorelei tilted.

"No, I don't. But you and Mary Ann can experience a Christmas . . . What did you call it?"

"Christmas forest." She raised her head high. "That's what it's called, right?"

He didn't want to admit it out loud, but a Christmas forest sounded a lot more fun than a Christmas tree farm. "Not exactly."

Everything sounded more fun with Lorelei. Even eating frozen pizza. The taste was nowhere near Uncle Steve's, but it worked in a pinch.

"Let's decorate the house for tonight. Then I'll be back bright and early to pick you and Mary Ann up. By the time we pick out two trees, get them back here and decorated, we can start on the feast prep."

"Are you always this kind to the renters of my aunt and uncle's place?"

No, yes, no. No. "I'm kind to everyone, but you're the first single person ever to stay here." *That doesn't sound right.* "For as long as I can remember, couples have been renting this place in December." *That doesn't sound any better.*

Lorelei pouted. "You must feel sorry for me."

"Not at all. I just know I couldn't do it all by myself in twenty-four hours, let alone with a baby. I couldn't be a single parent, way too much of a challenge."

"Being a parent is easy." She threw her hands up and chuckled. "No, it's not, but it's rewarding. At times it's easy but also scary . . . and joyful, too."

"This is not my place to ask, but did your parents give you a hard time with your decision to adopt?"

"Surprisingly, their desire for a grandchild overruled their judgment of an atypical family structure. Once I said the word grandkid, I'm pretty sure they blacked out on the rest until I brought her home. Yet, my parents are still standoffish; they treat her as though she's an heirloom. They really wanted me to be married and not parenting alone. It's a bit sad, but I'm hoping they'll come around once she is walking and talking and they see that I'm doing fine raising her." Lorelei weaved white lights around the garland she'd draped over the fireplace mantel.

"I'm sorry to hear about that. I'm sure they will come around."

"Do you want a family?"

"I do. And if I didn't, my parents remind me every chance they get how much they want grandkids. But, first, I need a solid relationship. I'm not as strong as you."

"Oh, I've cried myself to sleep some nights." She took a deep breath. "I naively assumed, as a doctor, that anything that happened with Mary Ann I'd be ahead of the game on. I wouldn't have to worry about a cough or a rash or the things I see a lot of parents worry about when I'm at work."

"What happened?"

"Reality hit me. Mary Ann didn't sleep through the night for months. She hated the formulas, hated it when I cut her nails, even if I tried to do it while she slept. Not to mention when she did sleep, if I so much as breathed loud, she would wake. When I put her on her stomach for tummy time, you would have thought the world was about to end."

"I find this hard to believe. Mary Ann is the most perfect baby ever." He pointed upstairs, where she was fast asleep.

"I think we needed to grow on each other. We didn't share a bond like a birth mother and baby can, and we needed more time together. That was my biggest fear and, ultimately, my biggest hurdle to overcome."

"When did you become a family, officially?"

"Three days after she was born." Lorelei's eyes watered at the edges.

He immediately wished he hadn't asked her such an emotional question. *It doesn't matter when she adopted her daughter.* "I'm sorry. I didn't mean to dig deep."

She wiped her eyes with the back of her hand. "No, I'm remembering the moment and all of its beauty."

"Do you want to have a bigger family someday?"

"Yes, I would love to. I don't want Mary Ann being an only child. What about you? Do you want a big or small family someday?"

"I most definitely want a big family. Especially now that I can take them to the Christmas forest." He chuckled.

"See, it's a much better name." Lorelei poked at the fireplace logs. "Christmas tree farm sounds like they're herding trees and milking them for sap."

The image popped in his head of Cider rounding up a herd of Christmas trees, and he started to laugh. "Oh, goodness," he said through the laughter. He couldn't remember the last time he'd laughed or smiled so much, let alone the last time he stayed up this late. Not that real estate agents and bowling alley managers needed to be up early, but for some reason, he'd always been an early to bed, early to rise type. And he knew he would sleep little tonight with the excitement of taking Lorelei and her daughter to their first ever tree-cutting adventure.

"We should finish up decorating for the night. I need to head home and get some sleep. We have a big day tomorrow." But he didn't want the night to end.

"There's one piece of pizza left. Do you want it to go?" She pointed at the kitchen island.

"Traveling pizza?"

"Yes, the best part about frozen pizza is that it's solid as a brick when it's cold. It's essentially a transportable meal."

"Not gonna lie, I'm worried about our feast tomorrow."

Lorelei shook her head, and all he could do was smile. And that smile remained plastered on his face the entire drive home.

Chapter 16

When they entered the town of Booth (as the crimson-and-gold sign proclaimed on the side of the road), the thought of the resume Lorelei had submitted to a local doctor's office pinged in her mind as though an email alert had gone off. But she quickly disregarded it and sent it into the imaginary trash folder. She'd never heard back, so no reason to ponder it a second longer. By the time Tyler parked his truck, the coffee in her hand had finally warmed her to the bone. A red-and-green Paul's Christmas Farm sign stood before them and supported a layer of snow across the top.

"See, this looks like a forest and not a farm." She leaned forward in her seat. "I don't see any John Deere tractors."

"I should hope not. There's two feet of snow on the ground."

Lorelei unloaded Mary Ann from the back seat and attempted to put her daughter's fleece hat back on. Mary Ann had disagreed with wearing it this morning by showcasing the range and volume of her vocal cords and grabbing at it with freakishly strong fingers for an infant.

"Can you help me put her hat on? Maybe she'll allow it if you do it." Lorelei carried her bundled-up daughter around the front of Tyler's truck.

"Let's put this super-duper cute hat on to keep your super-duper cute ears and head warm," Tyler singsonged. He beamed as he slid on Mary Ann's hat, and she replied with a shriek of joy.

"Thank you." Lorelei pivoted toward the entrance. *Another reminder of how amazing he is, thanks.*

A forest of Christmas trees flocked in nature's white powder surrounded the tiny parking lot. Off to the left sat a small ever-green-colored shed with a single-windowed door in the front.

"Do we have to check in with anyone?" Lorelei glanced around.

"Paul is here someplace, if not in the office, then out there." He pointed at the maze of trees beyond the sign.

Tyler held a saw in his hand as he led the way past the sign and into the forest.

Their boots crunched over the icy snow packed on the ground. "Shouldn't there be other people here?" Lorelei glanced back at the parking lot.

"We're here early. It just opened at 9 a.m. Most will probably show up later—it's supposed to be sunny this afternoon. But we have a long list for today."

She didn't need a reminder of all they had left to do for the Christmas feast tonight. Of course, she was grateful for Tyler's help and excited to be experiencing her first Christmas tree hunt adventure with him and Mary Ann.

"If you see a tree you like, let me know. I know with all the snow, it's not the best."

"I think it's beautiful, this place. With or without snow. And we're the only ones here, so it's almost as though it's all ours." The scent of balsam fir and crisp morning snow filled her nostrils.

"Like an empty movie theater." Tyler paused, peering down a row of trees. "Have you ever had an entire theater to yourself?"

"Never. Does Oakvale have a movie theater?"

"No, but they do here." Tyler winked and continued down the snow-covered path. "So it looks like, one of us has enjoyed a solo movie theater and one has not."

"Maybe I could join you sometime." Why did you say that? Lorelei thought. She didn't know if there will be a *sometime* since I'm leaving after Christmas.

"I would enjoy your company for a movie. And my mom would love to watch Mary Ann."

"Sounds lovely." The wind picked up, she shivered, and then walked on. "Did I mention I put a resume in with a doctor's office here? It was back in the summer."

"No." Tyler glanced over at her.

"They had an opening, but I never heard back from them. It would have been a great step in the right direction, career-wise. It's for the best because I would have had the same issue of my parents not agreeing with a move to a small town and leaving the ER."

"I'm sorry to hear that." Although Lorelei didn't perceive his voice as sounding sincere, it did sound almost grateful. "Maybe there's a reason you never heard. We never would've met or formulated a tag-team parent intervention."

Lorelei paused and pointed. "What about that one?"

While it was hard to see exactly what the trees looked like under the snow, the fact that she was freezing meant the sooner they picked out two, the sooner they could be back inside the warmth of Tyler's truck.

"Do you use the saw to mark it? Like a claim notch?" Lorelei followed behind as they went deeper into the forest of trees. With each step, Mary Ann seemed to grow heavier.

The sound of his chuckle drifted around them. "No, we have to cut it down and haul it back to the truck."

Lorelei glanced over her shoulder in the direction of the truck. "But I need two trees."

"And I have two hands. We got this." Tyler used the saw to point. "This one?"

Lorelei leaned toward it. "Yes, I think so."

Tyler reached through the tree's branches and grasped its trunk, giving it a firm shake. The snow fell from it, exposing its beauty.

"Yes, it's perfect indeed."

"Do you want to cut it down?" Tyler hoisted the saw in Lorelei's direction.

Her eyes grew in surprise and a little bit of fear, too. "I can't. I'm holding the baby. Darn." She overly frowned, the dramatic expression endorsing her faux disappointment.

"No problem"—he reached out for Mary Ann, who kicked her legs in excitement—"I'll hold her for you." He grinned.

Lorelei raised an eyebrow and swapped her baby for the saw. She wiggled her shoulders and flexed her muscles under the bulky coat. Tyler smiled impressively. Once she brushed the snow away from the bottom of the tree, she put the saw's teeth against the base of the trunk and started to move it back and forth. It was hard to keep her squat form, but she would surely freeze more than she already was if she went to her knees.

With each sawing motion forward and back, her feet began to tingle from lack of blood flow. By the time the tree was halfway sawed, she leaned forward and toppled backward into the snow.

"I'd help you out, but I'm holding the baby." Tyler chuckled. "Darn."

She returned to her squatting position and brushed the snow from her coat. "I can now say purchasing a Christmas tree in a parking lot, precut, is the way to go."

"Your daughter can hear you," he whispered, pretending to cover one of her ears.

"And she can see me struggling, too. Mary Ann is observant. She'll remember this. Someday, when she's an adult and someone tries to convince her to cut her own Christmas tree down, she can say no thank you."

The tree started to lean. "Should you be holding this?"

Tyler made his way over to Lorelei and the tree. Reaching his hand inside, he grabbed ahold of the trunk. "You're good.

Keep sawing all the way through. And you can't assume your daughter won't love the wilderness. She might want to live in a Christmas tree forest, maybe even own one."

Lorelei blew a strand of hair from her eye and continued to saw. The workout with the saw helped warm her upper body, but her hands had started to cramp and her knees grew weaker.

"You can cut down the next one, right?" she whined.

"Yes, I just want you to experience this adventure."

"I think you mean you want me to experience freezing and a workout at the same time. Something I never thought was a possibility. Almost an oxymoron."

While she wouldn't admit it, Lorelei was starting to enjoy this lumber-woman stuff. It wasn't as bad as she made it seem. Heck, she was cutting down a tree. A tree that she and her daughter could enjoy for the rest of their stay in Oakvale. A tree that Santa's gifts would sit under. A tree which she'd hang her daughter's first Christmas ornament on. As these visions filled her head, a rush of adrenaline kicked in and doubled the saw action. She powered through until the tree was detached from the earth in which it grew. Lorelei pumped her fist in the air as she leaped up to standing.

"Are you sure you won't be cutting down the next tree?" Tyler held the Christmas tree upright in one hand and Mary Ann in the other.

"I'm sure." Lorelei slouched. "I'm freezing, and my arms are already sore."

He handed back Mary Ann to her, and she held tight to the saw. If she dropped it, it'd be lost in the deep powder below.

"Hello there!" a deep voice called from the edge of the path.

Tyler gave the tree a good shake, allowing the last of the snow to fall off, and hoisted it up. "Paul, hi, how have you been?"

Paul stood at least six feet tall, clad in ski pants and boots with an oversize hunter-green jacket and matching ski hat. His beard, a silver-gray, nearly hid his entire face. His name fit him well;

he very possibly could be a descendant of Paul Bunyan. *Does he have an ox back at his house?*

"Who do you have with you?" His voice rumbled, nearly causing the land to tremble.

Lorelei stepped forward, Tyler directly behind her. "Hi, I'm Lorelei. This is my daughter, Mary Ann." She motioned to reach out and shake Paul's hand but realized she had her hands full.

"Nice to meet you. I'm Paul. Thanks for coming to my farm."

Tyler set the fir down in the thick snow. "Lorelei's staying in Oakvale at the Norths' place for December."

"Ah, nice. Welcome. Tyler, can I take that for you? Wrap it up?"

"Of course. We'll be getting a second tree, too." Tyler handed the evergreen off as though it didn't weigh much.

"I'll get this wrapped and loaded." Paul carried the tree back toward the entrance as though it were a miniature toy.

Lorelei handed the saw back to Tyler as they continued farther down the path. Above, the clouds started to part, and wisps of blue streaked across the sky. She thought about the last time she'd taken the time to observe the sky. The answer she knew, months at least. She tried to think of the last time she went to a park or explored something in the city away from work. Every question sent her mind shuffling through a blank calendar. The answer was lost in a busy career. Lorelei realized she didn't have her cell phone in hand; her mind didn't race with a list of chores. Breathing in deeply, she paused her steps and closed her eyes for a second before continuing.

"It's beautiful out here," Tyler mentioned.

"Did you come here as a child?"

"For as long as I can remember. I used to run between the trees with my dad playing hide-and-seek while my mom took her time finding the perfect tree."

"It sounds heavenly. What about as a teenager?"

"Oh, I still came out here, but less hide-and-seek." Tyler glanced at her.

Lorelei giggled. "Have you ever noticed this Christmas tree forest is your bookstore? The real estate business is your parking lot Christmas tree stand."

Tyler reached out his gloved hand, and Lorelei placed her matching one in his without hesitation. "We both have a large leap to take with our parents, and regardless of the result, we'll support each other."

She glanced down at their hands woven together and then back up at Tyler.

"We got this, one step at a time." He squeezed her hand, and together they continued on the path.

After another minute of walking, still, hand in hand, she spotted a tree to her left. "What about that one?" She reluctantly slid her hand from his and pointed.

"I think it'll be a nice contrast. The first one was short and round, and this one's tall and slender." He followed her direction and reached the tree. Kneeling, he pushed the snow away from the base and started to saw. Within only a few minutes, the tree was nearly cut.

"Would you please hold the tree up? It's about ready to fall." Tyler paused in his sawing motion.

"On it." She stepped deeper into the snow and reached past the limbs to the center. "This has been fun. I'm glad Mary Ann was able to experience this. Thank you." She wouldn't forget this little adventure and would hold it tight in her memory regardless of her plans.

"It's not over yet."

"What do you mean, is the saw stuck?" Lorelei tried to peer around the tree.

"No, I wanted to make wreaths with you, but we'll need to take the supplies to go. Since we have to get started on the rest of the feast preparations, there is not enough time."

"Do we have time to make another stop?" She took the saw from him as he lifted the tree.

"No, Paul has everything we'll need. Usually, we'd stay here and make them, but he can box them up for us. Christmas isn't only about trees. Everyone needs a wreath."

"Is that in the rental agreement, too?" Lorelei switched Mary Ann to her other hip and laughed.

"Nope, I triple-checked this time. It's in the Christmas contract, the general one. The one Santa wrote."

"Right, the one Santa wrote." Lorelei's eyes narrowed.

"He's the most important guy in December." He wrapped his arms around the tree.

"I'm pretty sure Mrs. Claus is the most important person in December." Lorelei hustled her steps to catch up. Even carrying a tree, he walked faster than her.

"How so?" His head pivoted back over his shoulder.

Finally, falling into stride with him, they walked side by side toward the truck, their bodies nearly close enough to bump into each other. Tyler held the tree against his right hip, and Lorelei held Mary Ann on her left hip.

"We all know Mrs. Claus is doing the laundry, washing his suits, making the meals."

"This is not the nineteen fifties. I'm sure Santa does his own laundry," Tyler declared.

"Okay then, the elves, they're the most important part of December. Without them, the toys wouldn't be made."

Tyler halted to a stop and pivoted toward her. "I think we discovered the most critical component of December, and it's not Santa."

"And it's not Mrs. Claus."

"The elves," they repeated in unison, laughing.

"Of course, this only works if we're not counting Christmas cookies. I mean, those are high on the list in importance, maybe even equal to the presents." Lorelei placed her hand on her hip.

"Christmas cookies! Sharon makes the best."

"I can't wait to try them."

Before they continued, an old-school ringtone, muffled from the inside of Tyler's pocket, sounded. He rested the tree against his side and removed his cell phone.

"Hi, Mom. Is everything all right? ... Yes, I'm with Lorelei and Mary Ann. We picked out two trees and are heading back into town soon. ... No, that should be fine. ... Yes, the turkey. A pound per hour. ... Great, then we can pull it from the freezer and preheat the oven." Tyler's face went whiter than the snow around them. "What? No, no, we didn't know that. Need to go, Mom, thanks, bye."

"What's wrong?" She moved in front of him.

"The turkey. We were supposed to thaw it."

"It's not like frozen pizza?" Lorelei's forehead creased, and her breathing halted.

Tyler shook his head no. "It's nothing like a pizza."

They pivoted and ran as fast as possible with a baby and tree in tow.

Chapter 17

"Do you think it'll fit in the microwave?" Tyler tightened a bolt on the tree stand.

"I may not know anything about cooking a turkey, but I know it doesn't go in the microwave, under any circumstances." Lorelei removed Mary Ann's layers of warmth and set her next to a few pillows on the living room floor with her toys and board books. "What about a water bath?"

"I think thawing it would be risky. There's a whole danger zone with the water being too warm or too cold. Let me call my mom again. She'll know." Tyler stood up and examined the tree in the living room. It appeared straight. As he made his way down the hall to the front door, he pulled his cell from his jacket pocket before hanging on the coat rack. By the time he removed the twine from the second Christmas tree resting against the wall, his mom had picked up.

"Mom, how do we cook a frozen turkey?"

Lorelei leaned back from the stack of ornament boxes, and he gave her a thumbs-up and nodded.

"Thanks, Mom. Great. See you tonight." He disconnected and slid his phone back into his jeans pocket.

"Good news! We can cook the turkey from frozen, but we'll need to add fifty percent more time. Based on our turkey's weight, normally we would cook for four to five hours, so seven to eight hours."

He counted in his head. "It will be ready at 6 p.m."

"When does everyone start arriving?"

Tyler winced. He knew it was just past 10 a.m. right now. "Five thirty."

With confidence, Lorelei lifted her head and declared, "I work in the emergency department. I've seen and handled things you would never want to imagine. I can most certainly handle a turkey and a few guests."

"There should be about forty."

She kept her head high. "All right, more than a few guests."

Tyler chuckled, which turned into full-on laughter. *Oh, she absolutely has this. How can she not?* She was determined, beautiful, and strong. He bet, if left to her own devices, she could have easily pulled off this feast without him. Regardless, he wanted to help.

He took the tree into the library off the entryway and wiggled the trunk into the stand as he thought of Lorelei and all she had accomplished to get where she was today. She clearly loved her daughter, being a mom, and being a doctor. Yet, everything was not as perfect as it seemed. The same went for him. He loved his life in Oakvale and his family and friends, but the bookstore was the missing element. He thought he'd already come to terms with not following the bookstore dream, opting to travel instead. If only he had enough money for both. After spending time with Lorelei on the tree lighting night, he noticed an ache in his chest whenever she wasn't around. Maybe it was more than the bookstore. Maybe his *life* was missing something.

As he screwed the last bolt of the stand into the tree, a loud thud came from the kitchen. Heading in the direction of the noise, he found Lorelei kneeling on the floor with the still wrapped twenty-plus-pound turkey.

"These frozen guys are slippery. I'm glad it's wrapped." She hoisted it off the floor and back onto the counter before he stepped in and helped.

"I'm glad Cider isn't here or she might've been fighting you for it." Tyler chuckled.

"Good point. I should have bought two turkeys. Not only is this a beast, but I don't think it will feed forty people."

"That's where the sides come in. Everyone will take a small slice of turkey and fill their plates with sides."

"Did I buy enough sides?" Her eyes widened, and her brow rose.

Tyler went to her and reached his hand out, placing it on her arm. "It's okay. This is not a contest where Oakvale residents will judge if they like you. They already do. The judging comes during the reindeer contest."

"For a small town, a lot is going on." Lorelei prepared the roasting pan and cut the turkey free from the wrapper. After flopping it onto the pan, she stood back. "Now, is that all I do?"

"There's a bag inside, that much I know, it has to come out." Tyler leaned around the counter and peeked at the turkey as though he was looking in a cave.

Lorelei tilted her head, following his glance. "Oh, okay." She reached inside and removed it like the doctor she was.

Tyler lifted the roasting pan into the oven while Lorelei scrubbed up.

"You're doing a wonderful thing by hosting this feast," Tyler said. "Don't cha know the town will appreciate the get-together? And it's a chance to get everyone even more into the holiday spirit. Not everyone has family here, and I think being a part of the activities helps. The fact that your parents are coming to town is causing a small commotion."

"Really?" She finished drying her hands on a dish towel.

"Of course, no one comes here for the holidays. We don't have a ski resort or shopping mall to entice people. In a way, it's nice."

"It keeps it cozy and familiar, like a small town should be." Lorelei set the timer on the oven.

"Your parents' visit will provide the town with an opportunity to show off. The usual types of renters who stay at the

Norths' house hide out. I think people come here to get away for a while."

"I know I sure did. Okay, ready to decorate the trees?" Lorelei asked.

"Yes, but first"—he held up a finger—"I have something in the truck." Tyler disappeared out the front door, and when he returned, he found Lorelei stringing colored lights onto the living room tree as the baby watched from her spot on the rug.

"This is for you, or Mary Ann. However you want to look at it." Tyler handed her a small rectangular box wrapped in snowman paper, and she tore it open, revealing a Hallmark Keepsake ornament box. Tyler's heart rate sped up; he'd never gifted someone something as meaningful as this.

Lorelei opened the box and pulled out a porcelain snowflake. Inscribed across the bottom in gold lettering read: Baby's First Christmas and the year. The middle of the snowflake allowed for a photo.

"It's perfect. Thank you." Lorelei delighted in the treasure and covered it tightly in her hand. "We need to find a photo to put in it." She leaned in and wrapped her arms around him.

His heart stuttered then raced faster, her hug completed him. Lorelei smelled like Christmas morning, joyful and sweet. When she let go, he wanted to pull her back in and keep hugging her.

"I think I have an idea for that." Tyler glanced at Mary Ann, who had gotten onto all fours in a crawl position on the floor. "For now, let's finish up these trees."

They wrapped the lights around the trees, then Lorelei finished stringing the colored strands in the living room, and Tyler added clear lights to the tree in the library. Next, they decorated the trees. Opting to divide and conquer, she handled the living room tree while he tackled the library one. As he grabbed another ornament from the box, he went to the edge of the doorway and observed Lorelei paused before the tree, finding a perfect spot for each ornament.

While he enjoyed decorating for the Christmas season, when he thought back on the process, he noticed everything he did was a routine, a rhythm without thought. Not to say that it was a mess or that he didn't care, but seeing Lorelei and her attention to enjoying the process and being in the moment made him realize maybe he'd been doing it all wrong. He needed and wanted to see Christmas through her eyes, in fact, everything through her eyes. For someone who worked in such a demanding and stressful field, he understood how she needed to be a part of something slower, something with a more personal connection.

Returning to the library tree, he took the time to learn from what he'd witnessed and hung the rest of the ornaments with a sense of joy, savoring the process. When he finished the tree, he stood back and took a breath. This Christmas would indeed be different.

"Have you thought any more about your decision?" Lorelei peeked around the door frame to the library. "Oh, your tree is beautiful." She entered all the way and placed her hands on her hips, admiring the tree.

He didn't want to admit she'd added to the complexity of his decision. "Thank you, and no, I should be, but . . ." He followed her out of the room and back into the living room, where Mary Ann wobbled on hands and knees.

"Oh, goodness!" Lorelei shrieked as she lowered herself to the ground, directly in front of her daughter. She clapped her hands. "Come on. Mary Ann, are you going to crawl?"

Mary Ann rocked her bottom back and forth and moved her arm like a robot, locked at the elbow. She lurched again, and the back knee jerked ahead.

"Come on, baby girl," Lorelei encouraged, propped up on her knees.

Mary Ann squealed in delight and inched forward again, wobbly on her arms but solid on her knees. Lorelei reached up and grabbed Tyler's hand. He flinched with surprise and delight that he was able to be a part of this first moment with them. Lowering himself to his knees, too, he joined Lorelei on the floor and cheered on Mary Ann.

Mary Ann kicked her feet back and laid on her stomach. Then she pulled her knees up and started the motion forward again, but the momentum was too much and she face-planted when her arms gave out.

"This is amazing to watch and rather funny." Tyler elbowed Lorelei.

Lorelei continued to hold his hand as she glanced over at him. "It's both, isn't it?" She turned back around and observed her daughter with a full-on smile. After a squeeze, she let go of his hand and clapped for Mary Ann.

After a few more crawls forward, Mary Ann's arms must have grown tired as she flopped forward and started to fuss. Lorelei picked up her daughter and rocked her until she quieted down. Tyler watched as her eyes grew heavy with each sway and struggled to stay open.

"Do you want me to start on the side dishes?" he asked, already heading to the kitchen.

"If you don't mind. I should put her down for a nap so she isn't cranky during the feast." Yet, she didn't head upstairs. Remaining in front of the living room Christmas tree, the crackling fireplace, and among a sea of Christmas décor, Lorelei swayed her baby, and he could do nothing to stop watching. He rubbed his eyes as though it would help, but he couldn't stop. If Norman Rockwell saw this, he would paint it for sure, and no doubt, it would be a bestselling piece of art. Tyler pictured such a masterpiece hanging in the bookstore. He would keep it up all year long, even with the Christmas theme. And he knew exactly where he would hang it, on the wall by the children's reading nook.

He blinked, pulling himself from his daydream. *Being an adult shouldn't be so hard.* Why did he continue to waver? It upset him. He'd pushed his dream aside because breaking the news to his parents that he didn't want to continue with the family's business gave him anxiety. Why were the best things in life the hardest? To him, this seemed backward. If life made good things easy and bad things hard, maybe the world would be a better place.

Being around Lorelei reminded him why he must obtain his goal. Not that he didn't want to hand the family business down, but he wanted a different legacy to leave for his children. Yet, only if they had the same joy as he did. His parents found happiness in real estate just as he did with books. And he wanted to have a job he loved, something which gave him absolute pleasure.

With excitement in his blood at the comforting thought, he threw open the refrigerator door a bit too hard, and condiments clattered against the shelf. Once he straightened them out, he removed the green beans, celery, onions, and carrots.

"Oh, no," he mumbled.

"What's 'oh, no'?" Lorelei asked as she headed to take Mary Ann upstairs.

"We didn't stuff the turkey with stuffing."

She paused as her lips formed a straight line. "I didn't season it either."

"This will be a Christmas feast to remember." He chuckled.

As she sighed and headed up the stairs, all Tyler could think about was that it surely would be a Christmas feast to remember because it would be the best one ever. Just like everything else since Lorelei and Mary Ann had arrived.

Chapter 18

T hankfully, no one noticed the turkey had been seasoned midway through the cooking process as they gobbled up their tiny slice. Tyler had a genius idea of whipping up more gravy than anyone could possibly eat—and any doctor (even her) would ever condone—to cover up the lack of flavors. *When in doubt, gravy up.*

The residents continued to pile through the door, and each one gave her a warm hug and introduced themselves. There would be no way to remember every single one of them, and she wished she'd thought to get name tags.

She couldn't help but wonder how it was that she didn't even know the names of her two closest neighbors in her building at home. To be fair, she didn't have lots of practice with having to remember names. At work, names were on the patients' electronic charts on her laptop, and employees wore badges. Lorelei wanted to remember everyone's names. She wanted to stroll the town and say hello to anyone she saw, get to know her neighbors, and then when they came into the doctor's office, she wouldn't have to glance at the chart to know who she was treating.

Every time the front door opened the blast of outside air caused the flame to dance in the fireplace. Mary Ann slept soundly upstairs in spite of all the commotion downstairs, and Lorelei couldn't believe it. She never would've thought this day would come. Any of these days, to be exact. Staying in the

Christmas rental house in a small town, her daughter learning to crawl and being there to witness it, and making a turkey for the first time, along with cutting down Christmas trees. Everything she ever wished for was coming true. And then there was Tyler—she never expected him, yet she felt at home around him.

"Delicious turkey, incredibly moist," Diane of Kim and Diane's Thrifty Finds mentioned. Her ruby-red coat hung off her arm, and a paper plate rested in her hand. Lorelei offered to put it with the rest of the coats, but Diane politely declined. Lorelei thought perhaps it was a security blanket for her, amongst the socialization. Diane remained at the living room window, gazing out at the display of Christmas lights in the backyard.

"Thank you. Please excuse me," Lorelei stated and left to mingle with the others.

Diane nodded but didn't turn around.

The kitchen island held the side dishes including mashed potatoes, a hot green bean dish, buttery rolls, cranberry sauce, stuffing, sweet potatoes with toasted mini marshmallows on top, and mandarin orange Jell-O salad, a family recipe and a staple at any Minnesotan gathering. Bowls, more like troughs, of gravy flanked both ends of the island. The platter of turkey, sliced as thin as possible, sat on the kitchen table next to the plates and cups. Tyler had brought over his blue cooler filled with ice and sparkling apple cider.

"Lorelei, this is delightful. Thank you for all your hard work." Jodi appeared out of nowhere. "I brought you my space heater." She set her plate on the island and tore into the roll.

"Thank you, you didn't have to do that," Lorelei said over the crowd noise.

"I hated the thought of you having another issue with your heater with the baby and all. Tyler put it upstairs for you already." Jodi raised her shoulder and beamed. "He's simply the best. He helped you today, right?"

"Yes, we went out to see Paul's trees in Booth," Lorelei mentioned. "Is your car running alright?"

"For the moment. It got me here." Jodi held up her hand. "Fingers crossed."

Tyler appeared from the end of the buffet line with a full plate. "Why are you crossing your fingers? This food is amazing. You didn't cook it." He elbowed Jodi.

Jodi rolled her eyes and forked some of the stuffing. "Let's hope you didn't either."

"I supervised, so we're good." Tyler winked at Lorelei, who focused on not blushing.

"We were discussing Jodi's unreliable car." Lorelei's stomach moaned, but she wanted to make sure everything was running smoothly before she filled a plate of food.

"Ah, yes"—Tyler nodded as he dipped his slice of turkey into the mound of gravy steaming over his mashed potatoes—"the beast with heart but no motivation."

Jodi giggled. "It does sound like a grumbly grumpy beast every time I start it up."

"I can always give you a ride home if you need it." Tyler raised his fork of green beans.

Yet again, Lorelei needed to switch her focus off Jodi and Tyler. They've both confirmed they're only friends, but even their witty banter made her heart slightly jealous. She wished she had someone like that back in Minneapolis. Someone to joke around with who was also there whenever they needed each other. Her job didn't allow much time for creating relationships of any kind, certainly not closely bonded ones.

As she took in the scene of everyone gathered around, chatting and eating, she wished her parents were here now to see this, to experience such a feast. And she needed it, too. She'd already forgotten the name of the couple holding their four-month-old baby boy standing near the kitchen table. The boy's name was Jack, that much she remembered. Hopefully, they could arrange a playdate soon.

With Garrison at her heels, Sandy finished filling her plate and gave a slight wave to Lorelei.

"Thank you for coming." Lorelei waved back.

"No, thank you," Sandy iterated as she and Garrison drew closer. "This is quite a feast. Where's your daughter?"

"Can you believe she's sleeping through all this? She should be waking up soon." Lorelei bent down and rubbed Garrison behind his ear. "She crawled for the first time today."

Sandy's eyes widened, a smile spread across her face and drew up her already rosy cheeks. "I'm happy for you, how great you were able to see her accomplish that."

Lorelei's shoulders raised in joy. "You're right. It's what makes life special, being able to be there for all those moments."

"Has Tyler convinced you to move here yet? Or do you not even need convincing?" Sandy forked her Jell-O salad.

Lorelei glanced around, checking that Tyler's parents were not within earshot. She spotted them with Tyler and Cider over by the fireplace. "Tyler and I have been busy getting to know each other, but I don't need to be convinced to stay. I need a place to live full time and courage. I'm hoping my uncle will be up for retiring." She leaned in closer to Sandy. "I'm trying to focus on giving Tyler the support he needs to gather the gumption to tell his parents he wants *you know what.*"

"I can't think of anything better." Sandy tilted her head. "Wait, I can, but that's a wish for a later time. Now, go mingle. We have plenty of time to chat later."

Lorelei weakly smiled and caught the red lines on the baby monitor rising up and down. Mary Ann was awake and probably babbling to herself about her feet. She hurried out of the kitchen and upstairs with a spring in her step.

Entering the darkened room, Lorelei found her daughter had rolled over and was wiggling her bottom as though a song played.

"Hi, Mary Ann. Did you sleep well?" she asked, lifting her out of the crib.

Lorelei held her close, breathing in that delicious baby scent she still had. Voices gently filtered into the room with the light from downstairs. As Lorelei swayed her daughter, she closed her eyes in hopes of capturing the memory for years to come. Déjà vu washed over her as the feeling of being at her favorite aunt and uncle's place in the country came to life. She'd visited a few times in the summer and occasionally in the winter when her parents traveled overseas. As her memories continued, a twinge of homesickness welled up inside her, and she knew why. She missed and yearned for such a lifestyle—and always had—but between work and her parents, she'd pushed it aside.

As Lorelei descended the stairs with her daughter on her hip, she paused, holding onto the railing. Standing in the perfect spot, she soaked up the gathering of the community below. The warm glow of Christmas lights filled the space, and voices of happiness floated up to her ears. This is what her parents needed to experience. This was why she'd brought Mary Ann there. She needed to find a way to make Oakvale home.

Lorelei's lips parted in a smile. For the first time, she didn't feel the need to race down the steps to do a million things. She didn't have the urge to reach for her cell phone to respond to texts or calls. All she needed was right in front of her to enjoy.

The sting of determination caused her to shiver as she continued down the stairs.

"There you are, and I see the princess has woken." Tyler placed his hand on Lorelei's back and guided her down the hall to rejoin the festivities.

With his hand on her back, although slight, it was enough to cause tingles to travel up the back of her neck.

"I wish my parents were here," Lorelei mentioned as they reached the island. "I'm determined now."

"Good! But don't worry. There'll be many chances to wow them and show them how important your dream is to you," Tyler encouraged. "I haven't seen you eat anything. Can I fix you a plate before all the food is gone?"

She switched Mary Ann to her other hip and nodded. "Thank you. Or, if you don't mind holding Mary Ann, I can get myself a plate. I can't believe how well everyone liked the turkey."

Tyler stuck out his hands, and Mary Ann leaned out of her arms. She happily accepted Tyler holding her and proved so with a raspberry-filled babble.

"Did you decide?" she asked, turning toward the island.

"I think so."

"Will you be talking to your parents tonight about the bookstore?"

Tyler shook his head. "No, I was excited earlier at the thought, and then I saw their faces and decided I need more time."

After filling up a plate, Lorelei stood next to Tyler and her daughter. "You decided on forgoing the travel? That's great! Sometimes you need to jump in with both feet. Would it help if I pushed you?"

"Lorelei, let's enjoy this evening. We've worked hard to put it together. The last thing I want is to ruin everything." Tyler's tone low and sharp.

Over her years working in the ER, she'd seen many causes of anxiety, not only with patients but the families as well. And Tyler's voice had a sense of tension and unease in it. She'd met Richard and Arlene, and they seemed like caring, loving parents. Maybe the anxiety Tyler felt was not from his parents, but solely from him.

"I'm sorry, I didn't mean to upset you," Lorelei whispered.

"No, I'm sorry. I think I'm on edge simply thinking about it."

"Excuse me," Sharon interrupted, stepping in front of them. "I have to say this feast is amazing. Such delicious food. You must tell me your secret for the turkey."

Tyler and Lorelei glanced at each other, eyes wide. Neither of them wanted to reveal the secret was being ill-prepared.

Sharon raised an eyebrow and stared them down. "Fine, don't tell me, but I brought my famous Christmas cookies. A nice full box I set on the entryway table." Sharon motioned to the front door without taking her eyes off Tyler and Lorelei.

"I'll tell you if you promise not to tell another Oakvale resident." Lorelei took a bite of Jell-O salad. Usually, people wanted her recipe for the salad when she made it for hospital potlucks.

"You cave so easily, Lorelei." Tyler leaned into her and gave her a bump.

"I want to try those cookies." Lorelei gave him a bump back.

"Good girl, I knew you were a keeper." Sharon took a long sip of sparkling apple cider.

"The trick is to cook the turkey from frozen and add the spices after one hour of cooking. Plus, shove a stick of butter into the cavity because you didn't put stuffing inside."

Sharon's mouth dropped into a gaping O shape, followed by a set of giggles rattled out in Morse code fashion. "My word, a doctor, putting a stick of butter on or in anything! And all the gravy you have out. Lorelei, you might be the best doctor ever."

"Thank you, but I'm not advocating for those meal choices. This is a special occasion, after all." Lorelei's forehead creased.

"Come on now. I'm stealing you away from Tyler. You can spend plenty of time with him later. Let's meet some new faces." Sharon wrapped her arm around Lorelei, directing her into the crowd of people.

As she mingled with Don and Kim and Uncle Steve and Ted, happiness welled inside her heart. She couldn't help but glance at Tyler holding Mary Ann as he chatted with Mrs. Wilson, who was without Mittens, and Paul, who ended up arriving about an hour into the feast. Her thirst to live her life here in Oakvale grew, even if it meant her parents would disown her. And as much as the excitement and desire rose in her, she couldn't stop thinking about Tyler's dream. A part of her didn't want to be happy if he was not happy. She was falling for him. She knew it even before she thought it. Lorelei pondered if possibly everything would find a way to work itself out. She needed to find a way, and deep down, she didn't want to fight her parents about it.

Chapter 19

Tyler closed the front door after saying goodbye to his parents, who lingered the longest after the pumpkin and apple pie plates were scraped clean. Entering the living room, he found Lorelei and Mary Ann on the rug. The joy of discovering to crawl continued in full swing.

"That was quite a turnout. You'd think everyone in town hadn't eaten in weeks." Tyler perched himself at the end of the couch. "I know you must be tired. I'll help you clean up."

"I'm wide awake, surprisingly, and Mary Ann took such a long nap she'll be up late." Lorelei glanced back at the island and kitchen table. "There's not much to clean up. I think a few pans, platters, and serving bowls need some soaking."

"I guess you're right. I thought for a second people would start licking the platters clean." Tyler made his way to the island, gathered the serving dishes, and placed them in the sink, pumping a smidge of soap into each one before turning the water on. Once everything was in position for an overnight soak, he dried his hands on the dish towel and snatched two mugs from the cupboard.

"Do you want to make Christmas wreaths and have some hot cider?" He filled the kettle with water and placed it on the stovetop.

"Yes, what a perfect way to end the night. Cider and wreath making."

The night was already beyond perfect from Tyler's viewpoint.

"I'm pretty sure my freedom days are numbered now that Mary Ann is somewhat mobile. She'll only speed up from here." She glanced up at the Hallmark ornament on the tree. "I'll wipe down the table, and you can grab the wreath kit. Oh!" Lorelei's eyes widened with anticipation. "Sharon's cookies."

"Cider, wreaths, and sugar cookies, the perfect trio." Tyler grabbed the white box with a red-and-green ribbon off the entryway table and the box containing the wreath materials and took them to the kitchen.

Mary Ann squawked and babbled away as she made it off the rug and headed toward the kitchen, where Lorelei wiped down the table. Cider finished searching for any remaining food on the floor, then located Mary Ann and observed her in her new skill.

"I can't thank you enough for all your help for the feast. Really, for everything." Lorelei smiled softly.

"It's been my pleasure." He set the supplies on the table and took notice of Cider.

His dog approached the baby with caution. First, Cider sniffed Mary Ann, and then lowered herself onto her stomach parallel to her. With each crawl forward, Cider copied, trying to mimic the motion.

Tyler took a seat at the table opposite Lorelei and undid the ribbon from the cookie box. As he opened the lid, Lorelei leaned over, glimpsing inside. Frosted green Christmas trees and red globe ornaments filled the box. When he and Lorelei reached for a top cookie at the same time, their fingers touched. A spike of adrenaline coursed through his hand.

"Sorry, you can have the first one. I'm acting as though I've never had one, and I've had enough to attend the ATSC meeting." Tyler grinned.

"ATSC?" She took the ornament cookie in her hand.

"Addicted to Sugar Cookies."

Lorelei laughed as the kettle whistled, and she moved to quiet it. After mixing the cider, she returned to the table with two steaming mugs. The scent of crisp apples and cinnamon filled his nose.

"I'm in the mood for a Christmas story. How about you." Tyler snatched the Christmas tree cookie from the box and took a bite.

"My Christmas story repertoire is probably nothing compared to yours." She bit the cookie, and her eyes fluttered. "Mm, that's delicious."

Running her fingers through her hair, she pushed it off the side of her face and glanced at the living room Christmas tree. "There was this one Christmas where Santa brought me the biggest chocolate-brown teddy bear I have ever seen in all my life. I couldn't even carry it to my room without dragging it on the ground the entire way."

Picturing a childhood-size Lorelei with the same determined face she'd had at Paul's Christmas Tree Farm, he smirked, holding the cookie up to his lips.

"See, since I can remember, I wanted to be a doctor. And this jumbo bear would be my first patient. I did a checkup which involved getting close to his eyes, ears, and nose. I then took scissors to his limbs and snuck my grandma's sewing kit into my room. Grandma Marie always carried a sewing kit with her in case something ripped during her stays with us. Anyways, I reattached each of the teddy bear's limbs, and he went on to become my first successful operation story. There was this pride I had knowing the teddy bear was whole again because of my work, even if I was the one who'd made him need the surgery in the first place."

Tyler finished the cookie and brushed his hands together. "Great story, but not Christmassy. What else do you have?"

Lorelei's forehead creased as she lowered her head in regret. "Fine then, I will think of a more Christmassy story, but you must tell me one first."

He reached back into the box and pulled out an orna-ment-shaped sugar cookie. "Has to be even. I can't eat a tree and not an ornament."

"I like your way of thinking." She reached in and removed a Christmas tree cookie.

With half a cookie hanging out of his mouth, Tyler unloaded the wreath supplies, laying them out on the table between them. Out of the corner of his eye, he could see Cider and Mary Ann inching around in a circle between the living room and kitchen.

"Let me think, a childhood Christmas story." He took a sip of warm cider. "Yes, the year Dad put me in charge of the Christmas tree. I'd recently gotten my driver's license, and my parents were big on the whole learn-to-be-an-adult stuff." Tyler rolled his eyes. "We always picked out our Christmas tree at Paul's farm, but this one year, my new shiny driver's license year, they sent me alone. I drove out, searched for probably an hour for the perfect tree so I could prove I was capable of this adult stuff."

"Did you end up picking out a horrible tree?"

"No, I picked out the perfect tree." He nodded his head in agreement with his memory of the tree. "My focus was on tree selection and driving, causing me to completely disregarded the most important part—tying the tree to the vehicle."

Lorelei brought a branch of greenery to her nose and inhaled. He watched as she closed her eyes, taking in the scent. "Oh no, this doesn't sound good."

"Exactly. How hard could it be to tie a tree to the vehicle? Apparently, more challenging than I'd thought. I must have pulled over five or six times on the way home to pick the tree up off the road and reattach it. Plus, back then, Paul didn't wrap them up like he does now, so the branches were flapping about in the wind and snapping off every time it rolled off the top of the vehicle."

"I would have gone back and bought another tree." Lorelei glanced over at her daughter and Cider, still within eyesight.

"I wanted to, but my father specifically only gave me enough cash for one tree on purpose, and my wallet was empty since I'd already spent my own money on my parents' Christmas presents. By the time I arrived home, the evergreen was bald in one section and broken in another section. My mom shoved the tree in the corner of the living room that year, showcasing the only good section left."

"See, you learned something, though. Both of these trees arrived perfectly here." She stood, going to her daughter.

"Indeed, I did." He arranged the bare wreath circle on the table, removed the wire gage, and set them next to it. "It's also why I now drive a truck with a bed and not a car."

"I feel like I'm ignoring her so much today." Lorelei picked up Mary Ann, who protested with kicking legs and flailing arms, so she set her back down next to Cider. "Sorry, continue." She returned to the kitchen table. "I guess with new skills come new protests."

Tyler chuckled and tilted his head, observing the duo on the floor. "I guess so. Alright, making a wreath is fairly simple. You'll make small bunches and then wrap the wire around it to secure it to the frame. It's simple enough for you to tell me Christmas story at the same time."

She gathered the greenery and holiday berries, making small bundles, then laid them on the wreath. With each one, she over-lapped the last one like a professional. "Let's see, okay, this is not a story from my childhood, but one from a few years back. I've always loved those vintage Christmas trees from the Victorian era with the candles and the draping of beads. Something my parents never did with their hip and modern city Christmas trees. The first year in my condo, and my first adult Christmas, I worked fifty hours or more a week. I decided what a great time to have the tree of my dreams finally." Her face lit up. "It was Christmas Eve Eve. I'd gotten off work somewhat early and made a mad dash to snatch up a Christmas tree from the grocery store lot. There were only a few left and they were rather dried out. I had this tiny car at the time, since I didn't have Mary Ann, so I took a cab there and back. Let me tell you how much cab drivers love hauling Christmas trees."

"Zero percent." Tyler glanced up from his wreath making.

"Exactly. So, I helped the driver attach the tree to the roof of the car, but I didn't have enough string, so I had to hold onto it with my arm out the window, while snow is falling inside."

He didn't want to laugh out loud, but picturing this story was too much, and his body shook as he buckled over with laughter. "I'm sorry, go on." Tyler clenched his jaw, but it didn't help as the laughter continued. "Okay, now I'm done."

Lorelei leaned toward the table. Her eyes glistened in the light as though the stars were created in them. "No, it's okay, it was hysterical. Thankfully, traffic was limited, and once we untangled the tree from the cab, I only had to drag it from the lobby door to the elevator. After I fought with the tree stand for forty minutes, the tree was up. Not straight, but up."

Tyler nodded. "Of course."

"I'd been collecting ornaments, candles, and strings of beads for a few years. Talk about planning, because I definitely had been. The tree leaned but was straight enough to hang decorations on, and while I was exhausted, I had to finish this tree. My parents were on their way, and I wanted to show them how great it looked since they'd refused my childhood requests all those years. I placed the candles on the branches and, because I have zero patience, I lit them. It was beautiful. The ambiance I'd dreamed of for so many years finally came true. Well, as you're aware, back in the Victorian era, those candles caught a lot of trees on fire, and my dried-up grocery store lot tree was no exception. The heater kicked on, and the tree was right near a vent. It blew a candle's flame up against a branch, and the peaceful glow turned into an inferno. I snatched the flame retardant tree skirt and threw it over the flames. Thankfully, I only lost a small chunk of the tree and nothing more, like my entire living room."

"They make fake, safe candles to put on Christmas trees," Tyler stated.

"Yes, but those don't look the same. Authenticity is hard to pass up."

"You have a point there." He noticed Lorelei had completed the wreath. She was authentic to him in every way. Something he didn't think he would ever find. It was like she was meant to be a part of Oakvale. And a part of his life, too.

She held up the wreath. "You know what would look great at the bottom?"

Tyler paused for a second. "A candle." He smirked.

Lorelei slapped her hand on the table. "No, most definitely not a candle! A bow." She shook her head, but he saw her blushing as she whispered, "A candle."

Chapter 20

U pon returning to the office the day after an unexpected day off, thanks to the Christmas feast, she burst through the door with more joy than anticipated. Jodi startled and jumped from her chair behind the reception desk.

"I'm sorry to startle you," Lorelei said with a rueful twinge and clenched her teeth at Mary Ann wrapped tightly in her arms. Her daughter babbled when she saw her mom making a funny face.

"Shucks, it's okay, Lorelei. Last night was such fun. I'd be all smiles, too." Jodi beamed, hurried over, and snatched Mary Ann from her arms.

"How many calls were on the voice mail?" Lorelei asked while handing over her daughter.

"Zero." Jodi tilted her head as though the question didn't make sense.

Every single day of Lorelei's career as a doctor was taken up by other doctors, nurses, and patients. Somebody required something from her every second it seemed. From the moment she parked her car in the hospital's parking garage until she started the car up to go home, someone needed her. Even lunch breaks were more of a catch-up-on-patient-notes-while-holding-a-sandwich-over-the-laptop affair than an actual break from working. Bathroom visits were often few and far between as well. Sometimes she swore her eyeballs were floating as she rushed down the hall.

"Zero?" Lorelei's face wrinkled with confusion.

"Yes, they knew we were closed because of the feast. You do have three appointments today. Anyone who needed something yesterday will come in today or would have called if needed. But let's hope not because everyone seemed healthy at your place last night."

Lorelei leaned forward. "Will it be bad? Everyone rushing in upset about the office being closed?" She glanced back at the door.

"Rushing in? Who's rushing in? No." Jodi shook her head and turned to make a silly face at Mary Ann in her arms. "Your mommy needs to remember this isn't the ER or the big city, now, doesn't she? Yes, she does." Jodi glanced up. "Can I put on some coffee for us?"

"I'll brew up some. You have your hands full." She sighed with relief that there was not a stack of messages to handle before coffee.

As she filled the carafe with water and leveled off the coffee grounds, Lorelei noticed how her shoulders felt. They were not tense or climbing up to her ears. Her jaw was loose instead of sore from grinding her teeth in her sleep. Her entire mood matched that of a spring morning with the warm sun coming up and a light breeze causing the flowers to sway.

Looking out the kitchen's French doors, she noticed snow drifting down in gentle flakes. While winter continued outside, spring happiness filled her as the coffee dripped into the carafe. Tyler sprung into her thoughts, and she allowed it. She missed him. Sure, the clock on the coffee maker read 9:05, and yes, she'd spent all of yesterday with him, but her heart missed him already. Should she miss him? Was it wrong to miss his company?

Lorelei didn't want to know the answer as she filled two Christmas mugs with coffee and walked out into the waiting room. She found Jodi sitting in the faux leather chair in front of the woodstove with a picture book on her lap, reading to Mary Ann.

"You're great with her. I can't thank you enough for all your help." Lorelei set Jodi's coffee mug on the small end table near the chair.

"Thank you. I've always loved children. And Oakvale is the perfect place to raise them."

"How long have you been working for Dr. North?" Lorelei wrapped her hand around her mug and sat in a chair near Jodi.

"Since I was seventeen years old." Jodi's eyes widened as though saying aloud how long she'd had the job surprised her. "I started coming over after school my senior year. I did little things. Filing charts, straightening the rooms, cleaning. Dr. North always saved the Christmas decorating for me, too."

"How nice it is to have found a job you love." Lorelei sipped her coffee.

Jodi's vision wandered the room around them. A smile warmed her face. "Indeed, it is wonderful."

Mary Ann started to fuss, and no amount of rocking from Jodi quieted her. Jodi handed the baby to Lorelei, who clumsily took her daughter, setting her mug on the hearth.

"Maybe I've lost my touch."

"She had a long night. Don't worry. She's still smitten with you. When I see you with my daughter, your entire body shifts. Your soul lights up. Mary Ann can sense that, too."

"Thank you. Say, do you mind if I mention something?" Jodi returned to her desk with a mug of coffee and flopped into the chair.

"Of course." Lorelei held her daughter on her left side, and between sips of coffee, scanned her cell phone with her pinkie.

"Don't take offense to this, but you need to relax." Jodi's lips formed a straight line.

Lorelei choked on her coffee. Jodi sprang up and ran to her. Lorelei set the mug down and covered her mouth with the cell phone as the receptionist patted her back. "Sorry," she finally sputtered, "what exactly do you mean?"

"Sorry, Boss Lady, I only meant that you are always go-go-go. Look, you're on your phone instead of enjoying your coffee and time with your daughter. Since you started here, you've created things to do that don't need to be done. Yesterday you dusted un-dusty items, your eyes are glued to your phone every free second, and you walk like you're always late."

"It's called multitasking. And look, I'm not wearing scrubs." Lorelei scrunched her nose up and glanced down at her puffy rose-colored sweater and jeans. "I feel less stressed, but I guess maybe old habits are hard to break, especially when I have no idea what January brings."

Mary Ann placed her infant fingers on her mom's hair and clenched her fist around the strands. "Ouch, baby."

Jodi came to the rescue, unwrapping Mary Ann's fingers from her mom's hair. "I've been thinking about the little pickle you're in."

"You have?"

"You still haven't seen the upstairs." Jodi snatched her coffee mug off the desk and waved Lorelei over. "Come on. There's plenty to see."

She shifted Mary Ann in her arms and followed Jodi up the steps with a wool broadloom carpet runner held down by brass stair rods. The darkly stained hardwood floors appeared well kept as they made their way onto the second-floor landing. The end of the hall boasted a stained-glass window with a small bench built directly into a nook. To her immediate right was a door, and off to the left three more closed doors. Jodi clicked on the hall light at the switch.

"This here is the first bedroom. It's empty, as you can see." Jodi turned the vintage brass-and-glass doorknob. "There are two empty rooms."

The room's two windows were a nice large size, allowing for lots of natural light. One window overlooked the front yard and the other overlooked the side yard and Don's Conveniences. Blue Victorian damask wallpaper covered the walls. As they moved out and down the hallway, Lorelei glanced through the thin banister rails to the first floor below. Jodi opened another bedroom door across from the first. There was one window with a view of the backyard. The Victorian damask wallpaper mirrored the other room, and she reached out to run her fingers over the textured embossing.

"These are nice size rooms," Lorelei commented.

"Yep." Jodi headed down the hall to an open door.

The narrow bathroom had black and white hexagon floor tiles with white polished subway tile running halfway up the wall, meeting the small window. A claw-foot tub was nestled off to the left, and on the right, a toilet and pedestal sink were situated.

"Wow, these pieces are gorgeous, not to mention in great condition." Lorelei ran her hand along the edge of the tub.

Jodi gazed around. "It's a weird feeling to love a bathroom, I think."

They wandered down the hall to Jodi's bedroom. The door was cracked open, and Jodi tapped it so it swung the rest of the way open. Light filtered in through the two windows. The backyard's bare maple tree covered in snow seemed outlined, as though in a picture frame, by the window;s molding—lovely! The other window overlooked the side yard. Floral striped wallpaper lined the walls in neutral beige. A fireplace of white-and-gray streaked marble decorated the opposite wall. A queen-size bed faced the fireplace, and a mahogany dresser showcased framed photos.

"I think I could've used this house for inspiration when I wrote my essay on interior design history." Lorelei pivoted around in a circle, taking it all in as Mary Ann started to fuss.

"I thought, maybe, if you don't mind being roommates, you could move in here." Jodi eyed Mary Ann on her hip, causing the baby to giggle.

"You want us to live here?" Lorelei's eyes widened. "But this is your home."

"Look, it's no secret that Dr. North is far beyond retirement age. Plus, I've spoken with Tyler and know there is not a single place for rent or sale."

"I guess I never thought of this as an option. I pondered maybe asking my aunt and uncle if we could stay with them until something came available, but I don't think I know them well enough to live with them. Heck, I'll know more about you by the end of December than anyone else in town."

Jodi giggled. "That's true. But you still need to break it to your folks first." Jodi turned her focus to Lorelei and then pivoted in a circle one more time before heading back downstairs.

"When I was thinking about it last night, I was reminded of my last attempt many years ago. I was ten years old when I presented my parents with: Why I Need a Dog."

She waved her free hand in the air as though pulling the memory from it. "I made a spreadsheet organizing the dog's walking and feeding schedule. I also created a chore chart to earn money to cover the cost of dog food, toys, and medical checkups. But my ultimate win, or so I thought, was my slide show of shelter animals in need of homes. It was the only time I've ever seen my prim and proper mother shed a tear outside of my graduation."

"Wow." Jodi reached for Mary Ann as she balance her mug, and held a squirming infant at the same time. "Sounds ambitious. How'd it turn out?"

Lorelei unfolded the king-size blanket off the corner of Jodi's desk and laid it out on the floor. "I adopted Jim. He was with me for about eight years. A fluffy white dog who weighed about twenty-five pounds. The veterinarian was never able to pinpoint what breed mix he was, other than the best dog ever." She took Mary Ann from Jodi and set her down to roam free.

"I bet he was the best." Jodi crossed her arms and took a sip of coffee.

"He was the best in every way. When my parents were out of earshot, I would call him Jimmy-Wimmy." Lorelei smiled, her eye twinkling with a trace of a tear. "They hated me doing anything babyish. But when I called him Jimmy-Wimmy, his tail would swish so fast I thought he was going to cool off the entire room like a jumbo fan on high."

"She's crawling!" Jodi cheered, pointing at Mary Ann, who was heading toward the edge of the blanket.

Mary Ann paused, stared at the floor, and then with a butt wiggle, continued. Jodi set her mug on the edge of her desk and followed behind Lorelei with her hands clasped together.

"I can't believe she's crawling. It's awesome to watch." Jodi nearly bumped into Lorelei's back, trying to catch a glimpse over her shoulder.

"Not sure about the dirty floor, but I guess it's good for her immune system."

"I can't wait until we're roommates." Jodi reached out her hand and placed it on Lorelei's arm.

"I do hope Mary Ann and I can stay. Miracles happen this time of year. 'Tis the season, after all." Lorelei half-smiled.

If Oakvale had taught her anything, it was that it was a town of hope. And she knew without hope there would not be any miracles. When she thought back on everything leading up to yesterday, all she remembered were amazing little moments fitting together. She thought of Booth, but it wasn't Oakvale. It didn't have the residents of Oakvale. It didn't have Tyler.

"You and Tyler looked awful cozy together last night," Jodi stated.

"We did?" She placed her hand on her chest. *Don't blush! Don't blush!*

"I caught him staring at you several times." Jodi touched her earring. "A man who stares at a woman over eating delicious food definitely has feelings."

Lorelei touched Jodi's shoulder. "He was?"

"Seems to me like you have a *few* things pulling you to stay."

Chapter 21

E ven after spending all day yesterday with Lorelei, Tyler wanted nothing more than to be with her right that very minute. Maybe he could invite her to lunch. *She has to eat.* He stared off at the empty bowling lanes. The office was vacant, except for Cider licking the last of the peanut butter from her dog toy in her bed. As Tyler swiveled his desk chair around, his eyes found three things: a small pile of travel brochures, his stack of to-be-read books, and out the window, Once Upon a Book.

His mind was like a teeter-totter. Either way, he would upset someone. Be it his parents, Lorelei, or even Sandy, who so desperately wanted him to be the one to take over the bookstore. The one person who might understand best was away for the month. Dr. North had mentioned he didn't want to leave the practice to just anyone, and he knew Sandy felt the same way. How had a woman and baby he'd only known a few days affected his heart this fast?

"Let's focus on something we can handle," he told Cider. "What Christmas book will I read to the children for story time?"

He always selected a new picture book each Christmas. Sure, he could read a classic such as *The Night Before Christmas*, but every child had heard that story a dozen or more times.

Before he dove too deep into thought, his mind drifted back to Lorelei and Mary Ann. *Her parents!*

"I need to think of what we can do to help convince them of her dream," he told Cider, who moved on to playing with her stuffed lamb by chewing on its arm. "Oakvale can help by showcasing its spectacular-ness."

Cider glanced up as she continued to chew.

"Their timing will be perfect, arriving the day of the reindeer decorating contest." Tyler's eyes widened.

He'd forgotten about what his decorating theme would be this year with everything going on. "Dad's making a Christmas-tree themed reindeer," Tyler said, remembering what he'd spotted in the box the other day.

As he stood, Tyler took in the bowling alley with its illuminated Christmas trees and lights strung up and down the ceiling. Rubbing his chin, he pondered what reindeer theme he could do that had yet to be done in prior years.

"I got it." He pointed his finger in the air, went to the beverage bar and poured himself a cup of coffee, and returned to his desk.

"Now, to think of how to help out Lorelei." He sipped his coffee. "Cider, do you have any ideas?"

Cider tilted her head up. The lamb's arm looked more like a soggy fuzzy stick.

Drumming his fingers on the desk, he glanced at the town outside his office windows. Twisting back and forth in the chair, he dove into childhood memories. In elementary school, he and his classmates would play hide-and-seek in town, spending an entire Saturday trying to find each other before quitting and grabbing lunch at Uncle Steve's. Every kid held a tab at the Oakvale Pizza Pie so their parents could pay later. But he didn't think Lorelei's folks would be up for a game of hide-and-seek. Tyler chuckled out loud remembering the time it took Jodi over an hour to find him hiding upstairs at Kim and Diane's. Or the time he and his best friend, Ian, hid in the park and ended up sitting on an anthill. They were easy to find once they started running around, smacking the ants off. He and Ian had been best friends throughout fifth and sixth grades, but his parents moved them to California, and the boys lost contact over the years. That was when Jodi and Tyler started to hang out more, and he was grateful for their long-standing friendship.

The bell on the door chimed, and Richard entered. "Hey, son. How's your morning going?"

"Morning, Dad. Another busy day." He smirked.

"Most people would love the opportunity to have days of leisure," Richard said sharply. "How's it going with Lorelei? Your mom said we could watch Mary Ann anytime. Of course, then she brings up how great it would be to have grandbabies to watch grow up and take over the family business."

Ignoring the same old conversation, Tyler asked, "What impressed you and Mom about Oakvale when we first moved here?"

Richard poured coffee into his travel mug and leaned against the bar top. "Trying to help out Lorelei for when her parents arrive, I see." He winked. "Well, your mom and I enjoyed talking to your teachers at any time. When you can track down a teacher in less than sixty seconds, it's a nice bonus. I think you or other kids, in general, behaved better in class when their parents end up sitting at the table next to them or waiting in the checkout line at Don's."

Tyler leaned over his mug. "Great point, Dad. As a parent, I mean, it's great, but I would think the one-to-one conversations would be helpful whether my child was struggling in an area or excelling in an area."

Richard nodded his head and shoved his hand in his jean pocket. "Yes, it's how we found out you were finishing the required reading before everyone else and needed a more challenging level of English."

"Ah, that explains why my homework became more complex." Tyler rolled his eyes. "Anyway, that's how Lorelei feels about wanting to have her own practice—to have a one-on-one, personal level of contact with each patient. Yet, her parents' focus is on the big picture career status."

Richard headed toward the closet and glanced up from the reindeer box. "Your Mom hasn't snuck a peek, has she?"

Tyler shook his head. His mother hadn't, but he had. "Have you disregarded the fact that we don't have any houses for sale?"

"Sandy and Ted might very well rent out their house when the bookstore sells. Then Lorelei has a house to stay in until something else becomes available."

He rolled his eyes at his dad's answer. "Where will the new owner of the bookstore live?"

"Details, mere details."

Richard strolled up to Cider, giving her several pets as she continued to destroy the lamb's arm. "It sounds to me like you like Lorelei."

Tyler's mouth fell open. "Dad! No, we only just met. I mean, of course, I like her. But not *like her* like her, it's too soon." Tyler crossed his arms with a huff. Was it too soon? It was, wasn't it?

Richard stood, raised an eyebrow, and placed his hand on his son's shoulder. "You know Santa might leave you coal in your stocking for lying."

"I'm not, a child, he would never do that." Tyler frowned. "Sure, I like her, yes. She's nice and beautiful, and Mary Ann is such a great baby. And of course I want a family and kids—I have to clean the lanes." He eased up from the chair as though his thoughts pinned him down.

Richard chuckled as he opened the door. "I need to run over to Sharon's before all of her sugar cookies are gone."

Tyler waved goodbye without turning around. He worked on dusting the lanes, gutters, and caps. Then it hit him like a ton of coal, he'd proven not only a way for Lorelei to have a place to live but an added incentive to buy Once Upon a Book. Cider approached where the carpet transitioned to wood and flopped down with her lamb.

"If I buy the bookstore, maybe Sandy and Ted will travel, and Lorelei can rent out their house." Not only did his dream depend on his decision, but also Lorelei's dream. "Of course, she still needs to confirm her uncle's retirement plans." He took a deep breath. "One thing at a time." But everything was finding its way, like Santa on a snowy night.

Chapter 22

The sound of a phone ringing caused Lorelei's right eye to pop open. She rolled over in bed and lifted her head, confused by the noise. The room remained pitch-black except for the soft glow of the backyard Christmas tree lights around the drawn curtains' edges.

Ring, ring, ring.

After throwing back the covers, she stumbled from the bed, shoved her feet halfway into her slippers, and threaded her charcoal knit sweater over her pajamas. Once in the hall, she picked up the landline on the thin console table.

"Hello?" She rubbed her eyes and leaned forward into the phone.

"Dr. Lorelei, it's Sharon. I'm at home, not the café. It's at 471 East Pine Lane," she said.

"Hi, Sharon." Lorelei rewrapped herself in her sweater. "I'm sorry. Why are you calling me?" She didn't know what time it was, but far from sunrise for sure.

"Doctor, you're on call. Same as Dr. North," Sharon replied.

"On-call." She scratched her head. "Right, yes, of course." Being only half-awake affected her memory of the contract. "What seems to be the problem?"

"I had a slight mishap with my Christmas decorations. Maybe it's best if you come over and check me out."

"Of course, how do I get to your place?" Lorelei found a piece of paper and a pen in the tiny drawer of the table. Excitement grew inside of her, her first ever on-call assignment, face-to-face in a patient's home.

"Take a right on Maple, then left on Birch, then another left onto East Pine Lane, I'm the house on the end, 471," Sharon stated.

All tree names. Let's hope I'm writing this down correctly, she thought. "Oh, my daughter. I'm afraid I don't have anyone to watch her," Lorelei hesitated.

"Bring her along."

"See you soon, Sharon." Lorelei set the receiver back on the cradle and pressed her lips together before they burst into a smile. *A medical bag, she needed a medical bag.* If her uncle worked on-call, he should have a bag around the house.

Lorelei returned to her room, opened the closet doors, and started to search for something that might be a bag. The type she'd only seen in movies, old movies. She spotted something black and picked it up. The bottom was worn, it had short handles with a golden clasp. She lifted it off the shelf and opened it up. Inside was everything she might need, or so she hoped.

Dressed and bundled up, she carried a barely awake Mary Ann to the car and loaded up herself and the medical bag. The clock on the dash came to life and read 11:15 p.m. She blinked and squinted her eyes. "I thought it was much later."

As she drove the five minutes to Sharon's house, she made a wrong turn on Oak, which was not a part of the directions at all. Thankfully, the streets were clear of snow, and the full moon made for extra light to read the street signs once she got on the correct tree's road.

With Mary Ann and the medical bag in hand, she marched through the snow-covered path to the front door and knocked.

"Come in!" Sharon's voice yelled from behind the door.

Lorelei shoved the slightly sticky door open and entered. To her right, was the kitchen, on the left was the living room.

"Oh, goodness," Lorelei gasped.

On the living room floor laid Sharon, and on top of her, a Christmas tree. But Lorelei didn't think it could've done any damage at all by falling on Sharon. Possibly an ornament breaking might have done more harm, so better to be safe than sorry. Lorelei laid Mary Ann on the nearby couch, placing pillows on the edge to keep her from rolling off, and went to Sharon.

"Why didn't you say your Christmas tree was on top of you?" Lorelei pushed the tree up and off Sharon.

"Because I didn't need you driving all speedy to come over. I might have twisted my ankle, and I didn't want to take any chances. I'm sorry to have bothered you so late." Sharon pushed herself up to sitting. "I might have overreacted, too."

"No worries, it seems I went to bed earlier than normal tonight." Lorelei knelt and checked Sharon's ankles. "It felt like two when I got your call. Why are you decorating your tree so late at night?"

"I had yet to decorate it, and it looked so sad sitting bare. I put a Christmas movie on and decorated it but was drawn to the movie and sat down for a bit. The next thing I know, I wake up and gather myself for bed when I notice I never put the star on top. And a tree is not complete without its final touch. I guess I was more asleep than I thought and lost my balance on the stepladder. Thankfully, I had my cell phone in my pocket."

"I'm glad you did." Lorelei took hold of Sharon's left ankle. "Is it this one?"

"Yes."

Lorelei didn't notice any swelling or anything at all. She gently moved it a little to the left and then the right, causing Sharon to wince.

"That hurts a bit."

"I don't think you twisted it because it moves fairly well, it'll be sore and bruise, but that's about it. Can I help you up?"

"Yes, please." Sharon gave Lorelei her hand, and with some support, Lorelei lifted her to stand.

"Keep off it as much as possible for a few days." Lorelei assisted Sharon to her couch.

"Thank you for coming all this way and for disturbing your daughter. I didn't want to take any chances."

"You did the right thing. Never can be too safe when it comes to important things, especially ones you use every day, like ankles." Lorelei sat near her sleeping baby. Glancing around, she added, "Beautiful home you have here."

"Thank you. I've been living here for over thirty-five years. I stay pretty busy with the café, but it was my lifelong dream to own it. I bought it when I was a teacher over at Oakvale Elementary. I was Tyler's second-grade teacher."

Lorelei tilted her head and awed to herself. "How long did you teach?"

"About ten years." Sharon observed the tree. "Would you mind fixing the star?"

Lorelei stood and stepped one step on the three-step ladder and adjusted the star. "And you gave it up to be a baker."

"Yes. I miss the kids, but I see them in my café. Of course, they are all adults now, and they bring their kids in. It was time for a change." Sharon gazed at the tree and smiled. "Everyone needs a good change once in a while. Especially when it means chasing their dreams."

"I wish it were as easy as it sounds." Lorelei perched on the edge of the couch, turned to her daughter, and watched her sleep.

"Oh goodness, you're correct, and it was far from easy when I left my teaching position. They found someone a school year later, and not one single person was honestly happy for me for some time." Sharon glanced at the floor. "But it doesn't mean that help was not there for the school. Other teachers pitched in, and they all made it work, so my dream could work too. I hosted field trip days where the kids would come in and help make something and learn about math and science once a week.

Overall, I think the kids learned more from me leaving than staying."

"I want that type of life for Mary Ann—a community where I know as many residents as possible. I want to immerse myself in the town. Be a part of something we can give back to."

"Oakvale is great for raising a family and for finding love." Sharon covered herself in a nearby cream knit throw.

"Let's not put the gravy before the potatoes." Lorelei crossed her arms. She was starting to feel a setup coming on.

"If you'd like me to watch Mary Ann while you and Tyler go out for a bite to eat, it'd be my pleasure."

"A date?"

"Doesn't have to be a date, could be supper. Make sure Steve doesn't light a candle in the middle of the table and it's supper. Light it and it's a date."

Lorelei threw her hand up to her mouth to keep the laughter as quiet as possible. "In that case, I've been on a lot more dates than I ever thought."

Sharon chuckled slightly. "You like Tyler," she stated, although it should have been a question.

"He is . . . yes, I do like him. But I like everyone here. And I have a baby, and my life is not . . . I'm not . . ."

"You're not what?"

Lorelei sighed as she observed Sharon's living room. Framed photos hung on either side of the wall leading into the kitchen. A small television sat on the corner of a long bureau, which looked like something casing an old record player. Although the kitchen was dark, she could make out some of it and was able to tell it had not been updated for centuries. Being in Sharon's home felt exactly like being in the café—cozy. "It's important for Mary Ann to have stability. You know the whole spiel about dating and kids."

Sharon nodded her head gently.

Lorelei ran her hand over her knees. "I want to at least know I'm going to stay in a town before I start putting my heart out there."

"You're *not* staying?"

Lorelei leaned back into the corner of the couch. "I want to, but as you know, it's not as simple as it might seem. Jodi did offer up the great idea of being her roommate. Although, my parents play a big role. As an only child, my support system is limited, and their opinion matters. I've struggled with disappointing them. I guess it doesn't matter how old you are, you always worry about what your parents think, and the desire to please them never goes away."

"I'd not thought of the extra rooms above the doc's office." Sharon readjusted the blanket. "I think we all worry about disappointing others, not only our parents. You should've seen this town throw a temperature when I announced my retirement from teaching. I was giving them a bakery, but still, they pouted. This town loves Tyler, and we see how he lights up when he is around you and Mary Ann."

"I do enjoy his company. And while I love this town, the reality is far from my dreams." Lorelei had experienced hospitality wherever she went, a continued warm welcome. Her heart quickly wrapped itself up in Oakvale, and she knew Tyler was a big part of it. "I do hope a Christmas miracle happens, and someway, somehow, everything works out."

"I'm grateful we have this time together." Sharon reached over the sleeping baby and took Lorelei's hand. "When I'm at the café, it's go-go-go. It was important for me to chat with you, even if it's rather late at night."

"Important?"

"Why, yes. We, the town, if we all pull together, I don't see any other outcome but a happy one. And if all else fails, I—we!—can win your parents over with a sugar coma of sweets."

Lorelei quietly laughed.

"Are you hungry, by chance?" Sharon tilted her head.

"Is it wrong if I say a late-night snack sounds good?" Lorelei instantly welled with nostalgia. The moment was mirroring a memory she had with her aunt and uncle on their farm.

"Never, I have leftovers from a hot dish I made yesterday."

"Give me directions, and I'll get it heated up." As she rose from the couch, Lorelei turned and glanced at Mary Ann, thinking, they'll find a way to stay. It was as though her heart finally spoke louder than her mind.

Chapter 23

T yler rarely went into work early, especially since most people didn't bowl or look for houses at the crack of dawn.
However, once in a while, he found himself arriving as the sun
rose over the pines. He parked his truck and patted his leg for
Cider to jump on out. As they strolled past the office, Cider
paused.

"Come on, girl, today we're going for a long walk before
work."

Cider caught up in a few steps, and they headed toward the
town's Christmas tree. Its lights were now on 24-7 until New
Year's Day. They walked past Oakvale Pizza Pie and then came
upon the doctor's office and Don's Conveniences. He paused,
wondering what his mornings might look like if Lorelei and
Mary Ann moved there for good. *Would they start dating?*

The sunrise shifted over the tops of the trees, and Cider's
breath cast tiny clouds in front of them with each pant. Glancing across the street, he saw Sharon's car in the front parking spot. Her café didn't open for another thirty minutes. She
would be in the back, mixing batter and starting the coffee.

Continuing down the street with Cider at his side, he turned
left into a small park surrounding Oaky Pond. In another few
weeks, the pond would most likely be frozen over and become a
fun little outing for the resident kids with their ice skates. Snow
covered the benches wrapping the path, but it was far too cold
to sit down, anyway. Making his way around, Cider discovered

a broken limb near a tree and picked it up in her mouth with a joyful romp.

As a kid, he and his dad would come out here and play a quick hockey game before school started. If it was winter break, they would play a longer game until his dad had to open up the office for the day. He loved his childhood and hoped to provide the same type of service for new residents or teenagers becoming adults. It drove him to want to run the family business, but soon he noticed it didn't make him feel the way the bookstore did, and he didn't even own it. Helping others find the perfect book gave him immediate, enduring satisfaction.

From the corner of his eye, he noticed Sandy and Garrison entering the park.

"Good morning," he called.

"Good morning, Tyler." Sandy waved and let Garrison off his leash.

Cider and Garrison dashed toward each other, the branch becoming a prize toy to be won.

"I think Garrison is getting a bit of cabin fever lately and figured a nice walk would do him good." Sandy wrapped his leash up around her gloved hand. "What brings you out here this early?"

Tyler fidgeted with his jacket's zipper. "Wanted to clear my head and see if any new ideas would come to me." He glanced at his boots, and when he looked up, Sharon was crossing the street. "I'd like Lorelei and Mary Ann to stay in town for good, but I'm afraid her obstacles are too big." He sighed. "I feel helpless."

Sharon waved as she approached, slowly limping. "Hi, everyone."

Sandy readjusted her scarf to cover more of her neck. "Good morning, Sharon."

"I saw you two and had to come over." Sharon buttoned up her coat. "I had the pleasure of spending time with Lorelei over a late-night snack last night."

"Sharon, why are you limping?" Tyler asked.

She batted her hand. "Don't tell the doctor. I'm taking it as easy as I can, my tree wanted to tango with me last night, and it won."

"Taking it easy probably doesn't involve you working, let alone walking over here." Sandy rubbed her gloved hands over her arms.

"Don't cha know, my hindsight's off?" Sharon bit her lip and cowered.

"Sounds more like your sight was lost at sea." He furrowed his brow in her direction.

Sharon shook her head. "It's not bad. I think I made the pain worse simply because I wanted to get some one-on-one time in with the doctor. Dr. North is great, but I already feel such a warm connection with Lorelei. And we all know the doc has been meaning to retire."

Sandy and Tyler glanced at each other and nodded in agreement.

"Let me know if there's anything I can do to help you or Lorelei. Maybe something the residents can all do together?" Sandy offered.

"Should we hold a town hall meeting to devise solutions to solve all our problems?" Tyler joked as he watched Cider and Garrison attempt to play takeaway with the branch.

"Not a bad idea." Sandy winked.

"You don't happen to sell a how-to book on this issue?" Tyler tilted his head and raised his right eyebrow.

"Sometimes, I wish there was a book for anything and everything in life. Or at least a pamphlet." Sandy reached her hand out and patted Tyler on the arm.

"Don't we all," Sharon mentioned. "Oh, did Lorelei tell you about Jodi's idea?"

Tyler shook his head.

Sharon clasped her hands together as she smiled. "Lorelei could be Jodi's roommate."

Tyler's eyes lit up. "The two spare rooms! Brilliant. But she hasn't talked to her parents yet."

Sandy and Sharon shook their heads in unison, and doubt spread over their lips.

Tyler crossed his arms. "Why do you think Lorelei and I are filled with such self-doubt that we can't speak our minds to our parents? We both want to, more than anything."

Sandy stared off at the pond. "I think we all struggle with self-doubt. I know I do. Take for example when I place my orders for books. I second-guess every single one as though I'm ordering my final supper. The bookstore thrives because I make the correct selections. Rarely, if ever, have I had to return unsold books to the publishers. And I've been running that place for so many years I've lost count, but long enough to know I shouldn't doubt each order."

Surprise spread over Tyler's face. "I had no idea. And sadly, it does make me feel better."

"I do the same at the café." Sharon shrugged. "Make too many muffins or not enough cookies."

Sandy glanced over at the dogs. "I do like Lorelei, and I hope she and her daughter can stay. And since I'm not your mother but your friend, I feel I can suggest you and Lorelei would make a wonderful couple."

"Sandy." Tyler's eyes darted to her.

"I second that," Sharon added.

"You know we're right." Sandy winked.

"And bold enough to say so." Sharon nodded.

He folded his arms over each other and rocked on the heels of his boots. "You're as bad as my parents."

"Tyler, need I remind you it's Christmas time. Isn't this the time for miracles?" Sharon asked.

"I sure hope so." Tyler sighed. "We have plenty of time at least to brainstorm before Lorelei's parents get here. I'm sure between everyone, we can come up with some great ideas to showcase the town and our community. Show them Lorelei doesn't need to be in a big city to be amazing."

"Oofta! My scones are in the oven!" Sharon yelped, limping off, waving her hand back toward them.

"Bye," Tyler called.

"Don't feel down about all this. There is still plenty of time left in December to get both of you on the right track. But I'm a teensy bit surprised you're having a change of heart. I know how much traveling meant to you."

"It does, but it just might be worth throwing away one dream for another." Tyler bunched up the neck of his coat.

"I'm itching for retirement, and by golly, if I have to drag you by your ear to confront your parents and tell them what you want, I will."

"Thanks for reminding me about the perks of a small town." Tyler chuckled.

"My pleasure." Sandy grinned. "Now, come join me for a hot-from-the-oven scone."

Chapter 24

Instead of walking over to the bowling alley and seeing if Tyler wanted to get lunch, Lorelei carried Mary Ann across the street to Kim and Diane's Thrifty Finds. She wanted nothing more than to spend time with Tyler but felt she was bugging him. With all the help he'd provided over the last few days, he probably enjoyed the time alone.

Thinking of Jodi's words from a few days back, she took a step and then another. She focused on walking slow, sauntering toward her destination with ease. The muscles in her neck relaxed, and her grip around Mary Ann loosened enough to lessen the strain on her shoulders.

Once she made it to the front of the store, she found herself glancing back at the bowling alley. The snow stopped last night, but the clouds remained, casting a dark atmosphere around her.

Back in the city, it would look different. She would head out of her condo and see people hustling to the upscale coffee shops or into buildings with soaring shadows. Lorelei would say hello to passersby, but they didn't know her, and she didn't know them. With everyone heading to and from work, there wasn't much time for small talk anyway. And forget about meeting up for lunch. Her work schedule made it impossible, and if she didn't have work, she was too tired to go out. Lorelei breathed in the crisp air and attempted to exhale her self-doubt.

Pulling open the door with her free hand, she wiped her boots on Kim and Diane's entry rug. Elvis's voice singing "I'll

Be Home for Christmas" filtered through the store. The scent of cinnamon and frosted pine mingled with the smell of dusty wood.

"Hi, welcome," Kim said, coming toward the front of the store. She wore a thick plum sweater, and her wavy dark-chocolate hair barely stayed tucked behind her ears. "Lorelei! You brought your daughter. May I?" Kim held her hands out toward Mary Ann.

"Yes, please. Carrying her any distance now is becoming a chore. She's growing so quickly." Lorelei handed her bundled-up daughter over.

Shaking her arms out, she glanced around. So far, she'd only been able to use the stroller once here. At least in the city they cleared the sidewalks so she could push the stroller and not have to carry her so much.

"Are you looking for something in particular?" Kim held Mary Ann on her hip as the infant grabbed hold of a chunky sweater button.

"I'm hoping to get some inspiration for the reindeer contest decorating thing Tyler mentioned." She loved everything about antique stores in Minneapolis, but with her schedule, she hadn't gone inside one in at least six months.

"Inspire away. I'll entertain Mary Ann. I must say, the Christmas feast was amazing. Thank you for hosting." Kim made an icky face at Mary Ann, and she belly laughed in return.

"Thank you. I loved having everyone over." Lorelei's cheeks warmed with a smile. "Do you know where my aunt and uncle go every December? It seems like an odd time to travel."

"Yeah, I know it does, but all everyone ever hears is that they head north. The Norths go north." Kim sighed a laugh. "They've never told you?"

"No, I guess I've never prodded enough to get an answer. Come to think of it, I've never seen pictures of their travels, either." Lorelei picked up a beaded blue glass bowl.

"Now that you mention it, they never talk about it." Kim's Minnesotan accent was much stronger than those in the city, and Lorelei took notice of the way she drew out her o's and a's.

"I'd love to chat with my uncle about his retirement goals." Lorelei browsed around the store, checking out the knick-knacks. "But without a phone number to contact them at, not much I can do at this point."

"If it helps you worry a bit less, the whole town is surprised he hasn't retired by now." Kim followed behind.

Lorelei glanced over her shoulder. "Really?"

"It's as though he reached a certain age and stopped aging." Kim switched Mary Ann to her other hip. Kim peeked around the store as though looking for someone. "You didn't hear this from me, but the Norths look the same as they did when I was a teenager. Plus, I think Dr. North worries about leaving the practice to a stranger. Not to mention, Jodi's been with him for years, and he wouldn't want to be the cause of her losing her job. However, I doubt he would shut it down. It would leave the town stranded for healthcare. Some people can't drive to Booth."

Lorelei moved on to the next display area. "Well, Jodi proposed the idea of Mary Ann and me moving into the two spare rooms above the practice."

"What a fabulous idea." Kim touched Lorelei's arm. "And you think you might like to stay for good, as our doctor?"

"I'd love nothing more, but I haven't discussed it with my parents, and I must speak with my uncle about his plans." Lorelei smiled slightly when she spotted a framed Norman Rockwell on the wall. In the painting, a man sat on a ladder, scratching his head, staring at the Christmas tree.

"It's not an original." Kim pointed at the painting. "But in my book, a print of it is better than not having it at all."

"It's perfect."

"For . . .?" Kim tilted her head, staring at it with Lorelei as though trying to find the answer.

"For the reindeer contest thing." Lorelei placed her finger on her lip. "Do you have some classic Christmas lights? The big colored ones that burn your fingers when they're on and if you dropped them, they shatter?"

"Oh, yes, let me think." Kim carried Mary Ann up and down the narrow aisles peeking around. "You know, I think they're upstairs."

"I can go look, if you don't mind." Lorelei touched Kim's arm as she moved past her.

"Be my guest. I'll be here with Mary Ann."

Lorelei took the stairs two at a time. When she reached the top of the landing, she paused, thinking of Tyler. In the daylight, the upstairs didn't seem as mysterious as it had been in the dark. And it didn't feel as cozy without him. She spotted the Christmas lights on a hook near the windows.

After taking the light strand into her hand, she peered out the window at the town below, blanketed in last night's snow. The Christmas tree lights were on, and the cloud cover made it dark enough that the lights could be seen rather well. Left of the tree, she spotted a person leaving Once Upon a Book and waving at a person over by Don's Conveniences.

Wrapping her hand around the window frame, Lorelei continued watching the town in motion below. She spotted Jodi exiting the office and hurrying across the street to Sharon's Café, all bundled up. Uncle Steve emerged from Oakvale Pizza Pie, holding the door for a couple who hugged him and waved before getting into their car.

The entire town, warm and friendly even on the coldest of December days, gave Lorelei goose bumps of joy. Then, out of the corner of her eye, she spotted a BMW without a single snowflake on its custom navy-blue paint, rolling into the center of town.

"No," Lorelei whispered. "It can't be. It's not the twentieth."

She removed her cell phone from her purse and checked the date. "No, no, no! They're early."

With the Christmas lights in hand, Lorelei rushed down the steps and halted at the cash register. "I'm leaving these here. I'll be right back."

She jogged past Kim and Mary Ann. "Can you watch her for two more minutes, please?"

"Sure thing," Kim's voice confused. "Is everything alright?"

Elvis's voice sang out "Santa Claus is Back in Town" through the store.

"No! My parents are here!" Lorelei pushed the front door open and headed toward the shiny BMW.

Chapter 25

It was a miraculous sight to see a car without any snow on it pulling into a parking spot in Oakvale, and Tyler took notice, especially since it was a fancy vehicle.

"They must be lost," he told Cider as he threaded on his jacket.

The BMW eased into a parking spot in front of Tyler's office window. A man with ash-blond-and-gray hair stepped out from the driver's side and rubbed his arms over his thick ski-worthy coat. The passenger window eased down, and a woman with blonde hair as straight as a book page said something and pointed at Tyler's office door.

He hurried outside, leaving Cider behind. "Hi, I'm Tyler. Can I help you? Do you need directions?"

The woman had already rolled back up the window.

"Hi there, yes, actually, we are looking for 8778 West Spruce Lane." The man walked over and reached out his hand. "I'm John."

Tyler took it gave it a firm shake. "That's the Norths' place. You know they're out of town his month?"

"Yes, we're here to visit our daughter and granddaughter. We arrived early since we were worried about her being in this tiny town all alone." John glanced around Tyler at his office behind him. "A bowling alley and a real estate office in one? You don't see that every day." He rocked on the heels of his wing-tip shoes.

"Yeah, wait," Tyler paused. "Are you Lorelei's parents?"

Before the man could answer, Tyler spotted Lorelei jogging as quickly but as safely as one could through the snow-covered street over to them.

"Dad!" Lorelei called out. "Dad, what are you doing here?" She halted to a stop, nearly sliding into Tyler and John. Her hand wrapped around his arm for support, and he reached out his opposite hand and grabbed ahold of her. Once she regained her balance, she straightened up and let go.

Tyler's eyes widened with the realization that Lorelei and he had yet to finalize their plans for Operation Assert Independence 101.

Lorelei hugged her dad, but when she glanced at Tyler, he noticed she looked anything but happy. She looked more like she was in shock, and he understood why. If his parents showed up early, especially if they were against his choices, he would be flustered too.

"Dad? Is everything alright? Is Mom with you?" Lorelei glanced over at the BMW.

Before John could reply, the car window rolled down, and a lilac-and-cashmere-covered arm reached out. "Hi, Lorelei. Come over here and hug me. I'm not getting out in my heels. Do they plow the roads here?"

"Dad, this is Tyler. Tyler, this is my dad, John."

"We met," Tyler mumbled.

Lorelei stepped off the sidewalk and went over to the passenger side of the BMW. She reached inside and gave her mom a meager hug. "And this is my mom, Joanne."

"Pleasure to meet you, Tyler." Joanne waved from inside the car. "I believe we've seen all there is to see, and this seems like a good little town. Small but cute."

Tyler shook John's hand and waved at Joanne. "Thank you?" He could not believe her mom wouldn't get out of the car for a proper hug, and Tyler reminded himself not to let his face show disapproval. *How could she judge a town she'd only been in for ten seconds?* His mind spun with concern. Convincing Lorelei's parents might be more challenging than he'd thought if they already disapprove of the town.

"Is Mary Ann at day care? Shouldn't you be at work?" John asked, stepping toward his daughter.

"I'm on lunch, and Kim is watching Mary Ann." Lorelei shoved her hands inside her coat pocket. "Why are you here early?"

Tyler noticed Cider had brought her lamb to the window, eager to meet new people.

"We were getting things ready for Christmas and received your voice mail about your stocking." John glanced over at Joanne.

"Yes, Lor, we figured why not come early and keep you company. Not sure there is much to do here." She held a hunter-green stocking with *Lorelei* stitched in red ribbon. "We bought one for Mary Ann, too. And I'm glad we did. It doesn't look like they have much of a selection of anything around here. But, honey, if you're working, why aren't you wearing scrubs?"

"First, there's more than enough to do here." Lorelei sighed a laugh and shot dagger eyes at Tyler. "Second, the work attire here is different."

"Moving on, your mom and I thought it best to come early, see if we could talk some sense into you, and have you back in the city by Christmas. Spend Mary Ann's first Christmas at home." John glanced around at the town before him. "We have tickets for *The Nutcracker* at the Orpheum Theatre and can catch a carriage ride there, too. Does this place even have a movie theater?"

Tyler took a step back toward the office door. Lorelei's folks managed to put the town down every time they opened their mouths. "I'm going to let everyone catch up. It was nice to meet you." As the words left his lips, he saw Lorelei tense up and stepped forward.

"Thanks for bringing the stockings." She all but lunged for Tyler, turning him toward the office and shoving him at the door just as he opened it. "Tyler, I needed to ask you something for a . . . patient. Be right back."

"What's going on?" he whispered once inside. Panic rose inside of him at the thought of how intense the last few minutes had been.

"I can't believe they bought Mary Ann her first stocking." Lorelei's lips dipped at the edges. "What am I saying? Of course, they overstepped. They always do. I wanted to be the one making or buying her first stocking." She turned to the window, faked smiled, and waved at her parents. Turning her head back toward him, her brow creased. "You're supposed to be helping me," she said, her voice taut.

"I froze up. I'm sorry. They're here early, and we have yet to formulate a plan. Besides, I didn't think I needed to be prepared to defend Oakvale. Are they always that sharp-tongued?"

With a fake smile remaining on her face, she talked to him through clenched teeth. "I know they're rough around the edges, but once you get to know them, it's not so bad, kind of, I guess. What are we going to do?"

He tugged at his ear. "We must show your parents how great Oakvale is. Because clearly, they already dislike this town. I don't know why, they just got here. Maybe you need someone who can whip up a better plan than me. I mean, wow, your folks."

"Did Jodi tell you we figured out a place for Mary Ann and me to live?" She grabbed his arm. "I was going to tell you yesterday, but I didn't have a free moment. Well, we did, but I was working on reeelaxxxinnng."

"No, but Sharon did." Tyler's brow furrowed.

Lorelei snorted a laugh. "More about that later. Look, I need you. We're a team. Let's not forget, we pinkie swore."

"Your parents frazzle me. Do you feel frazzled? I'm for sure frazzled. They. Are. Early." His eyes widened. "I feel like I'm losing before we've even begun."

Lorelei let go of his arm, and Tyler ran his hand through his hair. "Let's take them to Oakvale Pizza Pie tonight," he suggested. "I can meet you there after work. We'll immerse them into the town with food. Everyone loves food, right? And pizza?" Tyler paused and placed his hand on his chin. "They like pizza, right?"

Her face scrunched. "They like Italian dishes." She sighed. "Here's what I'll do. I'm going to have them follow me to my aunt and uncle's house. They can watch Mary Ann while I finish up my day at the office. Then, we'll meet up at Pizza Pie at six." She glanced back over her shoulder towards the window.

The BMW was there, but it appeared as though John had climbed back inside the car.

"Perfect." Tyler gave his hands a firm clap. "I'll spread the word around town that your parents are already here, and we need to—I need to—*we* . . . no 'me.'"

Lorelei lowered her head. "I don't think I can do this."

"You can, and we can." Tyler placed his hand under her chin and lifted her head. Their eyes met, and it took a great deal of strength not to pull her closer, hug her. Loosen the worry from her face. "We can't let them frazzle us. It doesn't change the goal. It's a blessing, a Christmas miracle."

"How is this, them arriving early"—she used her eyes to point at her parents—"a Christmas miracle?"

With his hand still on her chin, he said, "Because the sooner you talk to them, the sooner your dream starts."

A smile warmed on Lorelei's face, but he saw doubt lingering behind the blue of her irises. As he lowered his hands, she stepped back, adjusted her scarf, and headed outside. He watched Lorelei as she said something to John, when he rolled the driver's side window down. She pointed in the direction of the Norths' place. As the BMW backed out of the spot, Lorelei headed back over to Kim and Diane's store.

Glancing down at Cider, Tyler bit his lip to keep the doubt he'd developed from dropping out. When he looked outside, the reindeer decorating contest flyer taped to the office window caught his eye.

"That's it! We can move the contest up. Nothing shows a community coming together like a good old-fashioned contest, right, Cider? If they see how happy everyone is to have the doctor—their daughter—here, then maybe they'll be open to accepting Lorelei as a small-town doctor." His hands moved up slightly into the air as though displaying a banner that read, Small-Town Doctor Lorelei Parker. He could see it.

Moving to his desk, he took out a notepad and wrote down all that Oakdale had to showcase.

By the time he finished, the snow had begun to fall. Gathering up Cider's leash, he pulled the wool hat over his head and made his way to his first stop, Uncle Steve's pizza place.

Chapter 26

The drive back into town with her parents sitting on either side of Mary Ann's car seat dragged on. It seemed to last five hours not five minutes. Going home to change might have been a mistake. But she didn't want to show up for supper in clothes she'd worn to the office because her parents would indeed have a comment about it. The last thing she needed was to add more fuel to her parents' fire. Plus, with the continued snowfall, the BMW would not do well driving in it. She fluttered her eyes as she thought about it and parked her sedan in front of the Oakvale Pizza Pie.

"Are you sure there's not someplace else you would like to eat, Lor?" her mom asked, her seat belt still on. "Your father and I passed several in the town before this, Boone or Bone. It's a might bit bigger."

That town! "Booth. The town you passed was Booth. It's nice, but it's not Oakvale. Mom, you'll love Steve's cooking, trust me." Lorelei stepped from the sedan.

John lifted Mary Ann from her car seat and hoisted her over to Lorelei so he could safely climb from the car. Taking Mary Ann from her dad's hands, she led them to Oakvale Pizza Pie's front door. As she was about to reach for the handle, it opened, and Tyler appeared with a beaming smile.

"Why hello, perfect timing, Uncle Steve set us up at an excellent table." Tyler held the door while everyone entered.

"Is it next to your picture? I still need to find it." Lorelei winked. She needed something to take her mind off the nervousness and stress from her parents.

"You wish it were that easy." Tyler placed his hand on Lorelei's back, and it sent shivers through her.

Lorelei's cheeks flushed from the touch. Maybe all the distraction she needed from her parents was Tyler's company. No, because she liked him—and that only complicated her dream of staying in Oakvale. She knew if her parents thought she wanted to build a life here because of Tyler, it would be a high school lecture all over again. *She was an adult now. She could make her own decisions.*

She buckled Mary Ann into the restaurant's high chair as Tyler pulled out her chair. Simultaneously, John pulled out a chair for Joanne. With everyone seated, Uncle Steve strolled over.

"Welcome, Lorelei, wonderful to see you and your daughter again." Grinning, he turned to her parents. "We love having regulars here and new guests. You must be Lorelei's parents. I'm Steve." He reached his hand out and shook John's hand and then Joanne's.

"Thank you, Uncle Steve. Yes, this is my mom, Joanne, and my dad, John. They arrived early to spend some time with Mary Ann and me." Lorelei took a menu from Uncle Steve and immediately buried her face behind it.

"Nice to meet you both. May I start you off with some beverages?" Uncle Steve asked.

Mary Ann fussed. In her haste of rushing home after work, and her parent's early arrival flustering her, she'd forgotten to shove some toys into the diaper bag. "I don't have anything to entertain her with." She glared at Tyler.

"Here, I don't need one." Tyler handed his menu to Mary Ann, who took it and squealed with delight at the new toy.

Lorelei smiled shyly and noticed that the dimple on the left side of his cheek appeared in Tyler's return smile. Why did his smile make everything anxious inside of her melt away? *That only happens in the movies.* Her mind traveled to those classic Christmas movies she loved and the nostalgia of a small-town as a backdrop in a movie, particularly when it snowed at the perfect moment. Oakvale gave off that exact vibe, friendly and cozy. Like home sweet home. *She'd bet it's even cozier in the summer.* She thought of the lush green grass of a backyard, ice cream while strolling the town's street, and fireflies during a walk around the pond.

"Come here often?" John asked, directing the question at Tyler without looking up from his menu. His voice shattered Lorelei's idyllic daydream.

"Yes, several times a week." Tyler folded his arms and leaned back in the chair as Uncle Steve remained at the table.

"Why are you calling him uncle, Lor?" John asked.

"Because everyone calls him that."

"Do you serve red wine? A good quality red wine?" Joanne eyed the owner over the top of her menu.

"Yes, I like to think it's a delightful wine." Uncle Steve moved his pen over the pad. "I'll bring you a glass. And for you, John?"

"Red will also be fine," John said, still focused on the menu.

"I'll have some of your chilled apple cider." Tyler folded his hands together.

"I will as well, Uncle Steve. And would you mind—" Lorelei started to remove a bottle from the diaper bag on the floor.

"I'll bring out some warm water, too." Uncle Steve pivoted and hurried off to the kitchen.

"I do hope the wine is good," Joanne remarked as she observed the restaurant with a tightened jaw.

Lorelei rolled her eyes at Tyler, and he pushed his lips together as though to keep from winching with distaste. She glanced around the restaurant and noticed that for 6 p.m. it was not as busy as she'd assumed it would be. Only two tables were occupied. Before Lorelei could think anything of it, the door opened and along with a chill of outside air, Sharon and Jodi swept in.

The women, bundled up in jackets and scarves, approached the table, removing their gloves simultaneously.

"You must be John and Joanne. I'm Sharon." She hoisted a small white box with a green-and-red ribbon on it toward them. "I brought you my famous Christmas sugar cookies. You're more than welcome to come to my café, but I figured this would tide you over until then. Maybe as a midnight snack."

John stood and took the box. "Thank you. That's very kind of you, Sharon." He set the box near his utensils.

"I'm Jodi. I work with your daughter. She and Mary Ann are a pleasure to have in the office." Jodi began to reach out her hand to shake theirs but quickly retracted it.

"Mary Ann?" Joanne continued to study the menu. "What does she mean, Lor?"

"I take Mary Ann with me to work," Lorelei mumbled as her daughter swatted at the menu and sent it flying off her high chair.

"You must be kidding," Joanne inquired in a tone Lorelei associated with school report card day when she received a B instead of an A.

She noticed Jodi and Tyler gave each other a panicked look. Sharon picked the menu up off the floor and set it on a nearby empty table.

"Jodi is excellent with kids." Lorelei fanned herself with the menu. *Why was it so hot in there?*

"We don't doubt that, but it's a place of business, Lor. You can't have a baby in a place where you're running a business." John's eyes traveled toward Steve, balancing a tray. "What do you think your uncle would say about it?"

"Here's your wine." Uncle Steve set two glasses of red in front of Joanne and John. "And here's the warm water for your baby girl."

"Thank you." Lorelei smiled while watching her parents inspect the drinks in front of them as though they might contain poison.

"Oofta, your cider!" Uncle Steve declared and hurried back to the kitchen.

"If I may." Tyler eyed Lorelei as though checking for permission.

She nodded her head slightly with approval. Please save me, Tyler, she thought.

Tyler continued, "Dr. North wouldn't have an issue with Mary Ann being at the office. Oakvale doesn't have a day care center. Families help out families. The school is excellent and does have superb after-school activities for when Mary Ann is older."

John chuckled. "*When* Mary Ann is older? Why would you think she'll be here when she is of school-age?"

Tyler cleared his throat and ran his hand over his mouth. "What I mean is when Mary Ann is ready for preschool and if she happened to be here then . . ." He tugged on his ear. "I mean, clearly she isn't old enough. I just thought if this was in the future. And we might have a day care center soon. There is a need; just have to get everything in order."

Lorelei's heartbeat sounded like it was hooked up to a heart rate monitor in the ER that beeped for all to hear. She knew Tyler meant well.

"What Tyler means is that other kids here, that were once Mary Ann's age, are now in after-school programs, and the schools are great." *Well, that wasn't any better.*

"I love watching Mary Ann. The doctor's office is never busy to the point where I can't handle a child and answer a phone call or walk-in." Jodi knelt next to Mary Ann, who happily sucked away on her freshly prepared bottle.

"That's fine, but a baby doesn't belong in a doctor's office, regardless of the location's population." Joanne's posture was perfect in the chair, even at the end of a long day. "Not that any of that matters since you'll be back home shortly."

"Lorelei is a blessing to this town," Sharon marveled.

Another burst of cold air wafted in when the restaurant door opened, and Richard and Arlene shuffled inside. Arlene spotted the forming group around the table and waved.

"Hi," Richard cheered, approaching the table. "I'm Tyler's dad, Richard. You must be Lorelei's folks." He shoved his hand out with enthusiasm at John, shaking it.

Her parents' faces held perplexed looks.

"I'm Arlene, Tyler's mom." Walking around the table, she grasped Joanne's hand, cupping her other hand over the top. "Welcome to Oakvale. It's a wonderful place, especially to raise a family. We love having your daughter and Mary Ann here with us. We can tell how happy Lorelei is as the town doctor. Her knowledge continues to impress each patient she sees." Arlene moved toward Tyler and reached her arms around him, hugging him from behind.

"Thanks, Mom." Tyler patted her arm.

Joanne leaned forward in her chair. "That's nice, and thankfully she can use those skills where they're most needed, at the hospital. The patients at the hospital are the lucky ones."

"Our nearest hospital is over in Booth, about forty-five minutes out, so we're blessed more to have your daughter her to bridge the gap." Arlene encouraged sternly.

Uncle Steve made his way to the table and set down Lorelei and Tyler's chilled apple cider. She picked up her glass and took a long sip. The entire town slowly flooded through the restaurant, clearly trying to help her out. Tyler must have set everything up, but she still didn't have the courage she needed. She needed to be firm with her parents, but she wasn't ready yet. There were still shortcomings she needed to work out, and she refused to lay her dream out in the open for them to reject and insist she head back to Minneapolis that very night.

"We hope you'll be joining us for the reindeer decorating contest," Arlene encouraged.

"You decorate reindeer? Isn't that against some sort of animal law?" John asked, making a face as he sipped his red wine.

"Heavens, no, they're not real reindeer," Richard chuckled. "They are made of sticks and twigs."

Lorelei set her glass down. "I thought that wasn't until—"

"It's tomorrow," Sharon emphasized to Lorelei as all the residents standing around the table nodded their heads in agreement.

"We'll have to see. Now, if you will excuse us, we should be ordering supper. It's been a long day." John stood as though to dismiss the crowd.

"John." Joanne looked up at him. "It might be the only thing this town does for all of December and thus might be the only thing we'll have to keep us busy."

Suddenly, Lorelei wondered how well the Christmas feast she held would have gone over if they'd been there. Her dad would've chuckled at the thought of her cooking anything not from a box. Although technically, the stuffing had come from a box. And her mom would've insisted on hiring a professional chef.

Kim entered the establishment and shook the snow from her hair. "Hi, everyone," she beamed.

John's eyes widened as he sat back down, letting out a sigh.

Everyone standing around the table, including Lorelei and Tyler, wore jeans while John had on pressed gray slacks and Joanne a long navy-blue dress. *This is backfiring quickly.* Lorelei needed to get Tyler's attention but didn't know how to do it discreetly. Her parents were not happy. She'd caught them sharing a glance. A glance Lorelei had seen in the past when they'd discussed her dates. The opposite of what needed to happen was occurring. Every resident coming in to make them feel welcome was only causing them to feel bothered.

As Kim approached the table, Mary Ann decided she wanted nothing to do with her bottle and chucked it as though she were a pitcher in the World Series. The restaurant fell silent as they stood in shock. Lorelei lowered her head into her hands for a brief moment in hopes of gathering her composure.

"Hi, I'm Kim. My sister, Diane, and I run the thrift store across the street. It's more like an antique store," Kim paused, but Lorelei's folks didn't move a facial muscle. "Anyways, we'd love to have you stop by, browse around, and offer you a discount on purchases."

If there was one thing her mom liked, it was antiques. When she was a child, they'd go from store to store on a Saturday, searching for the latest finds. And Minneapolis had at least ten antique stores to satisfy Joanne's shopping habits. *Maybe there was a silver lining after all with Kim and Diane's store.* Lorelei needed them in a good mood for when she announced she was leaving the ER.

"Thank you, Kim. That sounds lovely." Joanne reached for her wine glass.

When Lorelei raised her head back up, Mary Ann's empty bottle sat on the table, and Tyler stood rocking her near the table. She stared at them, such a peaceful moment amongst a crowd of residents and her unhappy parents. *How could they look around and not have smiles on their faces right now?* Everything went silent in Lorelei's ears as she gazed at her daughter and Tyler holding her. *Okay, she definitely found him handsome, she could say that for certain.* She could admit it to herself as long as it wasn't said aloud because then things would become even more complicated.

"Do you know what you want?" Tyler's voice broke through her thoughts.

She nodded with a shy smile though she was unfocused, her mind fuzzy with contemplation.

"To order, for supper?" Uncle Steve asked, standing next to Tyler.

Lorelei squeezed her eyes shut firmly before opening them with a slight head shake. "Yes, supper, right. Let me try the pizza this time. Cheese only, please."

"And for you, John?" Uncle Steve turned to her dad.

"I'll try the chicken parmigiana."

Before Steve could finish writing down the order, Joanne said, "I'll have the bruschetta."

Steve scribbled faster onto the pad.

"And I'll have my regular, thank you," Tyler said to Uncle Steve as he continued to rock Mary Ann.

Kim joined the rest of the crowd around the table. The group stood there awkwardly until the sound of harmonizing voices grew louder and louder from somewhere in the distance. Lorelei spun around in her chair toward the restaurant's windows. A group of four people appeared, wrapped up in matching red scarves and donning black caroler hats.

When she turned back around, Tyler gave her a thumbs-up out of view from her parents, and his dimple showed.

Lorelei stood up at the same time as Uncle Steve headed back to the kitchen with their food orders. "Tyler, may I borrow you for a second? I had a question about a photo back here." She took him by his elbow and led him to the back of the restaurant.

She watched as Arlene, Richard, and the rest of the residents leaned forward toward the table, possibly attempting small talk with John and Joanne.

"What's going on?" Lorelei whispered as the voices of the carolers grew louder once they entered the restaurant, singing "Carol of the Bells." The scent of oregano, tomatoes, and fresh dough wafted past her nose.

"Too much? I thought this would be helpful, everyone coming in to introduce themselves. Show a real sense of community, and demonstrate how much we love having you here." He provided a clenched-teeth smile. "Sharon thought of the carolers."

Lorelei sighed and took Mary Ann from him. "Thank you for all of this, but it's coming off staged and not . . . real. And *I* know this town is real, but this"—she motioned with her eyes toward the growing crowd around their table—"is not Oakvale. I mean it is, but not this level."

Tyler's shoulders slumped. "Oh."

Reaching a hand out, she placed it on his arm, feeling his bicep on accident, causing her to forget what she was about to say.

"Don't let my bowling muscles fool you." He flexed. "I'm pretty strong."

"Funny guy. Look," she smirked, dropping her hand, "my parents might not like the wine, but they'll love the food. It's amazing, and this town is, too. And I didn't even think about Kim and Diane's store. My mom will be happy for at least a few hours. But maybe we need to ease them into everything slower than the current blitz happening at table four."

"That's table three." Tyler tilted his head and winced. "Sorry, not the time for jokes. You're right. Honestly, I had good intentions. Do you think the reindeer contest will be good?"

"Yes, I think it should help. We'll get a good meal in them, hope they sleep well, and then tomorrow we'll meet up for the reindeer thing. Where is the contest held? The bookstore?" Lorelei kissed her daughter's forehead.

"Let's do it at your place."

She glanced at her parents and the residents surrounding the table. "Yes, perfect."

Lorelei headed back to the table with a slight hop in her step, and Mary Ann bounced on her hip. The carolers stood near the door's entryway, continuing to harmonize.

"Is everything alright, Lor?" Joanne asked once the carolers ended their song.

"Couldn't be better." Lorelei set Mary Ann in the highchair. Never in her life had staying in a rental been so much fun.

Chapter 27

Tyler carried his Santa-themed mug of coffee to the living room window of his home. As he sipped, he admired the snowflakes trickling down, softly adding another layer to what was already on the ground. Hopefully, it would let up a bit so everyone could make it to Lorelei's in the afternoon for the reindeer contest.

Cider finished her breakfast and took up her spot on the faux leather couch. He set his mug on the coffee table, gave his dog a quick pat, and snatched a log from the rack. Opening the wood stove's door, he tossed it in.

Tyler glanced at the lit Christmas tree next to his overstuffed built-in bookcase. For some reason this year, the tree had huge gaps where more ornaments could fit. *The downside to upsizing the tree.* While he pondered how to fix the shortage, he glanced over at the breakfast nook. The box of décor for the reindeer contest sat on the table.

Hopefully, today would go better than yesterday with Lorelei's parents. They hadn't found the wine at Steve's to their liking, or so it seemed. But they'd enjoyed the food, which was a massive win, and had left the restaurant with huge smiles on their faces.

As he stood in the middle of his home, he could see the entire first floor and the staircase to the second floor. He thought back to when he'd bought the house. It'd been a complete gut job. The previous owner was a single woman who'd inherited it from a grandmother she'd never met. Town history showed the grandma as the original owner, and the builder of the cabin-like home had been her late husband. Once inherited, the woman from Texas moved in, but the Minnesota winters proved to be too much, and she put it up for sale the following spring before moving back to Texas.

He took another sip of coffee. The smell of balsam fir from the Christmas tree and the scent of cinnamon filled the room. Tyler always tossed a few cinnamon sticks into the wood stove to create a warm atmosphere during Christmastime.

Upstairs remained as bare as when he'd first moved in. There were a total of two bedrooms and one full bath upstairs. Most nights, Tyler found himself drifting off to sleep on the couch with a book rather than sleeping in the bedroom. The main bedroom had become more of a movie theater as it held the only television in the house. Cider and Tyler would munch on popcorn and kick back on the bed, opting to watch a classic movie over a new one. While the house was small, it worked for him, for now.

The wind howled outside, breaking Tyler from his thoughts before Lorelei and Mary Ann popped into them. Blowing snow passed by the windows, and doubt set into his stomach.

"Let's hope this passes, Cider. We need the reindeer contest to happen. Lorelei and Mary Ann need it to happen."

Cider lifted her head off the couch as though to ask why.

"The more we show the Parkers how committed the community is to Lorelei and how happy their daughter is running the doctor's office, the better chance Lorelei has to change their minds." He moved toward the couch and sat down, resting his elbows on his knees.

Something blue caught Tyler's eyes outside through the snow, and he stood up. Between the crackle of the fireplace and the wind, he didn't hear anything. Lorelei's sedan was parked next to his truck, and her fluffy scarf blew in the wind gusts with each step she made toward his porch.

Tyler set his mug down and bolted to the door, throwing it open. Snow drifted in as Lorelei made her way up the front steps.

"Tyler! Thank goodness you're home!"

"Lorelei, what are you doing here? You should've called." Tyler took her arm as she nearly blew away, walking up the steps.

Once inside, she said, "I tried to call on my way here but couldn't get a signal with my cell phone. The heater at the house went out again, and the firewood is nearly gone." She took a deep breath, shook the snow from her coat and stomped her boots on the doormat. "Your address was on the fridge. I hope you don't mind." Lorelei glanced at Tyler, but then her mouth fell open. "Wow, your home, it's . . . beautiful."

Moving her hand from her scarf to her chest, she stared. Cider jumped from the couch and greeted Lorelei by sitting at her feet. Without looking down at the dog, Lorelei gave Cider a few pets then stepped farther into the living room.

"It smells divine in here." Lorelei smiled and closed her eyes.

"Thank you." Tyler stepped up behind her.

He noticed she took a deep breath before she opened her eyes again. Lorelei being in his home caused nervousness to well up inside him. Since he rarely dated, his parents, Jodi, and a few neighbors were the only ones to ever to stop by. A desire to impress Lorelei came out of nowhere. But he knew it was not about himself or even the stature of his home. He wanted her to feel welcome and comfortable. He didn't want this to be the first and last time she came through his front door.

"Come in, have a seat." Tyler motioned toward the couch. "Would you like some coffee?"

Lorelei gazed around the room as she nodded yes. He poured some coffee into a snowman-themed mug. When he handed her the coffee, he noted the innocence in Lorelei's eyes spread over her entire face as though light grew from inside. Her eyes, a soft shade of blue with hints of sage at the edges, caught in the fire's glow.

"Beautiful," she whispered as though the house might blush to hear the news.

Tyler nodded. "Yes, you are."

Lorelei turned to him, wrapping her hands around the mug. "What? Sorry, did you say something?"

"The house, yes . . . thanks." Tyler took a drink of coffee, and tugged on his ear. "Please relax, have a seat."

She lowered herself onto the couch and took a sip from the mug as her shoulders raised. "Great coffee. I'm sorry about barging in, but I didn't know who else I should go to. I know Don can help me, but your house was closer than heading into town."

"I'm glad you stopped by. Of course you shouldn't be out driving in this weather. We don't have snow plows out here."

Lorelei leaned back into the couch. "I didn't want to venture out in this, but everyone is frozen back at the house. My parents insisted I leave Mary Ann with them. Yet, judging by the fear in their weak smiles when I left, I believe they're counting the minutes until I return."

Tyler sat next to Lorelei, but not close enough that their knees touched. Cider jumped onto the couch and curled up next to him. She leaned forward and set her mug on the end table and picked up a book.

"You're reading *Main Street*?" She rubbed her hand over the cover.

"Of course, you said it's your favorite book. I had to find out why." Tyler shyly smiled. "It's alright, right? Or is it weird?"

"Not at all. I picked up *A Far Off Place* from Sandy the other day but have yet to start reading it. I've been rather busy with the Christmas feast and decorating and trying to relax and enjoy time with Mary Ann. Relaxing is hard work." She smirked.

He chuckled. "Sorry." Tyler continued to chuckle. "Sorry."

"It's not funny." Lorelei set the book down and frowned but started to giggle. "Maybe it's a little funny."

Once the laughter faded, Tyler said, "'Tis the season for celebration."

"And memories. Don't cha know I've made a ton with Mary Ann already. I'm forever grateful for everything." She picked up her mug again. "It's the best December I can ever remember having."

"Even with the continuous lack of heat?" Tyler questioned.

"The company makes up for it." She winked.

"We should probably head into town, see if Don can come over. I have plenty of wood here. I'll load it up into your sedan. If we put it in the bed of my truck, it will get damp from the snow."

Lorelei remained cozied up in the corner of the couch near the wood stove. "Your home is like a classic Christmas card scene."

"Thank you."

Lorelei brought the mug to her lips.

"Tell me more about this possible plan to be Jodi's roommate. She is ecstatic about it." He wrapped his hand around his mug, warming his fingers.

"Jodi and I get along. And it would solve a big problem. Not the *biggest* problem, but one of them."

"Plus, she loves Mary Ann."

Lorelei pushed a strand of hair behind her ear. "She does. I just hope I can stick to my guns with my parents. Of course, I need to speak with my uncle, but overall, everything else seems to be falling perfectly into place."

"I would agree, so we should get started." Tyler retrieved the small box of décor for the reindeer from the kitchen table and set it by the front door. With Cider's leash in hand, he threaded on his coat. "I don't mean to feel like I'm kicking you out, but we should get the heat fixed in the house or at least a fire going. I can only imagine how bad this is looking to your parents."

"Yes, I fended off several 'in the city' stories before I left." Lorelei set the mug on the coffee table and slowly stood up. "Your house is peaceful. Sorry, I hope this doesn't make me look like a horrible mother lingering here when my house is freezing. But my parents . . . I'm not sure I can convince them. Everything they've said has been incredibly negative, and it's starting to turn my thoughts in that direction and believe it all. Being around them right now, when they're grumpy, it's tiring."

Tyler placed his hands on the outsides of each of her arms. "You're a wonderful mom to Mary Ann. You're giving her an amazing life. Be it in the city or a small town, what matters is that you're her mom. And her first Christmas will be filled with love. Her life will be the best regardless of what you decide—ER, here, or someplace else. Convincing your parents is only one step on the staircase. It's not the entire flight."

Lorelei gazed into his eyes and nodded. Even with the scent of cinnamon in the air, he could smell the same floral peach scent he first noticed during their lunch at Pizza Pie. Tyler fought the urge to close his eyes and kiss her lips. She leaned toward him. *That's not helping!*

The dog barked, causing them to separate.

"Cider," he grunted. "She gets bossy when I have her leash and don't put it on right away."

Was she blushing? Tyler's hand remained on the edge of her shoulder, and their eyes met again. "I'm beyond happy if you can stay."

"Me too," her voice low and soft.

Cider barked. Tyler waved his dog off and leaned in. Cider barked again. This time he couldn't ignore her. They separated, and he sighed. *It's probably for the best.*

"We should go." Tyler stepped forward and opened the door. She reached for his hand, her fingers grazing his palm. Accepting it, he wrapped his hand around hers, grabbed hold of Cider's leash in the other, and stepped out into the developing storm.

Chapter 28

As Lorelei stood rubbing her hands near the fireplace, all she could think about was how she and Tyler almost kissed. Her stomach fluttered with butterflies, and she found herself staring at him. But she knew better than to daydream. Come the end of December, this Christmas fairy tale would end. *Unless...*

Closing her eyes, Lorelei counted what still needed to happen, yet again. *Convince her parents Oakvale was the perfect town to raise Mary Ann in and get my uncle to retire.* Honestly, she was tired of the overthinking. She needed to take the leap.

Tyler placed another stack of logs on the fireplace hearth and brushed off his hands. Mary Ann napped upstairs with the space heater Jodi had loaned her while her parents sat on the couch, uncomfortable expressions plastered on their faces while bundled up in their jackets. Cider had stretched out on the living room rug just below the fireplace.

"Hopefully, Don will be here with supplies to fix the heater in a few minutes," Tyler announced.

"I'm grateful for the small heater Jodi lent us," Lorelei commented.

"This house is far too large to have that heater do any bit of good unless you're directly in front of it," Joanne snarked. "We should all go get a nice hotel room in Bone."

"Booth," Lorelei and Tyler said in unison.

Lorelei had driven them into town and let Don know what was going on. Although there was a storm raging outside, Don needed to grab supplies, close the store up, and carefully head over. They continued on their way after Don refused their offer to wait and give him a ride. He didn't want to bother them for a lift back to town.

"I hope the reindeer decorating contest will still be on." Lorelei glanced at the stove's clock. "I'm rather excited about it."

"How about we focus on not freezing first," John snapped, rubbing his hands on his arms.

"Mom, how about we make some cookies or a crisp? Using the oven will help warm up the house." Lorelei entered the kitchen and preheated the oven. While her mom had not taught her how to cook, Lorelei's grandma showed her how to bake all sorts of desserts from cookies to apple crisps to her famous Pflaumenkuchen. Thinking of it made her mouth water. The dessert called for special plums that were only in season in August or September for about one week, and not every grocery store carried them. Lorelei remembered standing on a kitchen chair, watching her grandma create the dish, and helping with simple tasks here and there, like stirring or sprinkling. There was no recipe card handed down when she passed, but Lorelei didn't need it if there had been one. Pflaumenkuchen and apple crisp were the only things she could make by memory and the only thing she made from scratch. Soon, her mind wandered to all the things she might try baking if she were not working so much. When Mary Ann got older, they could be baking queens, having fun, and making deliciousness together.

"Why don't *you* bake something," Joanne replied. "I'm staying here under the blankets. If this happened in the city, a repairman would have been here already to fix it."

Lorelei placed her hand on her hip. "Well, Mom, we're in Oakvale, and the slower pace is lovely. Besides, if I was back home, I'd be working and have a stranger in my condo. I know

Don, and he is not a stranger. The last time he was here, he locked up when he finished."

Tyler gave her a hidden thumb-up and smiled. She smiled back and straightened her posture.

"We understand the importance of safety, Lor," John mentioned. He turned his head and glanced over the back of the couch at his daughter.

"It's not only about that, John," Joanne interjected. She pivoted on the couch toward the kitchen. "Lor, you're five hours away from us, away from your career. You change lives working at the hospital. What do you possibly do here at the doctor's office? Treat a runny nose?"

"Mom, you can't compare a doctor's office to a hospital regardless of its location. They're completely separate work environments. Hopefully, if a doctor does their job well in the office, there will be fewer chances of patients ending up in the hospital." Lorelei angrily peeled a Granny Smith apple from the bowl sitting on the island.

"She makes a good point, Joanne," John agreed.

"Thank you, Dad." Lorelei moved on to the next apple, and Tyler took a seat at the bar stool opposite her.

"We only want you to be happy, Lor, and it sounds to me like you're trying to convince your mom and me that you want to move here to this tiny town. But let's not get into this in front of your guest." John eyed Tyler before he turned back to face the fireplace.

"Tyler is not a guest." Lorelei glanced at him as though she wanted permission to go on. "He's . . . a friend."

Joanne let out a not so silent huff.

"He *is* a friend, and so is everyone in this town whom I've met." Lorelei swallowed so loud she thought Mary Ann could hear it upstairs. "That's how it works in Oakvale."

The wind continued to howl outside, and the lights over the kitchen flickered as snow flurries floated in the wind.

"I hope you don't lose power, too," Joanne complained. "Although if the heater isn't fixed, I don't see why it'll matter."

Lorelei slammed the knife into another apple and chopped it up, allowing her anger to simmer. "Because we don't lose power in the city, Mom. Ever." She rolled her eyes, and Tyler placed his hand over his mouth to keep from chuckling.

"I don't need attitude. This is not high school," Joanne huffed. "Is something going on at the hospital with your position?"

"No, Mom."

The doorbell chimed, and Tyler jumped up to answer it. Lorelei continued to chop the apples and placed them in the rectangular dish without responding to her mom's question. Soon, Don's voice mixed with Tyler's and traveled down the hall. *They must already be inspecting the thermostat on the wall.* Wiping her hands on a nearby dish towel, she took it with her as she met up with the men.

"Hi, Don. What do you think it is this time?" she asked.

"Not sure. Fixed everything last time." Don hit some buttons. "But yep, it's not working again."

"Can you fix it, again?" Lorelei asked.

"Might need a whole new thermostat this time." Don rubbed his chin.

The lights danced in the kitchen, threatening to shut off.

"Have the Norths had this issues in the past?" Tyler asked.

"I don't believe so." Don threaded his thumbs around the buckles of his overalls, underneath his unzipped jacket. "At least, I was never called out to repair it."

The three stood in silence, staring at the thermostat, until finally, Lorelei asked, "Don, are you saying you're not going to be able to fix this one?"

"Correct, you'll need a new unit."

Lorelei wrapped the dishtowel around her hand. "Do you have one in town?"

"Nope, it'll be a while before I can get one in."

"What's 'a while'?" She dragged her hand through her hair and sighed.

"A few days." Don nodded without taking his eyes off the thermostat.

Lorelei wide-eyed Tyler. "Is there anything you can do to fix it temporarily?"

"Nope." Don rocked on the heels of his boots.

"Maybe Booth will have a thermostat in stock at that big chain store," Tyler suggested.

Don nodded his head. "You're probably right."

Right now, Lorelei didn't have the patience for this meandering back-and-forth. Returning to the kitchen, she finished cutting up the apples and sprinkled them with lemon juice. Next, she got out her frustration by making the crumble topping for dessert using the pastry mixer.

"Any good news on the thermostat?" John asked from the couch.

"Sounds like a trip to Booth to find a replacement." As the words slid from Lorelei's mouth, regret smacked her in the chest like a poorly caught salmon at Pike Place Market. Only this was not doctors' work conference in Seattle, and no one was laughing.

"Good to hear Booth can save the day." Joanne's voice wafted into the kitchen. Lorelei could see the smirk on her face without even looking.

By the time she slid the apple crisp into the oven, Tyler had entered the kitchen. "I'm going to have Don drop me off at my place since I rode here with you. I'll get my truck and head into Booth to see if I can get ahold of a new thermostat. It's far too dangerous for you to be driving in these conditions."

"You can't be out driving in it either. It might be worse in Booth." Lorelei poured herself another cup of coffee.

"I'll be careful." Tyler gathered Cider's leash.

"You can leave her here." Lorelei leaned over the counter, her hands wrapped around the mug.

"Thank you, I appreciate it. Are you sure she won't be a bother?"

"I'm sure Mary Ann would love to wake up from her nap and explore the floor with Cider." Lorelei warmly smiled.

"Be safe out there. It sure doesn't look good," John perked up.

Tyler glanced out the kitchen windows and back at John. "Thank you, sir."

Lorelei took her coffee mug and walked Tyler to the front door, where Don waited. After their near kiss that morning, she suddenly felt awkward about what to do. *Should I hug him?* Tyler moved his hands forward and then drew them back toward his sides. He half-waved and reached for the doorknob.

"See you when I return," Tyler muttered. "Of course, you'll see me when I return. I'm not sure why I said that. Sorry, I'm leaving now." He did another half-wave and walked out into the blowing snow.

"Be careful!" Lorelei called out as Don and Tyler stepped off the porch. Bringing her hand to her face, she closed the door and spun around to rest her back against it. If she didn't know better, Tyler appeared just as confused with how to say goodbye.

She made her way back into the kitchen as the lights danced once more.

"Lor, if you were home in Minneapolis, people wouldn't have to be running all over in this storm to get your heater working." Joanne readjusted the blanket over her shoulders.

"I know, Mom." Lorelei swung open cabinet doors looking for another baking dish. "It's not my house, remember."

"You're upsetting her, Lor. She's well aware of the challenges in a small town." John stood up from the couch and brought his coffee mug into the kitchen. "We know small towns seem great from the outside and maybe for a nice little getaway, but it's not practical to live here. Especially for a talented ER doctor who's a single mom moving up the hospital's career ladder. You have the opportunity to be what I never was able to be—the Dean of Medicine."

Frustration spread through Lorelei as she located a dish and set it on the counter. She reached for the bowl of apples and started to peel another. There was no reason why she should respond to her parents. They didn't want to change their viewpoint.

"Your dad's correct on several levels. Everyone who's important to you lives in Minneapolis and Chicago." Joanne glanced over the couch. "And you know how much we want you to be so much more than a doctor. The Dean of Medicine, can you imagine how wonderful that will be?"

Apple peel flew into the sink with each angry swipe Lorelei took. "I can't even begin to imagine it, Mom." Because when she did, it made her stomach hurt.

John poured himself more coffee and returned to the couch. "Maybe now is not the best time. I think once we're all warmed up, we can calmly discuss this."

The sound of wood crackling in the fireplace and the noise of the apple peeler were the only things to be heard outside of the howling wind. As she glared at the back of her parents' heads, she wanted to give them each an MRI. Find out why they were so strong headed against what she clearly wanted. She'd never spoken of the way they always overlooked her desires in her life. She just didn't understand them sometimes.

As she cut up more apples and mixed another batch of crumble topping, she thought of Tyler. Her eyes closed as the memory lingered.

"Lor?" John's voice broke through.

"Sorry, yes?" Lorelei asked.

"I hear Mary Ann. She must be awake." John pointed upstairs as he sat on the couch.

After sliding the second apple crisp into the oven and removing the first one, Lorelei headed upstairs to her daughter. *How dare they be judgmental about her not wanting to raise her baby near them if they didn't even want to get their granddaughter up from her nap?* Courage like she'd never felt before welled up inside of her as she opened the bedroom door. Mary Ann sat in the crib, smiling wide when she saw her mom.

"Hi, baby girl." Lorelei reached in and wrapped her up in her arms. "Did you have a wonderful nap?"

The room was the warmest in the house, thanks to the space heater. She felt blessed that Jodi had the foresight to lend it to her just in case there was another issue with the thermostat. Lorelei turned it off as she neared the window overlooking the front yard. The snow blew in the wind, and she could barely make out anything across the street.

"Let's hope Tyler and Don are safe," she whispered to Mary Ann and kissed her head. "Cider is downstairs waiting to crawl around with you."

Mary Ann squealed and squeezed her hands together.

Lorelei giggled. "Do you know the dog's name?" She paused and looked into her daughter's eyes. "Cider," she repeated.

As Mary Ann squealed again, Lorelei beamed with pride.

Chapter 29

T yler couldn't stop thinking about his embarrassing attempt at being casual upon leaving Lorelei. As he replayed it over in his mind, he cringed yet again. *Why didn't he give her a high five and call her* dude *while he was at it?* Putting his truck into park, he took a deep breath and leaned over his steering wheel facing the Norths' home.

Thankfully, the snow had stopped during his drive into Booth, and therefore upon his return, the driveway was lined with residents' vehicles for the reindeer decorating contest, including his parents' SUV.

Drumming his fingers on the dash along to the beat of "Run Rudolph Run," he tumbled headlong, lost in thought about the doctor who'd stolen his heart without even trying. Being around her, sharing an apple cider—or even, dare he say, frozen pizza—sent joy racing through him. None of that mattered when the Parkers didn't like him, and it was apparent in their distaste they showed earlier. Tyler shut off the truck, grabbed the new thermostat off the seat, and headed inside to join the festivities.

"Son! Here, help me carry in some more firewood," Richard called out, stepping out of the front door. "Did you find the thermostat?"

"Hi, Dad, yes. How's it going inside?" Tyler shoved the bag under his arm as Richard loaded his arms up with several logs.

"Other than the visible tension between Lorelei and her parents, it's great. I think we have everyone here for the contest, and now that you're here, we can start. Your mom is chopping at the . . . décor." Richard chuckled at his joke.

"Good one, Dad." Tyler headed inside with the bundle of wood.

The scent of baked apples and sounds of joyful conversation welcomed him into the kitchen. Even though the house was without heat, warmth surrounded Tyler as he said his hellos and set the wood next to the fireplace. He spotted Lorelei pouring refreshments into Sharon's and Jodi's glasses. Cider had taken up residence at the base of Mary Ann's high chair while Lorelei's daughter sat wide-eyed, taking it all in.

Nearing the kitchen island, he noticed five apple crisps lined up on cooling racks.

"Oh yeah, I got in the rhythm while you were out. Helped the house warm up some," Lorelei waved a half-full bottle of sparkling apple cider at him. "And kept me from losing my cool with my folks."

Tyler nodded, and she poured some into a glass. He accepted the glass and took a swig. "I'm guessing you haven't put your foot down with them yet."

"This close"—she held up her fingers in a pincher grasp—"when Mary Ann woke up, but by the time I walked back downstairs, I lost my nerve like a balloon in the wind. Up, up, and away. Look at my father, the way he stands with his hands in his pockets." Lorelei glanced over her shoulder. "He's already on the defense."

Tyler pivoted toward the living room. Watching as Lorelei instructed, he did indeed notice what she mentioned.

"Do you see how uninviting they look right now versus how welcoming everyone from town appears? How can they be so standoffish? Oakvale is magical. I felt it as soon as I arrived. Why can't they understand I don't want to be a big-hospital doctor? I want to be a small-town doctor."

"Then tell them that. Now, don't wait another second." Tyler elbowed her gently, and his fingers found hers resting at her side. She was clearly on a sugar rush, and she might as well take advantage of her blood sugar level.

She squeezed his hand in return. "Thank you."

He felt her heartbeat pulsing in the palm of her hand. Just then, John glanced over at the kitchen, gave a nod, and headed straight toward them.

"Tyler, were you able to locate a thermostat?" he inquired with one hand in his pocket, the other around his glass of red wine.

"I did." He turned to Lorelei and squeezed her hand. "I'm going to install it. It'll give you two a minute, unless you need me here."

Lorelei released the grip on Tyler's hand, letting him know he could go. At least, he figured that's what it meant. But as he walked off, he glanced back to smile at Lorelei and noticed her forehead was creased, her lips drawn down. *Maybe not.* It was as though he took all her courage with him when he left.

"Tyler, where are you going? We need to start the contest," Arlene called out.

He froze between the kitchen and living room. "Right, every-one, please, start without me. I need to get this thermostat installed first."

"It feels warm in here. Let it wait. Everyone! Collect your reindeer and supplies and find a spot," Arlene stated. "Not any different than last year. Lorelei, once everyone is set, will you please start a timer for thirty minutes."

Lorelei nodded and moved to get her reindeer and supplies. Though Arlene may have halted Lorelei from facing her parents right this minute, Tyler hoped she kept her resolve and only postponed her conversation until he was back at her side.

Sharon and Jodi occupied the living room with Uncle Steve while Arlene and Richard prepared in the kitchen. Kim and Diane set up between the living room and kitchen nearest to

Mary Ann and Cider. Sandy, Ted, and Garrison were arranged near the French doors to the back patio. That left Lorelei, her parents, and himself to organize a work space in the library off the foyer.

"My parents will share a reindeer. I hope that's not against the rules?" Lorelei questioned.

"Of course not; we're happy to have them join in on a Oakvale tradition any way they wish." Tyler smiled and opened his box of décor items.

"This seems rather childish." Joanne approached the reindeer as though it were real. "But we always try to be supportive of Lorelei and her . . . things. Lor, I hope you're grateful to Tyler for going out in that storm to get you a new thermostat. Small-town life is not for everyone. Imagine, what would you have done if you didn't know him?"

"On your mark!" Arlene called from the kitchen. "Get set! Reindeer decorate!"

"But, Mom, Tyler was here. And so was Don and anyone else I might have needed." Lorelei removed the strand of classic Christmas lights from her box and started to thread them into the deer's twig structure.

"Your mom is right, Lorelei, but it's not the time or place to discuss this. We're in front of guests." John stared at the reindeer. "Our apologies, Tyler. We already stepped out of line earlier."

"Nothing to apologize for, but if I may, Oakvale is not just a small town. It's a community." Tyler glanced at Lorelei, who focused on her reindeer.

He arranged red felt on the top of his reindeer. "Now, John and Joanne, if you want a chance to win the competition, you'd better start decorating."

Lorelei's parents glanced at each other and started to dig through their box. She'd let Tyler know yesterday she'd taken her mom to Kim and Diane's while her dad puttered around

Don's Conveniences to pick up some décor for the reindeer in preparation.

The Parkers removed spools of evergreen and cranberry ribbons from their box and began weaving it through the gaps in the reindeer's twigs.

"I know you're completely against me raising Mary Ann outside of Minneapolis, but I love it here." Lorelei peeked over at Tyler, and he nodded his head with a smile. "And I want to raise my daughter in Oakvale. I have no desire to climb the corporate ladder at the hospital and be the Dean of Medicine. Dad, that's your dream for me; my dream is to be a small-town doctor, and I hope to find a way to do so here. You're more than welcome to come and visit anytime you wish. I'm sorry if you disagree with my decision, but I'm doing what's best for Mary Ann and me."

Laughter and conversation filtered into the front room from the back of the house. Tyler watched as Lorelei took a deep breath but remained focused on her reindeer.

"I'm confused." Joanne tilted her head up as her fingers paused on the ribbon. "It sounds like you're giving up on the best career you can have and throwing it away." She laughed in a humorless sort of way.

"I'm not throwing any career away. I'm doing what's best. For *me*," Lorelei stated.

"Lor," John glanced over at his daughter. "We supported your decision to be a single mother, but this has gone too far."

"On both levels," Joanne added. "Oakvale is too far from us, and you're not thinking clearly. The holiday spirit has put you in an unrealistic snow-globe perception of life."

"No, Mom." Lorelei stopped threading the lights. "It's more than Christmas. I've kept silent—for years—to please you, but now I have to consider Mary Ann. Don't you remember my favorite times of childhood were spending time in Wyoming with—"

"If you're set on working as a family practice doctor, then open an office in Minneapolis," John interjected.

"How exactly will that work, Dad?" Lorelei threw her hand up.

"We'll talk to some business owners. See who is looking to sell." John's voice was sturdy as a tree trunk, confident.

"How does that make it a small town? How could I raise Mary Ann in a small town if my office is in the city?" Lorelei continued. "This is more than a building. It's about knowing the patients."

"Weekend home, Lor," Joanne stated. "You can come out here on the weekend."

"Let's not forget Chris is already the town's doctor, Lor." John stood up from the reindeer, his hands back in his pockets. "I agree with your mom, though. How about we take as many trips out to any small towns you wish, even back here to Oakvale?"

"Dad, you're not listening to me." Lorelei's body slumped, her hands rested over the back of her decorated reindeer. "It's not about vacation breaks. It's about everyday life. I'm going to live my dream. I'm leaving Minneapolis and my job."

Tyler moved to Lorelei and placed his hand on her back, and she instantly straightened up.

"We can discuss this after everyone goes home." Joanne threaded another ribbon around the reindeer's front leg. "You're only a temporary doctor here."

Lorelei turned and gazed at Tyler, he beamed, his hand still on her back. I'm so proud of you, he tried to telepathically communicate. He couldn't wait to tell her aloud once they were alone.

"I'll speak with Uncle Chris as soon as I can reach him. There is nothing more to discuss." Lorelei focused on a small, delicate wreath and placed it around the reindeer's neck. "I don't have all the answers, but I have one: I'm leaving Minneapolis."

Tyler's hand pulled away from Lorelei's back, and he returned to his reindeer. His mind raced as he added the black belt and golden buckle. Not only was he joyful for Lorelei's assertion of independence, but for Mary Ann's prospective childhood, she'd be able to grow up where everyone knew her name. And he needed to step up to bat and follow through on his part of their pinky promise.

Chapter 30

U ncle Steve grinned wide enough that Lorelei could see his missing molar. "This year's contest, by far, is the greatest to date."

Everyone gathered in the kitchen, their reindeers decorated and placed in front of them.

"We know you already made your decision," Arlene stated, giving him a wink.

"Not so fast, missy. You have a great reindeer but were met with stiff competition this year."

"From me!" Richard boasted.

Arlene raised her eyebrow at her husband and pulled him in for a hug.

As Lorelei glanced around, everyone wore smiles. Even her parents sported half smiles, though their hands were shoved into their pockets.

"This year's winner, who gets a gift certificate for dinner at my fabulous restaurant—dessert included—is . . . the reindeer who took a page from a Norman Rockwell painting, Lorelei."

She did a little hop and clapped her hands in excitement. For a few seconds, every worry about what had transpired during the decorating contest disappeared from her mind.

"Thank you, Uncle Steve." Lorelei hugged him and pretended to hold a microphone in her hand. "I'd like to thank Kim and Diane for allowing me to shop their wonderful store for inspiration. I want to thank my daughter for her determination to sleep through the night so I had ample rest. And most importantly, I'd like to thank the residents of Oakvale, for without you, I would have been relaxing and watching a movie in my pajamas right now." Laughter erupted, and Lorelei bowed as everyone clapped. "Now please, have some apple crisp."

The crowd headed for the crisp as though there was only one piece instead of five casserole-sized dishes. Mary Ann, still in her high chair, smacked her board book on the tray before shoving the corner of it into her mouth. Arlene's hand touched Lorelei's elbow, and she turned toward her.

"Why don't you and Tyler go grab some ice cream in town? Let us watch Mary Ann for you. I'm sure you could use the break." Arlene eyed the Parkers, who appeared to be having a private conversation in the corner of the kitchen.

"Ice cream? It's winter." Lorelei's forehead wrinkled.

"Tyler loves to eat ice cream, *especially* in the winter. Even as a child. He would sit all bundled up, so all I could see were his eyes, nose, and mouth as he licked away at his chocolate ice cream cone." Arlene observed her son and smiled. "I know you told your parents. We could hear bits and pieces." She pulled Lorelei in for a quick hug. "Richard and I would love you and Mary Ann to become residents."

"Thank you, Arlene." Lorelei sighed. "I needed to hear that."

Arlene rubbed Lorelei's back and said, "It's not easy for any parent to hear a truth that they disagree with. Give your folks time. They do want the best for you, even if it's hard for them to accept in the moment."

Richard approached with a heaping slice of apple crisp. "Is my wife giving you a hard time? She has never been beat before."

Lorelei's mouth made the shape of an O. "Hopefully, me knocking the champion off her throne doesn't make me an enemy."

"Now you must stay so I can beat you next Christmas." Arlene winked, and Lorelei saw where Tyler got his charm. "I offered to watch Mary Ann so Tyler and Lorelei can take a break, head into town."

As if hearing his name, Tyler approached. "It's a tradition to go get ice cream afterward."

"I don't want to encroach on a family tradition." Lorelei raised her hands slightly.

"It's not encroaching if I invite you as part of a new tradition." Tyler ran his hand through his hair. "Besides, parents always spoil the fun."

She couldn't help but giggle. As Tyler reached for her hand, she nearly choked on her laughter. Lorelei needed the warmth of his fingers wrapped around hers. This afternoon had been fun, stressful, and a weight off her shoulders all at once.

After everyone finished their apple crisp and collected a piece to take home, the house emptied steadily until only Tyler and Cider, Richard and Arlene, and the Parkers remained. Lorelei prepared a bottle for her daughter as Tyler gathered their coats and clipped Cider's leash on.

"I'll install the new thermostat while you're gone." Richard waved the box.

"I already completely forgot. Thanks, Dad."

Between the guests, the oven, and the fireplace, the house didn't feel as chilly as it had in the morning.

"We'll talk when you get back," John stated with an arm around his wife.

Exhausted from the thought, Lorelei stepped out into the crisp air and closed her eyes. She thought about Oakvale being home and smiled as the chill touched her cheeks.

"Come on, Thinking Beauty, let's get some ice cream." Tyler directed her toward his truck.

Lorelei didn't say a word the entire drive into town until they were at the counter of the ice cream parlor putting in their order.

"I'll take peppermint chip on a sugar cone, please." Lorelei licked the edge of her lip.

"Chocolate for me and vanilla in a cup for Cider." Tyler pointed toward his dog lying on a rug in the corner of the tiny pink-themed ice cream shop.

With cones in hand, they sat as Tyler set the cup of ice cream on the floor for Cider.

"I'm surprised more of the town didn't show up for the reindeer decorating contest." Lorelei took her first lick.

The pink peppermint matched perfectly with the 1970s Christmas tinsel spread about the store. Cider managed to chomp at her ice cream in grand delight as the shop played Frank Sinatra's "White Christmas."

"It's usually the same group of participants. For at least the last five years or so." Tyler eased a lick of chocolate into his mouth.

"Your mom is amazing. The way she spoke to me right before we left . . . I must ask, why are you so apprehensive to talk to them about leaving the family business?"

"My parents are great, but I'm their son, and it's a whole other ball game regarding me and the business. As you know, being an only child means it's on us exclusively to live out our parents' wishes and what they think is best for us."

Lorelei studied the cone in her hand. "I did my part, and now it's time for you to do yours."

"Your parents were not happy about your news. I thought it would go over a little better. But I'm proud of you. I can say that, right?" Tyler's eyes lingered on her.

"Thank you, and yes, I genuinely accept it. I should feel pleased, not guilty, right now." She glanced at Cider, who now held the empty paper bowl in her mouth as a chew toy.

"Are you having regrets?"

She shook her head. "Of course not." A smile broke out on Lorelei's face, and she reached her hand out and set it on top of Tyler's hand. "Thank you. I couldn't have done it without you. I guess I just hoped they'd be joyful—as though realizing they were wrong all along."

"They'll come around. It'll take time, but they will." Tyler flipped his hand over, and Lorelei's palm touched his.

She licked the peppermint ice cream and shivered, unsure if it was from the cold of the dessert, the thought of her parents' disappointment, or Tyler's touch.

"You don't want a career change, do you? I heard there'll be a bowling alley-real estate business up for sale soon." Tyler winked.

She shook her head and let out a whisper of a laugh. "I think I'll pass. I love being a doctor." Glancing around as though she was about to tell a secret, she said, "I simply hope my uncle will be up for retirement."

Tyler nodded. "I believe he will."

She studied her ice cream cone after each lick. Thinking back on when she first drove through Oakvale and everything appeared like the perfect dream. And she should have known it might be too good to be true. As soon as everything started to come together, it showcased its cracks. *Why couldn't she simply lick away all the problems?*

"Seeing you today, standing up for your dream . . . it gave me courage. And it's time to come through on my end, too." Tyler twisted his ice cream, licking some chocolate before it dripped down the cone. "I'm not waiting until the Christmas book reading to tell my folks."

Lorelei glanced away from her cone to study him. "You're not?"

"I'm doing it when we get back to the Norths'. I don't want to wait any longer. Traveling is not as important as being here in Oakvale and owning the bookstore. Having my dream come true. Plus"—Tyler's cheeks flushed—"I don't want to be away from you for six months."

Her face warmed, mirroring Tyler's, and when their eyes met, they didn't need words.

"At least we can each rip off the Band-Aid today and deal with the outcome together." Tyler brimmed with energy as he beamed, but Lorelei's facial expression switched to a pout. "Why the long face? You did it. You told your parents." Tyler tilted his head.

"Because it's not over yet. If they'd been all happy and accepting, I'd feel relieved, but as soon as I get back home to pack up, it will only be lecture after lecture. Plus, no one seems to know how to get ahold of my uncle, and he plays a final role in this, too."

"Don't give up." Tyler bit into the top of the cone.

"No, I'm not."

"Come on, Pouting Beauty. Let's go for a walk." Tyler gathered Cider's leash.

As they made their way outside, they continued to eat the remainder of their ice cream cones.

"I'll be right back. I'm going to drop off Cider with Ted." Tyler opened Once Upon a Book's door and slipped inside.

Lorelei turned toward the center of town where the Christmas tree lit up the area, casting a colorful glow around its snow-covered branches. Tyler stepped back out onto the sidewalk and held his elbow out. She wrapped her hand around it, and they walked on, finishing their ice cream. Once they crossed the street, a store caught Lorelei's eye.

"How have I missed this before?" She pointed at a tiny thin building, which almost resembled a New York City brownstone, with a sign that read Herb's D&B.

"Ah, yes, how did you?" Tyler winked. "It's the dentist and barbershop. D and B."

"Real estate and bowling alley. Dentist and barbershop. I'm feeling hopeful for the doctor's office and day care now." Lorelei chuckled. "Please explain to me how a dental barbershop works."

Tyler pivoted and faced the shop straight on. "Herb Winford, the dentist, and lifetime Oakvale resident, worked as a barber during his college years. He attended UMN and during that time this building became available." Tyler pointed at the sign hanging from the building. "Upon graduation, Herb realized that a customer lying back for a shave in the barber chair was no different than a patient coming in for teeth cleaning."

Wonderment spread over Lorelei's cheeks, drawing her lips into a smile. "That's ingenious!"

Somehow, hearing about Herb's brilliant connection between a dentist and barber caused Lorelei to keep dreaming. Tyler no longer dreamed of traveling because he didn't want to be away from her and Mary Ann. Her eyes twinkled with delight.

Chapter 31

"**M**om? Dad?" Tyler called as he and Lorelei walked through the front door.

"Tyler, we're in the living room," Arlene answered.

The Parkers sat on one side of the couch while his dad sat at the other end. His mom was on the floor with Mary Ann looking at a board book. Cider greeted the baby with a few licks before flopping down next to her.

"Mom, Dad." Tyler clasped his hands together as he stood in front of them.

He closed his eyes, took a deep breath, and when he opened them, Lorelei was in his line of sight, and he told himself, *I can do this if I only look at Lorelei. Focus. You want your dream. You deserve it, and Lorelei needs your help, too.*

"Christmas goose got your tongue, son?" Richard chuckled.

Tyler's forehead creased. *Maybe he couldn't do this!*

"He has something important to tell you," Lorelei chimed in. "And I know how important it is for him to tell you because it's important to us both." Her smile warmed.

Wiping his sweaty palms on his pants, he said, "Yes, it is." He squeezed his hands into fists and then released them. "Lorelei was bold enough today to let her parents know she wanted to follow her dream, and I want to do the same."

Arlene put her hand on her chest. "You don't want to be a doctor, do you?"

"You don't want to move to the city, do you, son?" Richard stood up from the couch.

"Mom, Dad, I'm not moving." He sighed. "I . . . I want to buy Sandy's bookstore. I don't want to run the family business anymore."

A log on the fireplace popped, and everyone in the room jumped.

Tyler continued, "I don't mind being a real estate agent, but it's not my passion. It's your dream for me, but not mine."

Trying to gauge what his parents might be thinking, he glanced back and forth at them as though watching a tennis match.

"We should give you some space," John stated, standing up.

"No, please, stay." Tyler motioned to the couch. "Lorelei was bold enough to speak to you during the middle of a contest. I can surely handle this."

When he glanced over at Lorelei, she smiled sweeter than peppermint chip ice cream. His mind went to their closeness this morning and how much he wanted to spend more time with her.

"Your father and I don't want to see the family business disappear, Tyler. The bowling alley, well, that's another story. But our name, we don't want it to end." Arlene moved to her knees. "You're supposed to hand it down to your kids and then them to their kids."

"I know you and Dad worked hard to build the company and to operate it from the bowling alley, so they worked together cohesively. And I'm sorry, but . . ." Tyler hung his head, the weight of it too hard for him to bear.

"What about your plan to travel?" Richard interjected.

Everyone's head turned to his father. Lorelei's lips parted, and her eyes went to his parents.

"I don't have the money to do both, so I won't be traveling. Traveling to all the bookish places would be amazing, but I can only have one. And I must go with what has always been my dream, the bookstore."

He observed his parents as they remained silent. Tyler turned to Lorelei as she picked up Mary Ann. The silence allowed Tyler to hear his heartbeat thump in his ears.

"This is what you want, son?" Richard asked.

Lorelei gave Tyler a thumbs-up. Mary Ann reached out and tried to pull it to her mouth as a teething toy.

"It is." Tyler brought his hands together.

Arlene and Richard shared a glance but didn't say anything. He didn't know what to expect from his parents. He hoped it wouldn't be the same outcome Lorelei had to deal with. The fire died down, but the room remained warm, which meant the heater was up and running again.

"Mom?" Tyler asked.

She stood up, using the coffee table for leverage, and walked toward him. "Your dad and I will always support you."

Here comes the but.

"But we had no idea you felt this way about the bookstore or our business," Richard added.

"I didn't want to disappoint you and Mom. I don't want our legacy to die."

"We know how much you have loved reading since you were a child. Although back then, you were more into chewing on them than reading them." Arlene winked. "You should have come to us about this a long time ago, regardless of how you thought we would handle the news."

His parents came together and held each other by wrapping their arms over each other's shoulders. "If you want to buy Once Upon a Book, we'll support you." Arlene glanced up at Richard, who nodded in agreement.

Tyler's hands dropped to his side. "You do? I can?"

Richard approached his son and placed his hand on his shoulder. "Yes, we only wish we'd not been blind to your dreams before and that you'd spoken to us about it when the store went up for sale. I see it now that it's in front of us, and looking back, I should have known."

Tyler hugged his dad and then his mom. "Thank you."

Lorelei was at his side when he stepped back, and he immediately embraced her, careful not to squish Mary Ann between them. When he pulled out of the hug, Tyler paused, staring into her eyes.

"We should celebrate," Lorelei announced. "How about some apple crisp?"

The room erupted with laughter.

"I've had plenty, but I can't turn down a small slice." Richard patted his stomach.

"Dad, thanks for putting in the new thermostat." Tyler made his way into the kitchen for a slice of dessert. While he didn't have room for much more dessert after ice cream, he couldn't pass up trying Lorelei's crisp.

"Yes, you're most welcome. It seems to be working fine." Richard followed behind. "Lorelei, we had a nice chat with your folks while you were out."

She glanced over at her parents, making their way off the couch. Tyler reached his arms out for Mary Ann, and she happily went to him. Lorelei scooped servings of apple crisp onto small plates and dispersed them around the island.

Taking Mary Ann over to the Christmas tree to look at the lights and ornaments, Tyler tried to be as out of the way as possible. He wanted Lorelei to have her space but be there for her also. But he wanted to know what his parents said to the Parkers and if they'd gotten anywhere positive with it.

"We did have a nice discussion with Richard and Arlene," Joanne declared. "But your father and I would like to talk more in private with you, Lor."

"We do value our daughter's opinion, but we've been around longer than you and can see the entire picture from an outside perspective," John added.

Richard and Arlene picked up their plates of apple crisp and hurried to the Christmas tree, as though using it as a shield from the parental disapproval. As he glanced over his shoulder, Tyler noticed Lorelei overly washing the serving spoon as her parents took bites of their dessert. The frustration on her face and the defeat creasing her eyebrow was noticeable from a distance. There must be something I can say to help her out, he thought. Who would have guessed they'd experience such opposite reactions from their parents.

Mary Ann lunged for an ornament on the tree, catching Tyler off guard. The plate of apple crisp in his hand went crashing onto the rug. As he glanced around, all eyes were on him.

"Cider really wanted that piece. She saw you made five batches of it," Tyler joked.

"Sharing is caring," Lorelei stated.

He figured the mess would cause her folks to roll their eyes or make a comment about something city-like. Instead, for the first time since the Parkers arrived, they actually had smiles on their faces. Maybe the reindeer contest was not what Lorelei's parents needed, but a conversation with his parents to see how important it was to live your dreams.

Chapter 32

E xhaustion settled into the depths of Lorelei's bones, or so it felt like once she sank onto the couch. Mary Ann was fast asleep in her crib upstairs. All three of the McCains had left shortly after Cider won the spilled apple crisp for a snack. The dog had managed to clean up the rug to the point that she didn't need to scrub any stains out.

"We need to talk." Joanne sat next to her on the couch.

Lorelei sighed and leaned her head back into the plush pillows. *Not now, Mom!*

Why couldn't she be like Tyler's parents? Lorelei couldn't help but whine to herself like a teenager again. Her mom hadn't changed in all her years. Whenever it came to something Joanne disagreed with, they had to talk. It could've been about buying a dress with her allowance, the music she listened to, or what electives she picked in college. Lorelei had never known a decision to be final with her mom around.

"The McCains . . ." Her mom looked up as John entered the room. "Well, they just didn't understand our point of view. It's not that we don't want you to be a small-town doctor, but you won't have the opportunities you have at the hospital. We want to see you continue to succeed in your career."

"Dead horse, Mom. You're beating a dead horse at this point," Lorelei groaned, covering herself with the blanket up to her chin.

"This is why we can never have a conversation because you're always on the defense." Joanne crossed her arms.

The couch cushions moved as her dad sat next to her. "Why can't you be like Tyler's folks? Did you see how open they were? How accepting?"

"The McCains did a great job of letting us know how wonderful Oakvale is and what they have to offer," John stated. "We'd love to vacation here, and we support you remaining friends with those you have made. But Oakvale is not for you, Mary Ann, or your career."

"What your father is slowly getting to is you can look at other small towns—ones like Booth, with a hospital. That's where we can compromise, as Tyler and his parents did."

"Booth is forty-five minutes away from here. Plus, you're still talking about a hospital. This is not a compromise. I've made my decision." Lorelei stared at the fire dying down in the fireplace.

"Where will you work? Where will you live?" John stood, and his hands immediately went in his pockets.

"Mary Ann and I will be rooming with Jodi above the doctor's office. It's a converted home with plenty of space. And I need to get a hold of Uncle Chris."

"You're going to raise our granddaughter in a tiny rented area of an office?" John stated, pacing the living room.

"Temporally, until a house comes up for sale. With Sandy selling the bookstore to Tyler, maybe they'll need a renter if they plan to travel." Lorelei tossed the blanket to the side. "Look outside. Look at what a magical place this is. And not just here in this house, but around town. Look at how great Tyler is with Mary Ann."

"I told you this was about him," Joanne huffed. "You only just met him."

Lorelei spun around, facing her mom. "Remind me how you and Dad met again?"

"These are different times," John mentioned.

"Dad, you're not from the twenties. You and mom met walking across the Bow Bridge in Central Park. And it was love at first sight."

John's eyes drifted off as though searching for the memory. "We did. I saw her and couldn't walk by without saying hi, without finding out her name, without introducing myself."

Joanne went to John and took hold of his hand. Lorelei saw the way they looked at each other, even now, after thirty-some years of marriage. "When I saw him, I knew."

"The most magical moment, as though we were the only ones on the bridge." John took his wife's hand and brought it to his lips for a kiss.

"We *were* the only ones on the bridge, it'd started to pour, and everyone else ran for cover. But not us."

Joanne and John stood face to face, the Christmas tree lights glowing around them. Lorelei gazed at the scene in front of her as the anger regarding their disagreement faded. She watched her parents remember their love for each other.

Lorelei's folks were lost in each other's eyes. She wanted that very kind of love herself. A long-lasting, heart-skipping love. Instantly, Tyler filled her mind and didn't doubt why. She thought about him as often, hoping she would run into him in town or that they could meet up for lunch or dinner. Not to mention how much her heart palpitated when Tyler held Mary Ann.

"Lor?" Her dad's voice broke through her reverie. "Your cell phone. It's vibrating on the counter."

She answered it swiftly. "Hello . . . Yes, this is she . . . Really? I'd never heard anything back, so I just figured . . . Well, yes, of course . . . Thank you, yes tomorrow . . . at ten . . . thank you. Bye." Hitting end on the phone, she set it back on the counter as her mouth gaped open.

"Is everything alright?" Joanne asked.

"That doctor's office position I applied for in Booth over the summer, it was them. They said my resume was misplaced. And they're still looking for a physician. They invited me in for an interview tomorrow morning."

"That's wonderful. See a Christmas miracle." John provided a weak smile. "Compromise."

Yet, to Lorelei, compromise shouldn't feel like heartburn. At that moment, she realized why so many emergency room patients thought they were having a heart attack when it was heartburn or too much stress. If she landed the job in Booth, it would solve her job situation. *But it wasn't Oakvale and it doesn't have Tyler.*

The monitor on the kitchen island transmitted Mary Ann's baby babbling, notifying Lorelei that her daughter was awake. Thoughts about the job interview tangled in her mind as she made her way upstairs, leaving her parents alone in the living room.

"Hi, baby girl." Lorelei entered the room and switched off the monitor. She lifted her out of the crib. "Did you sleep well?"

Moving to the glider rocker, Lorelei sat down and placed Mary Ann on her knees, facing her.

"Mommy received a phone call about an interview in Booth. What do you think about Booth?" Lorelei leaned forward and kissed her daughter on the forehead. "Mommy will go because it's important to take every opportunity given to you. But I already feel as though my heart isn't in it. Do you think we should tell Tyler?"

Mary Ann squeezed her hands together, brought them to her mouth, and drooled over them.

"Mum's the word, I think, since everything is going well for him. I'd hate to tell him something if nothing comes of it. He needs to focus on his bookstore. Who knows, I'm probably overthinking this. Tyler and I aren't . . . together. Although the thought of being together is a nice one."

She leaned back into the rocker's padded cushion, glanced around the room, and then back at her daughter, who was still impressed with her hands.

The desire to tell Tyler remained strong, but she pushed it aside. Christmastime was not the occasion to be worried. It was a time for miracles, love, and joy. Part of her hoped she could land the job in Booth because she didn't know what would happen with things in Oakvale.

"I think I should wait until I know for sure. No point in discussing what we don't have answers to."

Chapter 33

Tyler's morning started perfectly with a warm apple nutmeg muffin and aromatic black coffee at Sharon's Café. He lingered over the hardback copy of *Main Street* as Sharon poured him a to-go cup of hot cider. Once he left and headed across the street to his office, the sunshine warmed the icicles from the store's eves. Even Cider appeared to have a spring in her step and an extra *va-voom* to her hind-end swish.

Once Upon a Book didn't open for another thirty minutes, and Tyler would take the time to prepare the offer for Sandy. After unlocking the door and turning on the lights, he took a seat in the desk chair and faced it toward his dream.

"Can you believe it, Cider? We're going to do it."

The dog stretched and took her bone in her mouth.

"Don't get too excited." Tyler chuckled and took a sip of cider. "It wouldn't have been possible without Lorelei. I might be a grown man, but parents are still parents."

He spun the chair around and began typing up the offer as his thoughts drifted to Lorelei. When he left, the tension was still as tight as a violin string between her and her folks. A part of him had wanted to stay in case she needed him, but he didn't want her to feel she couldn't be strong enough on her own. She'd stood up to them, but it hadn't resolved any of what she needed; it seemed they may never accept their daughter's dream. He honestly couldn't believe how the Parkers continued not to support Lorelei. She'd accomplished plenty in her life so far.

Maybe they'd come to some type of agreement last night or perhaps even this morning after a good night's sleep. But since he hadn't heard from her, he wasn't convinced. *She would have called, right?*

As his fingers typed numbers into the offer of purchase form, the sides of his mouth rose into a slow smile. He was about to buy Once Upon a Book. Tyler glanced behind him at the bookstore when the office phone rang.

"McCain Rental and Real Estate," Tyler answered.

With each sentence from the caller, Tyler's hand gripped the phone's receiver tighter. As he hung up the phone, his email alerted him to a new message in his inbox. His chest tightened as he hit print on both the new document and his own. The printer spit out the pages, and he went to gather them without the pre-phone-call spring in his step.

"Let's go see Garrison." Tyler hooked the leash onto Cider's collar, and they made their way outside. "Then, we'll stop in and see Lorelei."

Crossing the street, he glanced over at the doctor's office but didn't see her familiar sedan parked out front. A sense of worry drifted deeper over him as he opened the door to the bookstore.

"Tyler, lovely to see you," greeted Sandy from behind the counter. "Need your next book already?"

Garrison trotted over, and Cider wagged her tail with delight.

He held up the papers in his hand. "I'm here with an offer on the store."

Sandy's mouth nearly fell into her teacup. "What? Oh my! Oh, Tyler!" She hopped off the high stool and hurried toward Tyler, wrapping him up in a hug. "You did it. How did it go with your folks?"

"Not so fast. I just received a phone call from another real estate agent."

Sandy's arms fell to her sides. "What do you mean?"

"I'm here to present my offer and an offer from another buyer."

"Of course, we'll go with your offer, Tyler." Sandy held her hand out for the paperwork. "That's not even a question."

"They're offering over your asking price." He swallowed and swore he could hear it echoing on the bookstore's speakers between lines of "Have Yourself a Merry Little Christmas."

"Why would they do that?" Sandy took the paperwork in her hand.

Tyler shrugged his shoulders as doubt rushed through his upper body and down to his fingertips.

"You know I hate reading contracts, so tell me what I need to know." Sandy fanned the papers in her hand.

"My offer is at your asking price, but I can't do any more than that. I did add a bonus of a thirty percent discount for you and Ted on all future purchases from the bookstore. Their offer is ten thousand over asking." He glanced back at the store's front window, Lorelei was still at the edge of his mind. Tyler needed all the hope he could gather, and Lorelei made him more hopeful whenever he was with her.

The bookstore's bell dinged, and Tyler turned around. "Jodi, good morning," he said.

"Good morning to you, too." Jodi removed her gloves.

"Lorelei hasn't made it in yet?" He glanced out the bookstore window.

"She'll be in after her interview. I thought you would have known?" Jodi bit her lip, but it was too late—the cat was out of the bag.

Tyler's heart raced. "Interview? What interview?"

"I probably shouldn't say." Jodi avoided eye contact. "Okay, alright. She has an interview in Booth at a doctor's office."

"Did her parents make her? How'd they get something set up so quickly? I don't understand. She didn't tell me she had an interview."

"I'm not sure. All I know is she said she would be in later today. Tyler,"—Jodi tilted her head—"I don't want her to leave. I want Lorelei and Mary Ann to stay. But can we blame her for going to the interview in Booth? I mean, I heard her parents aren't in favor of her choice, and it's better than heading back to the city. Or maybe she'll try to live here while she works in Booth."

"Did she tell you she wanted to live in Booth?" Tyler leaned on the nearby counter containing the register and checkout display.

How quickly his day had gone from joyful to gloomy. *Why hadn't she told him? Maybe that was the only compromise her parents allowed.* He rubbed his fingers across his brow as though trying to summon a genie from a lantern. The thoughts of their near kiss sank into his mind, making him doubt where they might have been heading. Maybe he'd read everything wrong this entire December.

Shaking his head, he stepped forward.

"I'm sure there's a reason she didn't tell you," Jodi offered, trying to sound cheerful. "Do you want me to have her call you when she gets in?"

"No, thank you." Tyler patted his leg and called for Cider. The clouds shifted, blocking the sunlight that came streaming through the bookstore's windows.

"Sandy, take the other buyer's offer." He clipped on the dog's leash but remained hunched over, the weight of sadness and confusion swirling around him like a snowstorm.

"Tyler?" Sandy's hands rested on top of the two offers.

"I can't believe how I got everything so wrong. Take the other offer."

"Tyler, wait," Sandy huffed.

He waved her off as he passed Jodi and exited the bookstore. Tyler silently scolded himself with each step through the snow. Thankfully, he'd saved the travel brochures. Unfortunately, Oakvale was the last place he wanted to be.

Entering his office, he removed Cider's leash, then grabbed a bowling ball and shoes off the rack, and clicked on the lane lights. Once he'd switched his shoes, he took to the lane and heaved the ball down it like a frustrated teenager. The ball nearly bounced over into the other lane but eventually knocked over four pins on the far right. By the time the ball came up the return, Tyler was pacing.

"I'm so confused," he said to Cider. "I thought she and I had . . . something. I thought she wanted to live here. I mean, yesterday she told her parents exactly what she wanted. She wanted to be here in Oakvale. Maybe after more discussion with her parents, she decided we don't have enough to offer her. Maybe we're not a good enough place to raise Mary Ann."

He took the ball and chucked it down the lane, scoring a spare. Pausing, Tyler observed the bowling alley and office around him, full of Christmas decorations. It was a time for hope, joy, and laughter, family and friends. But right now, Christmas didn't seem like any of those things to him.

Chapter 34

With her emotions more mixed than a bag of various greens, Lorelei parked her sedan in front of the Norths' place and shut off the engine. Mary Ann had spent the day with her parents.

"Do I accept the job they offered in Booth?" she asked the empty air around her. "If only I could talk to my uncle."

After the interview, she'd returned to the office and saw three eagerly waiting patients. There was a three-year-old by the name of Mike with a crayon in his ear; Linda, who had a bug bite in the shape of a T-Rex; and Patty, who'd slightly burned her hand on her oven.

Lorelei had zero time to discuss anything with Jodi since she had to hurry off to babysit the twins and after spending five minutes trying to get her car started. Lorelei wanted to talk to Tyler about the interview, but by the time she left the office, the only lights on at the bowling alley were Christmas ones. His life moved forward, after all. She assumed he was probably over at Once Upon a Book going over the offer details, but Lorelei hadn't spotted his truck anywhere in town.

"If I take the job in Booth, I can have the small*ish*-town life and make my parents happy . . . ish." She stared at the sedan's ceiling and noticed something for the first time—a coffee stain in the shape of a star on top of a Christmas tree. Lorelei squinted and refocused her eyes on the stain. She couldn't remember seeing it there before.

"If I was to wish upon it, what would I wish for?" Lorelei continued to stare at it. "I would wish for my life, and my daughter's, to be here in Oakvale—no commuting to Booth—and for my uncle to retire and turn the practice over to me." As the words left her lips, she glanced out the front windshield as the snow started to fall.

Lorelei willed herself out of the sedan and reluctantly entered the only-for-the-month-of-December Uncle's home to face her parents.

"Did you hear back on the interview, Lor?" her mom called out before she put her purse on the entryway table.

"Yes," she answered, pausing, "they called about two hours ago and offered me the position."

"Congratulations," John announced from the kitchen, where he wiped his hands on a towel. "Let's go out and celebrate. How about that pizza place? Maybe we can bring a nice bottle of wine?"

"First, you know it drives me crazy when you bring your own wine into a restaurant."

"We pay the corkage fee," John reminded her.

Mary Ann babbled on a blanket in the living room.

"To me, it seems like you're putting down the restaurant's wine selection. Second, I have yet to accept the offer." Lorelei went over and kissed her daughter's forehead.

"Why not?" Joanne asked.

"Because, Mom, I'm doing what's best for Mary Ann and me."

"But we discussed this last night," Joanne whimpered as her brow creased.

Lorelei removed her jacket, tossed it over the back of the couch, and plugged in the living room Christmas tree lights. The instant the glow of lights came on, she felt a smidge of joyfulness amid her gloomy emotions.

"Yes, Mom, we did." Lorelei ran her finger over the ornament Tyler had gifted Mary Ann. She had yet to fill it with a photo.

"You and Dad decided what to compromise on. But I'm not happy with it. I went to the interview because you've raised me never to disregard an opportunity. However, that doesn't mean I agreed."

"Lor, Oakvale is simply too small a town. You can't grow here." John entered the living room. "How about you plan to retire here instead?"

Lorelei's hands dropped, and she cupped them around her waist. "Retire? I have at least forty years to go on that one. And I can most certainly grow here. I'll have time to grow my family."

"What about vacationing here?" Joanne offered.

Lorelei continued to stare at the Christmas tree with delight, despite the frustration going on around her. The scent of fresh fir danced in her nose, and she smiled at the memory of cutting it down with Tyler. She sighed, went to the light switch by the French doors, and flipped on the backyard display. It didn't matter how many times she gazed out at it, every time felt like the first.

"Miracles happen still, right? Especially during Christmastime." Instantly she covered her mouth. Lorelei had not meant to say it aloud. Or maybe a part of her had. She turned around to face her parents, who both sat on the edge of the couch. Mary Ann rolled over and crawled to her board book laying at the edge of her baby blanket.

"Is that a rhetorical question?" her mom asked, tilting her head.

"It's not. It's not a question at all. I'm here in Oakvale. I'm not taking the job in Booth. I'm sorry if that upsets you, but I love this town. I like the residents and Tyler, and so does Mary Ann. I'll find a way to make it work. You can disagree all you want, and I know you're disappointed, but I still want you to know that you're always welcome to visit. So it's final: I'm not staying in Minneapolis, and I'm not moving to Booth."

John and Joanne sat there, lips in straight lines.

Finally, John stood up. "I guess there's nothing else to say then. We disagree with you, but we accept it."

"John?" her mom squawked. "We *do not* accept it. She hasn't even spoken with your sister and Chris about him retiring."

He looked back at his wife. "I don't want us to end up like the Noblins and their son. Do you know how many family outings and birthdays the Noblins have missed with their son and grandchildren?" John sat back down next to Joanne. "It's not perfect, but nothing in life can be."

"But—" Joanne started.

"Mom, why did you want me to be a doctor? Why did you and Dad support my career?" Lorelei picked up her daughter's board book and used it to keep her hands busy.

"Well, because it's what you wanted, and we loved how big you dreamed." The hope appeared to drain from Joanne's face.

"And now my dream is to switch focuses. I'm still a doctor, I'm still helping others, but I get to be so much more than a ten-minute doctor. In the hospital, I see dozens of strangers every day. I don't find out what happens with them and their illnesses. I don't learn about their families or interact with them on a personal level."

A smile formed on Joanne's face as though she thought about the relevance of what her daughter described. "I guess I've never thought about it that way. It probably makes you a better doctor when you know more about them."

Lorelei sat upon the edge of the couch and faced them. "Mom, I'm happy here. Honestly happy. And I'm not at the hospital. I'm exhausted."

Joanne wiped a tear from her eye. Lorelei reached over to her and set her hand on her arm.

"Mom, I have a daughter now, and I don't want you to think that I don't value your opinion, but sometimes you have to let hope step in and take control."

Joanne moved her hands, placed them overtop her daughter's, and gently nodded with a weak smile. "I love you."

"I love you too, Mom."

Lorelei pulled her cell phone from her pocket and brought up Tyler's number. Watching Mary Ann crawl close to her, Tyler's voice mail clicked on, and she hung up.

"I'd rather tell him in person that I'm staying. It seems impersonal to leave something important on a voice mail."

"I agree," John said.

"Yes, and I'm sure he has good news to share with me. I bet he and Sandy have been hashing out the details of his newly acquired bookstore." Lorelei went to the kitchen and prepared a bottle for Mary Ann.

"I can't believe you're not able to reach the Norths." Joanne glanced at John.

"I wish Candace and I had a better relationship, but there was such an age gap between us that we didn't have a normal brother-sister relationship." John looked at the photo of the four of them on the mantel. "She'd moved out and left for college while I was still in elementary school. I was her annoying younger brother. I should've done better to keep in touch with her, and taking her up on visits."

Lorelei sighed, testing the formula temperature on her wrist. "You can always start, Dad. I'll be living here, and you'll be coming to visit. It seems like the perfect time to make it happen."

She saw her mom glance through the French doors at the falling snow outside. "Let's hope for a Christmas miracle, then."

As if on cue, the doorbell chimed. They all looked at each other, eyes wide.

"I'll get that." Perplexed, Lorelei headed to the front door. When she pulled it open, a man and woman stood in front of her, a classic cherry-red pickup truck was parked in the background. "Hi."

"Lorelei," the man with a white-as-snow beard said.

She nodded, taken aback. "Uncle Chris? Aunt Candace."

"Yes, indeed." He chuckled.

She'd never seen such rosy cheeks in all her life, even on patients with a fever.

"Goodness, come in." Lorelei stepped behind the door, allowing them inside. She hadn't seen them since she was a little kid and didn't know if she should hug them or not. "You surely don't need to ring your own doorbell."

"You must be wondering why we're here," Aunt Candace said. She wore a dress of crimson red with buttons running from neck to toe.

"Is everything okay?" Lorelei led the way into the living room. "It's a miracle you're here. I've needed to speak with you, Uncle Chris, but no one seems to have your cell number."

Uncle Chris chuckled, "Oh yes, everything is dandy. And we don't have a mobile phone. Candace needed a recipe, and well, it was important enough to come home and get."

"Plus, we wanted to meet our grandniece." Aunt Candace's eyes twinkled.

"I think you know John and Joanne." Lorelei motioned to them, standing near the island.

Candace beamed upon seeing her brother and hurried to him. "John, what an amazing surprise!" She wrapped her arms around him.

"You have the most magical timing." Lorelei picked up Mary Ann from the floor.

Candace stepped out of her brother's arms while Chris hugged Joanne, then moved to John and gave him a big hug, too.

"We didn't know we'd have such a wonderful family reunion." Uncle Chris wrapped his hands around the opening of his winter coat.

"And this is must be Mary Ann." Aunt Candace approached the baby, and Mary Ann's eyes lit up, her tiny grin spreading wide.

"I wanted to talk to you about your practice." Lorelei wrapped her hand around her daughter's fist as she tried to yank on her mom's hair. Candace held out her hands for Mary Ann, and Lorelei handed her daughter over to her grinning aunt.

"Yes." Chris followed his wife to the kitchen, baby in tow, and opened the nearby cupboard, removing a small wooden box.

"I decided I want to move here, and Jodi said she'd love to have us as roommates. I'd like to rent out the two other rooms above the office for myself and my daughter. The issue is this town isn't busy enough for two doctors." She bit her lower lip in anticipation.

"I couldn't agree more." Uncle Chris beamed. "You've been good this year."

Okay, then. "What I'm wondering is, if maybe you had any plans to retire soon, or shortly. I know this is unbelievably forward of me to ask." Lorelei caught Candace giving her husband a look.

"Chris, you've been trying to find a replacement for the last few years." Candace turned her attention to searching the wooden box of index cards.

"Yes, but I didn't want to leave my patients to just anyone."

Lorelei's shoulders slumped. "I know."

"And luckily, you're not just anyone—you're family." His voice was friendly but deep when he said, "It has been a long time coming."

"Oh?" Lorelei's posture straightened.

Candace held up a recipe card and returned the box to its spot in the cupboard.

"Let me make sure I have this straight because it . . . it's almost a Christmas miracle for you to show up like you have and then to make my dreams come true." Lorelei watched as Mary Ann continued to fixate on her great-aunt.

"I've been waiting for you to finally come and visit so you could have this very discussion," UncleChris said.

"Wow, I'm honored," Lorelei gushed. "Thank you."

Lorelei's parents remained standing near the island without saying a word.

"You decorated beautifully, probably the best we've seen in all our years." Candace observed her home. "Don't cha think, Chris?"

"Indeed." He nodded his head in agreement. "Now, let me hold my great-niece before we have to go."

Candace handed Mary Ann over to Chris, and Lorelei expected a fuss or two, but instead, her daughter gazed at him in delight. Her great-uncle chuckled from deep in his belly, and Mary Ann giggled with joy from hearing the noise.

Lorelei brought her hands together in anticipation. "So, it's settled?"

"Yes, it's settled. As soon as we return at the end of the month, we'll finalize everything." Uncle Chris winked. "Oakvale is blessed, isn't it, Candace?" Chris handed Mary Ann back to Lorelei.

"Indeed, we are." Aunt Candace kept her eyes on Lorelei and smiled.

The reality of her uncle's words sank in, and Lorelei leaned on the kitchen island. In her greatest moment of joy, she wanted nothing more than to have Tyler by her side, his hand in hers.

"How is everything else going?" Uncle Chris's eyes moved around the room. "The heater probably went out a few times."

Lorelei laughed. "Yes, and a hole in the roof."

"Oh my, we're so sorry." Aunt Candace's forehead creased. "I believe Don did a great job of fixing it up."

"Yes." Lorelei nodded.

Chris turned to Candace. "We should be on our way. Everyone is waiting on your Christmas dessert."

"I can't believe we forgot it," Aunt Candace stated.

Chris took her hand in his. "I can't believe you don't have that recipe memorized."

"I'm glad I didn't." She winked at the Parkers. "We have a lot of catching up to do."

"So sorry we have to run," Chris added as they began to head toward the front door. "We look forward to many family visits in the new year."

"You can't stay a bit longer?" Lorelei followed. "Seems like a long drive from . . . up north just to turn around."

The Norths paused at the door and softly laughed. Candace beamed at Chris as though they weren't all that sorry for making the trip.

After closing the door, Lorelei carried Mary Ann back to the living room and looked at her parents. "Is it me, or do they look an awful lot like Mr. and Mrs. Claus?"

Chapter 35

Tyler searched through a stack of Christmas picture books, desperate to find the perfect tale for O Come, All Ye Reader, but came up short. He sighed and set yet another book back on the display table of the bookstore. Every thought went to Lorelei. *How could she not tell him about her interview? He should never have allowed himself to spend so much time with her and Mary Ann, knowing they wouldn't stay. He should never have allowed himself to . . .* He knew exactly where that thought was going, but he wouldn't let himself finish it.

"Trying to find the perfect book for the reading?" Sandy stepped to his side.

Tyler ran his fingers over the raised font on a hardcover. "I should have selected it by now."

"You can always go with a classic," Sandy suggested.

Garrison and Cider lay near two twin kindergarteners nestled in the children's reading corner. Between them, their mom read from a pile of books they'd selected from the shelves.

With his voice low, Tyler said, "You know I like to pick something special and new each Christmas."

Sandy motioned for them to step away, allowing the boys to focus on their mom's reading. He followed her with his arms crossed.

"I hate to address the For-Sale-elephant in the room, but Ted and I need to decide on an offer. Are you sure you want us to take the other offer?" Sandy brought her cardigan sweater into her hands and closed it over itself as though she might be chilly.

"How could she not tell me about the interview?" Without letting Sandy answer, Tyler continued. "I thought I understood her dream. After she confronted her parents, I thought she would move forward. But instead, she went to an interview in Booth and didn't mention a word to me. I thought — I thought we were a team." Tyler shoved his hands into his pockets, but it reminded him of John, so he slid them back out.

"Have you spoken to her?" Sandy offered. "Asked Lorelei why?"

He shook his head. "I should go. I'll come back later when my head is clearer, and hopefully, I can find a book. Can I leave Cider here? She seems to like this story." He pointed toward the dog.

"Of course." Sandy patted his back and provided a weak smile.

Tyler gave her a half-nod and made his way out of the bookstore, across the street, and back to his office door. Then, he spotted Lorelei's sedan pull into a parking spot. She waved and smiled at him before climbing out of the driver's seat.

"Tyler." She approached, her face beaming with joy. "I've been trying to reach you. I called, but you didn't answer. I have great news."

He opened the door to the office but didn't hold it for her, instead he headed inside without a word.

Lorelei followed, catching the door before it closed. "It's best I tell you in person, anyway."

How can she be so happy?

"I'm busy right now." His voice was sharp; cold as an icicle. As he eyed her, he noticed the joy evaporate from her lips.

"Oh." She murmured the word soft and low, then her brow furrowed. "Sorry, I didn't mean to interrupt your . . . work."

She glanced around the empty, silent bowling alley.

"I'm sure you're busy as well." Tyler shuffled papers on his desk and clicked the mouse to wake the computer. He thought, I'm not busy at all, but I'm upset, and I don't want to talk to you at this moment. "Maybe I'll see you later," he said instead.

"Sorry, I disturbed you."

He continued to stare at his computer until the sound of the bell on the door chimed. Closing his eyes, he sighed. Sandy had told him minutes ago to talk to Lorelei, to find out what was going on with the interview in Booth, but he couldn't. Once he saw her, his heartache doubled. He couldn't get on a plane to start his trip fast enough.

Tyler swiveled in his chair and spotted Lorelei heading into Once Upon a Book. Mary Ann must be with her parents back at the Norths'. Obviously, she left her daughter with them because they were all getting along now that Lorelei compromised and was moving to Booth. Watching her enter the bookstore made him realize he'd developed the same feeling for her as he did for Once Upon a Book. Like a favorite story he'd read over and over again. Too bad he never wanted to see that book again now.

Staring at his computer, he tried to focus, but his mind wandered since he didn't have any work to do. He kept his thoughts on Lorelei as he mixed himself up a cup of hot cider. *Maybe she does have another option than to agree with her parents and compromise. Maybe that's what she'd showed up to tell him. To tell him about Booth; to tell him she didn't have a choice. But she'd said* good *news. How could Booth be good news?*

The bell above the door made one jingle as it slammed against the frame. He spun around in his chair to find Lorelei stomping back into the office and up to his desk. She hoisted a Once Upon a Book paper bag at his chest. "I got this for you. Sorry to bother you." Lorelei didn't wait for a response as she pivoted.

Holding the gift in his hands, he couldn't make his mouth form the words. *Stop, wait.*

Lorelei flung open the office door and speed walked to her sedan. He watched from the window as she backed out of the parking spot. Then, reaching inside the paper bag, he removed a picture book. A Christmas-themed one. One he had not heard of before. *The Twelve Days of a Minnesota Christmas.* How had he never seen or heard of that book before? Sandy must've ordered it, but he hadn't seen it on the shelves earlier.

He carried the book to his desk where travel brochures were spread out, and resting up against his computer monitor was a photo. The picture he'd taken during the Christmas feast where Lorelei and her daughter posed in front of the Christmas tree with the warmest smiles he'd ever seen. Tyler held the photo in one hand and the book in the other. He tried to fight it, but a smile overcame his lips, warming his cheeks. Lorelei had managed to select the perfect book for him to read to the children when he couldn't find a single thing in an entire bookstore. He had to find out why she'd gone against her dream. He couldn't book his travel until he knew the answer.

With the picture in hand, he grabbed his jacket and hurried out into the cold.

Chapter 36

E ven though the snow was already off her boots, Lorelei continued to stomp them on the foyer rug. She tossed her purse on the entry table and made her way into the living room. Mary Ann attempted to crawl under the Christmas tree while John and Joanne tried to distract her with her toys.

"Is everything alright, Lor?" John asked from all fours.

"No." She threw her head backwards. "Men!"

Going into the kitchen, she set the kettle on the stove and prepared a mug for hot apple cider. She picked up Mary Ann, kissed her, then set her back on the floor to play.

"Did something happen with Tyler? Did you tell him your news?" Joanne asked over the crackle of the fireplace.

"Apparently, he's too busy."

Lorelei drummed her fingers on the island until the kettle whistled, and she poured the steaming water into the mug and did a quick stir. "I'll be out back. I need to calm down."

Leaning against one of the pillars, she took a sip of the warm apple cider, nearly hot enough to burn her tongue. How badly she wanted to speak with Tyler, to tell him the great news. *Everything was going so well, and now Tyler wanted nothing to do with her.*

She didn't turn around as the sound of the French doors opened behind her. "I'm not in the mood to talk, Mom."

"Good, because I'm not her."

Tyler.

Her heart skipped, regardless of how upset he'd made her feel. Continuing to stare at the beautiful Christmas tree light display, she heard Tyler's boots on the patio, stepping closer to her. She clutched the warm mug in her hand. As she exhaled, the steam from her breath and apple cider mixed.

"Thank you for the book. It's perfect. I can't believe I've never heard of it before." Tyler's voice came from just over her right shoulder.

"You're welcome."

"Look, I need to know why you gave up on your dream. Jodi said you went for a job interview in Booth. I need to understand—"

"I'm not taking it." Lorelei didn't look at him. She couldn't. "Maybe if you hadn't been so rude earlier, you could've given me a chance to tell you."

"You're not taking it?" He rejoiced. "The job in Booth?"

She shook her head. "I went because I never pass up an opportunity. They lost my resume that I submitted over the summer. If I didn't take chances in life when given to me, I would never have ended up here. Oh, and I met with my uncle and aunt, and he'll be retiring. So, I'll take over his practice for good come the new year, not that you care."

"Chris and Candace were here?" Tyler inquired.

"Yes, they stopped by earlier today. They needed a recipe. It seemed rather odd to drive from wherever they're staying, but . . ." For a second, she dropped her defense and glanced over at him.

His vision was focused squarely on her, and it melted her heart in an instant.

"I was upset you didn't tell me about the interview after everything we did together. I thought you didn't stick with your dream."

She turned to him. "My dream remains the same. I would have taken the job in Booth if I wanted to, but I didn't. It wouldn't be the same as being here, in Oakvale . . . with you."

Taking a sip of cider, she bought herself a second to gather her thoughts. "I'm looking for a place for Mary Ann to grow up, for me to slow down and spend time living life. A place to get to know my patients."

Lorelei caught that dimple flex in his cheek, and she felt her cheeks blush.

"That's great." He moved his hand out toward her but paused and withdrew it. He reached into his jacket pocket and pulled out the photo. "For your ornament."

Lorelei set her mug on the railing and wrapped herself up tighter in her jacket. She took the picture in her hand. "It's perfect."

Tyler ran his hand through his hair, unsure of what to say, then reached for her again. This time, his hand rested on her arm.

"We're staying." Her lips lifted in the corners.

"You're staying." Glancing down at his hand, he pulled back yet again. "I'm sorry. Honestly, I should never have brushed you off. If I've learned anything this December, it's been from you, and you taught me to have the courage to be aware of what's important. And you, Lorelei, are important."

This time, she was the one who reached out for him, taking his hand in hers. When their eyes met, she knew once again that Christmas miracles do come true. They smiled softly at each other.

She couldn't help but blush when he inched closer, taking her in his arms. "I'm pleased you're staying."

She pressed her lips together and glanced down before meeting his eyes again. "You have no idea how pleased I am."

The sound of laughter inside the house caused them both to turn their heads toward the French doors. On the living room floor, her mom and dad sat with Mary Ann, and her parents were *laughing*.

"Are they . . . ?" Lorelei asked, her tone confused.

"Laughing?" Tyler chuckled. "Why, yes, your parents are laughing. And look, no one's hands are in their pockets."

"I'm happy we both made our dreams come true. I'm staying, and you own the bookstore."

His eyes widened. "Oofta!" He reached for the door handle and flung the door open. "I told Sandy to take the other offer."

"What other offer?" Lorelei's heartbeat raced. "I thought you bought the bookstore already?"

"I bah humbugged myself!" Tyler jogged through the living room.

Before Lorelei could ask him what he meant, Tyler was out the front door, and his truck's engine roared to life over the sound of the crackling fireplace.

Chapter 37

T yler yanked open Once Upon a Book's door hard enough that the bells threatened to fall from overhead where they rang.

"Sandy!" he shouted, his eyes scanning the store.

She stood at the counter, talking with a woman he'd not seen before.

"Tyler!" Sandy turned in Tyler's direction.

"I tried to call you, but the line was busy." He approached the women, breathing heavy. "Take my offer. I still want to buy the store."

"Sorry, we haven't met." The lady wearing a cream tweed jacket and black gloves stuck out her hand.

Tyler halfheartedly shook it. "I'm Tyler. Nice to meet you."

"Jeanette. I'm afraid I've already put an offer in on this wonderful bookstore. And far above asking price."

Tyler's shoulders tensed up, and he clenched his teeth together. Jeanette was no doubt the buyer whose agent sent over the offer that morning.

Sandy looked at Tyler, then back to Jeanette. "I have yet to sign any paperwork. Tyler is my real estate agent."

"Yes, right." Tyler's pointer finger shot into the air. "If you'll excuse us, Jeanette." He took Sandy by the elbow. "I need to speak with my client."

As Tyler directed Sandy toward the fiction section, he felt Jeanette's eyes on him and swore he heard her fancy black high heeled boot tapping the floor in nervous anticipation.

Sandy spun around, facing Tyler, whose face scrunched up with worry. "You remember you're my agent, right? I can't accept an offer without your assistance. You would have to file it."

He ran his hand through his hair. "I did seem to forget that part." Tyler sighed a laugh. "Lorelei, she didn't take the job in Booth. I completely overreacted."

Sandy crossed her arms and pressed her lips together. "You don't say."

Tyler glanced over his shoulder at Jeanette, who remained precisely where they'd left her, with her impatient stance still intact. "As your agent, I advise you to take the higher offer, but as your friend—a long longtime friend—I advise you to take the offer from the person who knows this town and store."

"You don't say." Sandy tilted her head at Tyler and then toward Jeanette, who gave a half-smile and waved.

Tyler huffed and closed his eyes for a second. As he popped an eye open, he asked, "Well?" He opened his other eye and saw the hint of a hidden smile forming on Sandy's mouth.

"Of course Ted and I will take your offer. I'm glad you came to your senses. I can't believe the buyer showed up in person." She peeked around Tyler at Jeanette. "What do we do now?"

Tyler pivoted. "You tell her you won't be accepting her offer."

Together, they made their way over to Jeanette.

"I'm so sorry you drove out here, but I won't be accepting your offer." Sandy scurried behind the counter. She lifted her tea mug and took a long sip.

"What? I'm a little confused." Jeanette held her hand out in a stopping motion. "You're not accepting my offer? It's over asking price."

Sandy nodded. "I'm accepting another offer."

"Why would you do that?" Jeanette glared at Tyler.

"Tyler is a longtime friend and resident of Oakvale. And my husband and I want to sell the business to someone we know."

"Well, this is ridiculous," Jeanette snapped and slid on her cat-eye sunglasses. "I hope you know you've made the wrong decision." She stomped to the door just as a customer opened it.

Jeanette pushed her way past, and the moment her heel hit the snowy sidewalk, she wobbled. Tyler and Sandy hurried to the window as Jeanette plopped swiftly into a pile of freshly fallen snow.

"Should we help her up?" Sandy asked.

Before Tyler could answer, Jodi was at Jeanette's side, but the angry woman waved Jodi off as she attempted to stand. They watched as Jeanette ended up rolling over, going to her knees, and then standing. Jodi continued to reach her arms out in an offer to help stabilize the out-of-towner but was batted away. Finally, Jeanette was on her feet and staggered to her car, climbing inside.

Jodi entered the bookstore and removed her pink gloves. "Who was that?"

"A potential buyer for the bookstore." Sandy returned to the counter and her hot tea.

"Oh?" Jodi's eyebrow arched.

"I'm buying the store, and she wasn't pleased with the news." Tyler watched as Jeanette peeled out of the parking spot.

Jodi squealed and hurried over, hugging Tyler.

"This is the best Christmas ever!" Jodi cheered. "And it's all thanks to Boss Lady."

"Come on, now," Tyler complained, "I should get some of the credit."

"I only give credit to those who don't make fun of my car." Jodi smirked.

"Alright then, it's more important that I continue to be able to make fun of your car, so all the credit can officially go to Lorelei." He nodded his head, and secretly, Tyler would have to agree. This Christmas would go down as the most miracle-filled one he'd ever experienced.

"What will happen to the real estate office and bowling alley?" Jodi asked. "Maybe the slip-and-slide lady would want to buy it?"

"I don't think so." Tyler laughed, and Sandy joined in.

"Then there is only one more thing on the list." Sandy picked up her mug.

"There is?" Tyler questioned.

Sandy waved papers at him. "To sign and officially accept your offer."

"Right!" Tyler's mind was on Lorelei.

"Tell me what's happening because I feel like I'm missing something." Jodi leaned her elbow on the counter.

"I confronted my fear of being honest with my parents and told them I've decided to use the money I saved for traveling to buy the bookstore. And Lorelei's uncle and aunt stopped by, and Dr. North will be retiring."

"Boss Lady is for sure staying?" Jodi's eyes widened with delight.

Tyler grinned. "She is indeed."

Jodi hugged Tyler. "I'm so excited. How awesome."

"'Tis the season for great news." Tyler clicked his pen.

Chapter 38

After Tyler called and invited Lorelei to supper, she spent about fifteen minutes getting ready, her nerves dancing with excitement. Once at Oakvale Pizza Pie, she spent another forty-five minutes locating the photo of him from childhood on the wall. *The last thing on the list.* There were so many photos! Lorelei grinned, checked the time, and waved Uncle Steve over.

"Can we sit here?" she asked.

"Yes, please have a seat. Will Tyler be here shortly?" Steve slid a pen behind his right ear.

She spotted Tyler enter the restaurant and gave him a slight wave. "There he is right now."

Steve pivoted toward the door. Snow fluttered around Tyler as he brushed it off the shoulders of his jacket. As he approached the table, his smile grew.

"Hi," he said, his voice soft.

"Hi."

He pulled out a chair for her and then sat across the table. Lorelei's eyes traveled to the framed childhood photo on the wall behind him.

"I see you found my photo. The final thing off your list." Tyler glanced back at it.

"Your dimple is more pronounced now." Lorelei leaned forward.

"Ready to order?" Uncle Steve appeared and removed the pen from behind his ear.

"Sure, I'll have my regular." Tyler leaned on the table.

Lorelei looked over the menu. "I'll try the fettuccine alla Bolognese."

Steve scribbled on the pad with his pen. "Perfect, and to drink?"

"Sparkling cider," they said in unison.

Steve beamed and headed to the kitchen.

Tyler took a breath. "You know, we needed each other as much as we needed a couple of Christmas miracles."

Tilting her head, she found herself thinking back on her December adventure so far. "My uncle and aunt coming to town was the icing on the cake, at least for me."

"I can't imagine how very different my December—this town's December—would've been without you and Mary Ann." Tyler reached his hand out and took hold of hers. "For a long time, I wondered if I would ever meet someone as intelligent, kind, funny, and amazing as you are. I mean, this town is small, after all."

"You might've had to go to Booth to find one." Lorelei bit the side of her lip to keep her laughter from seeping out.

Tyler chuckled with a nod. "Honestly, I don't think I'd have my dream without you, and now you're a part of my life, and Mary Ann, too. I mean, we each leapt, but—"

"But we couldn't have done it without the hope and drive we provided for each other. We were each other's harness in the jump."

"You're exactly right." Tyler gave a squeeze to Lorelei's hand. "If I'd fallen, at least I'd have had a good doctor to patch me up."

"I think we're like a snow globe . . . how we worked together, how we needed each other." Lorelei pushed a strand of hair behind her ear. "A scene in a snow globe is calm and pretty, but when someone comes along and shakes it up, they make it beautiful because they've revealed the dormant sparkle."

Steve came out with napkin-wrapped utensils, set them on the table, and then lit the candle in the middle of the table.

Lorelei and Tyler shyly glanced at each other.

"Sharon insisted," Steve declared. "Oh, your drinks!"

Lorelei giggled. A feeling of comfort floated over her like a single snowflake breaking free from a cloud.

"I hope my parents grow to love visiting Mary Ann and me here." Lorelei draped the napkin over her lap.

"Give them time." The dimples in Tyler's cheeks showed as he rubbed his thumb over her thumb before leaning back in his chair.

"What do you think will happen with the bowling alley?" She glanced over his shoulder and out the window.

"I hope someone will have a passion for keeping it the same but find a way to make it their own, too."

"True." As her lips rose into a smile, the restaurant door opened, and in walked her dad and mom, carrying Mary Ann. "My parents are here."

Tyler pivoted in his chair toward the entrance.

John approached their table. "We're not here to interrupt your date, but your mom and I were hungry."

"We'll have Steve seat us over in the corner, as not to disturb you." Joanne beamed. "Tootles."

Lorelei shook her head in amazement. Her parents appeared happy. Taking in the restaurant around her, she closed her eyes for a second and smiled. Everything this month had come together like a true Christmas miracle. And the opportunity to take over permanently for her Uncle Chris was like a Christmas star lighting the way. She was so grateful for so many things: the fact that Tyler had still been running the real estate business long enough to be her contact person; the fact that her parents were watching Mary Ann while she was about to enjoy some of the finest food she'd ever experienced; and the fact that she sat across from a man she couldn't wait to spend more time with and learn more about.

"We've earned our dreams," Tyler said and stood up.

He took her hand and pulled her to stand next to him. "Have Yourself a Merry Little Christmas" drifted through the speakers as Tyler placed an arm around her waist. *Okay, so they were going to dance in the middle of the restaurant. No prob.* She swayed along to the melody with him until the song ended, and their eyes met. He leaned in for the kiss she'd been waiting for, and it was every bit as magical as the Christmas season.

Epilogue

One Year Later

"**W**hen's the couple arriving to sign the rental contract and pick up the keys to the Norths' house?" Lorelei walked up to the counter at Once Upon a Book, and Mary Ann walked next to her. While Tyler had sold the real estate agency and bowling alley to Jodi's boyfriend, who'd since relocated to Oakvale from Booth, he still helped out every once in a while.

Once Upon a Book looked stunning as ever with this year's Christmas décor while an instrumental version of "Jingle Bells" played over the store's speakers. The Oakvale Christmas Tree Lighting would happen any minute, and Lorelei didn't want to miss it, especially now that Mary Ann was older. Hopefully, it'd be even more special on her second go-round.

As if summoned, the bookstore door flew open, and in dashed a couple in their late forties, grinning and holding hands.

"Hi, welcome to Once Upon a Book," Tyler announced.

"Hi, we're the Janeys, here to rent the house. I'm Mike." The man reached out to shake Tyler's then Lorelei's hand.

"I'm Donna," his wife said, though her scarf nearly hid her entire face.

"Perfect timing, welcome to Oakvale." Lorelei thrust her hand out. "I'm the town doctor, Lorelei." She scooped up her daughter after a firm shake of Donna's hand.

"Wow, see honey, I told you this town would be the perfect vacation spot." Donna beamed.

"I have the rental contract right here." Tyler handed them the document. "Do you suppose you might want to host the Second Annual Christmas Feast?"

"Oh, that sounds wonderful." Mike took a pen from the counter and started to flip through the pages. "What do you think, honey?"

"Yes, we'd be delighted." Donna wrapped an arm around her husband.

"Perfect, we can go over the details once you're settled in." Lorelei eyed Tyler.

"Last year's was a real big hit, and this town loves nothing more than its holiday traditions," Tyler added.

"Sounds great." Mike scribbled his signature on the page and laid the pen down. "What about something to do tonight for fun?"

Tyler handed over the keys. "The tree lighting is about to happen if you have the time. It's not to be missed."

"Now, that we must see. The pictures online look like magic happens here." Donna wrapped both her hands around Mike's.

Tyler took Mary Ann from Lorelei, set the toddler on his forearm, and followed the renters toward the front door with his hand on Lorelei's back. Cider jumped up from her bed and joined them.

"We'll be seeing a lot of each other this month." Tyler locked the bookstore door as they all stood outside. "Go ahead, gather around." He pointed toward the town's Christmas tree.

"Thanks," the Janeys said in unison and dashed off like two schoolchildren headed for the playground at recess.

"Are you ready?" Tyler asked, sticking out his hand for Lorelei.

She nodded, and together, they made their way over to Kim and Diane's store, up the stairs to the second floor, and across the space to the window. From above, they saw the residents gathering around the unlit tree.

Tyler let go of Lorelei's hand and, as she stood gazing out the window, he reached into his jacket pocket. With Mary Ann resting her head on his shoulder, he turned to Lorelei and got down on his knee. Cider continued to peek at the town from the window's ledge.

"Lorelei, it's been an amazing year of adventures and watching Mary Ann grow, but I can't do it from afar anymore." Flipping his hand palm up, he opened his fingers to reveal a diamond ring. The din of the town below counting down from ten sounded outside the window. "Lorelei, will you marry me?"

She gasped and covered her mouth. "Yes! Oh goodness, yes, I'll marry you." Bending down, she kissed his lips.

As he held Mary Ann in one arm, her head lolling sleepily on his shoulder, he slid the ring onto his fiancée's finger just as the Christmas tree below lit up Oakvale's idyllic main drag. And now, *finally,* the last of Tyler's dreams were as perfect as the shining star upon the tree.

The End

Did you love this story? Maybe it wasn't right for you? Either way, I would love to hear from you!! A quick minute to write a review would mean a great deal to me and help future readers discover this book. Please and thank you!

Thank you readers...

...for sharing my books with your friends, family, coming to see me at book signings, and book club meetings, and leaving reviews.

Grab *GROUNDED IN JANUARY* here!
Grab *GROUNDED IN JULY* here!

Acknowledgments

A big long-distance hug and thank you to my *Happy PAWS Readers* ~ Sam Alvarez, Caroline at Page-Turners, Carol Harris, JoDena Pysher, and Carrie Thompson.

A big SHOUT OUT to Linda Martin, April Greer, Bambi Rathman, Joyce Stewart, Durene Adams, Starla DeKruyf, Tina Meyers, Rachael Bloome (and Mariposa Coffee), Dyana Hulgan, Annette G. Anders, Jamie Rutland Gillespie, Denise Birt, and Betty Taylor for your continued support for my books.

Thank you to my editor Krista Dapkey, your suggestions and editing really helped the book shine. I'm delighted to be working with you!

And all my love to Ransom and D.S. (who didn't get stuck reading this manuscript five times).

About the Author

Savannah Hendricks (born in California, raised in Washington, and resides in Arizona) is a full-time social worker and fills as much of her weekends as possible with writing. She loves all things dog-related and has a passion for red wine. Savannah enjoys gardening, baking, and creating yummy recipes. You'll often find her hollering at the TV during restoration shows when they paint over red bricks.

If you'd love a digital personalized autograph or bookplate, you can request one by visiting: savannahhendricks.com
Please discover more about Savannah by interacting with her on:

Instagram: savannahhendricks_author
Facebook: AuthorSavannahHendricks

Also By Savannah

Heartfelt Coming of Age/Women's Fiction
Sun City, 85373
The Album (Multi-Award-Winning)
I Adopted My Mom at the Bus Station (Multi-Award-Winning)

Humorously Wholesome Romance
Route to Romance
A Hearts of Woolsey series: A Desert Restoration, A Desert Romance, A Desert Rivalry
The Christmas Rental
Grounded in January (Award-Winning)
Grounded in July
To Work Out or to Wed

Meaningful Picture Books

Where Does "I Love You" Go?
The Needle-less Christmas Tree & Other Tree Tales
Winston Versus the Snow (Multi-Award-Winning)
Nonnie and I (Available in English, Spanish & Bilingual)

www.ingramcontent.com/pod-product-compliance
Lightning Source LLC
Chambersburg PA
CBHW021952170626
46808CB00001B/126